Crossroads
of Bones

A Katie Bishop Novel

LUANNE BENNETT

For Sharon Marden. Girl, the things you do for friendship…

1

SAVANNAH, GEORGIA – SUMMER

I f the night sky were any brighter, I would have thrown my bloody hands in the air and waited for the Chatham County police to drive by and question me about the hole I was digging. But it was just dim enough to conceal my activity under the massive live oak with the botanical veil hanging dangerously close to my forehead.

"Don't mess with the moss," I kept repeating in a distracted mantra, minding the rules about one of Savannah's trademark features, choosing to swat the swag of Spanish moss away from my face instead of ripping it from the low hanging branch and tossing it into the grave next to my feet.

With a mean stab and push against the shovel with my bare foot, I hurled another load of dirt at the growing pile next to the hole, a cold tear running down my cheek as panic collided head-on with the sorrow filling my chest. The light from the moon was like a spotlight, interrogating my actions and recording the crime for the day when I would face a jury of my peers, just before I was sentenced to rot in hell for what I'd done.

"Why did you make me do this?" I asked, shaking my head as I tossed the shovel a few feet away and dropped to my knees. I bent down toward the shallow grave and plunged my fingers into the Georgia clay, gasping from the pain of my fingernails yielding to the hard dirt. The blood was running up my arm, spreading from my hands to my elbows in dark crimson tendrils, continuing all the way up until it wicked into the fabric of my tank top.

A cold sensation shocked me. I sat back on my heels and looked down at the blood covering my chest and stomach, turning the white fabric into a deep red pool of carnage glistening wet under the moonlight. The blood kept flowing over me, somehow seeping from his wounds into the pores of my skin. I turned and gazed at the lifeless form lying on the ground behind me, watching the black lines emerge on his bare back and continue to crawl into curved shapes, the design filling with shades of ruby and sapphire. The tattoo grew into a neatly executed work of art that I would have been proud to display on the walls of my own shop, next to all the other tattoo art, if it hadn't triggered my urge to vomit the second I looked at it.

That tattoo was just wrong.

The body moved and I fell backward trying to scurry away, careful not to fall into the shallow grave. Then his head lifted off the ground and turned toward me, pinning me with a cold and lifeless stare.

"Jesus," I whispered, vaulting straight up on the mattress, my shirt soaked in cold sweat. I swept the hair away from my damp face as the flash of heat dissipated like an explosion, from the center of my chest outward through the tips of my fingers.

They'd started over a year ago, while I was finishing up my last year at Columbia University. Although the tattoos in the dreams that kept me awake at night were usually unfinished, this one was rendered completely.

The ink embedded in my own back began to quiver in a restless stir, lifting from my skin but settling back into place before it could break free. I knew a bad sign when I saw one, and that dream was a bona fide omen. My beast knew it, too. I was a magnet for the worst kind of shit that sailed right over the heads of normal people and made a beeline straight for me, because most people didn't share their souls with a dragon.

3:17 a.m. glowed from the face of my phone on the nightstand. How was I even functioning on two or three hours of sleep each night? My blue eyes were beginning to look gray and dulled from fatigue, and my posture had lost its grace.

I slipped my hand over my shoulder to soothe the stirring lines on my back. I'd gotten good at controlling my beast. Not an incident since moving to Savannah six months earlier. Good thing, because this place was different. Savannah had its own subculture of the strange and unusual, but it didn't come close to what was prowling the streets of Manhattan alongside its mundane inhabitants. But based on those dreams that kept me awake at night, I had an uneasy feeling that Savannah just hadn't shown herself to me yet.

Deciding it was futile to fight for a few more hours of desperately needed sleep, I went to the kitchen and swung the refrigerator door open. God, I wanted to climb inside and perch on the wire shelf. New York had nothing on the low country when it came to the sweltering heat of summer. The air conditioner—that useless box wedged in my window—hadn't worked for over two weeks, and my landlord was full of excuses every time that day came and went when he promised to have it replaced. What did I expect for the low rent?

With my boyfriend at the time—Elliot Fleming, bestselling author and rising star—I'd moved from New York City to Savannah with big ideas of opening a tattoo shop. He was working on his next book about a powerful Southern family living in Savannah, so his argument to move here started out purely as a research mission. I liked the idea, too. Don't get me wrong, I loved living in New York, but starting a business in Manhattan is cost prohibitive.

So here I was, standing in front of the fridge in the early hours of the morning when normal folks were still in bed. I'd managed to open that tattoo shop, but the boyfriend was long gone. I guess it wasn't Elliot's fault I couldn't stand the thought of moving to L.A. We were here for barely four months when he got the Hollywood bug, with his book optioned for film and that option looking more and more like it might get the green light. But after working my tail off setting up shop here, I was staying put for at least a few years.

God, I was such a cliché. When did Katie Bishop become such a cliché? I'd moved eight hundred miles from home for a man. *But* . . . I was on my way to rectifying that cliché. I was a perfectly intelligent woman with a degree from Columbia University. Granted, environmental engineering was a world away from the path I took, but it was something to fall back on if the shop failed or I got sick of drawing on other people's skin. Nothing wrong with a corporate job and a steady paycheck, but the thought of sitting in a cubicle—or even a fancy office—made me queasy. I just didn't believe I was put on this earth for that.

Another round of sweat was beginning to collect between my skin and the tank top I was wearing. I grabbed a bottle of cold water and headed for the patio. At least there was a breeze outside to push the intolerable heat around instead of stewing in a stagnant house the size of a shipping container. The house wasn't bad, just small. I'd rented the old bungalow right after Elliot left for the West Coast. It had history and charm, not to mention a few ghost stories that had never been substantiated. At least I'd never met any of them. The oddest thing I'd seen since moving in was the occasional disappearance of my hairbrush. But it always showed up eventually, right where I'd misplaced it.

I made myself comfortable in one of the cool metal chairs and propped my feet up on top of the table, listening to the bugs and tolerating the humidity painting my skin. I thought I might actually doze off when I heard the bushes rustle a few feet away from the patio.

"Damn it, Sea Bass!" I bolted out of the chair, suddenly realizing I had nothing on but that tank top and a ratty pair of underwear. "What the hell are you doing out here in the middle of the night?"

"Well, you weren't supposed to find me," he said. "What are *you* doing out here?"

Sea Bass—short for Sebastian—McCabe was my number one employee at the shop. Despite his party boy appearance and lack of backyard etiquette, he was an amazing artist capable of conceptualizing just about anything a client verbally presented. I'd seen him take a woman's animated description of a post-apocalyptic metropolis and turn it into a blazing ball of fire circling the Emerald City of Oz. Never once had a customer walked away less than ecstatic about his work, which was more than I could say for my number two employee, Mouse. She was also a talented artist but tended to take artistic liberty with the client's skin. Although the threat of unemployment had improved that bad habit remarkably.

"You're not staring at my ass, are you?" I grabbed the dirty towel draped over the back of the chair and wrapped it around my waist.

His skin flushed as he averted his eyes. "Hell no! Jeez, Katie! Not that your ass don't look good, but Maggie would cut off my balls."

The visual of his girlfriend reprimanding him lessened my annoyance. She was not one to mess with on a good day, and God help the woman who tried to hit on her man.

"Look, I was on my way home from Mojo's, and you did mention yesterday that something's been creeping up on you at night. I just figured—"

"You figured you'd swing by and defend me against my nightmares?" He scratched his head and muttered something I couldn't make out. "Sit down," I ordered, tossing him my bottle of water. "Mojo's, huh? You do know tomorrow is a work day?" Mojo's was the local dive known for cheap drinks, drunken brawls, and less than savory patrons. No discretion at all about who they let inside.

"I ain't drunk, if that's what you're worried about." He leaned over the table and opened his mouth wide, forcing a hot breath in my direction.

I jerked back to avoid the unmistakable smell of pepperoni and peppers. "Yeah, that's a little much, Sea Bass. I don't need these drive-bys. I can take care of myself." If he only knew how true that was, that the beast hidden under my clothes was more than capable of deterring any threats. The ink serpent that sprawled over my entire back was more than a tattoo; it was a birthmark, my heritage, my scarlet letter that never let me forget what I was. My birth parents were a mystery to me. The only thing I knew was that my mother was Russian and my father was a zmaj. That's dragon, for laymen. I'd spend the first twenty-two years of my life not knowing that I was the child of a dragon, the beast remaining silent until a couple of years ago when it came out in full glory to defend my best friend who was being attacked. That's when I learned how protective it was of the people I loved.

"I'm not trying to crowd you, boss, but this ain't Ardsley Park. Sometimes I wonder if all that commotion you been dreaming about ain't coming from right outside your bedroom window." He nodded firmly, punctuating his theory. "You just keep the neighborhood in mind."

"My neighborhood is just fine." I considered whether it was time to confide in him. I'd been putting it off for weeks, finding every excuse in the book to delay the inevitable. But he was the best friend I had in Savannah, and with that friendship getting stronger by the day it was only a matter of time before the dragon took a real shine to him. Better to prepare him for it. "Sea Bass," I started, still debating the sanity of disclosure. "I've got something to show you, but first you have to promise me you won't freak out and do something stupid."

He sighed and practically rolled his eyes at me. "Just put it out there, Katie. Say what's on your mind."

Instead of explaining it to him gently, I decided to just rip the Band-Aid off and show him. "Just keep that mind of yours open." I stood up and turned around, grabbing the edges of my shirt.

"Now hold on, Katie," he said, scrambling out of his chair and backpedaling as I began lifting my tank top. "I didn't come here for anything like *that*. You're my boss, and Maggie's gonna—"

He went quiet as I slipped the shirt over my shoulders and held it against my breasts, completely exposing my back. "You see that?" I could feel it coming to life, moving and undulating over my skin as my heart beat wildly and my adrenaline surged. I'd come out in public before, but the strangers on the streets of Manhattan never connected the flying beast to the girl with the dragon tattoo. Except for a few trusted friends who were bigger freaks than I was, no one else had ever seen it move on my back. Not even Elliot. That had been difficult, especially during sex when it liked to spread its wings.

"Jesus H. Christ," he whispered with a tremble in his tone. "What the fuck is that?"

I pulled the shirt back over my head and turned around. "That's the reason you don't have to worry about me. I'm not what you think I am." I could smell his fear and hear his feet shuffling for traction on the concrete patio, like he was about to bolt. "Jesus, Sea Bass," I said, pulling my shirt back on. "I won't hurt you. It took a lot of trust to show you what I am. Don't make me regret it."

He swallowed hard and froze. "What are you?"

"Let's see . . . how do I put this?" I thought about the description I'd been given by my friend, Ava—a witch who'd helped me answer that very question two years earlier. Dragon's child, demi-dragon; which would incite the least amount of panic? "My father was a zmaj." Seemed less crazy than the other labels. "But my mother was an ordinary woman," I quickly added to defuse the absurdity.

"And a zmaj is—?"

"A dragon," I said, cutting to the chase. "A Slavic dragon, to be specific."

Without saying a word for a solid minute, he stood there reading my face. "You wouldn't be fucking with me, by chance?"

"No, Sea Bass, I'm afraid this is very real."

He bobbed his head thoughtfully, appearing to have a complete change of heart about that fear he was harboring a minute earlier. "Okay. I can handle this. I'm cool with it."

I stared at him cautiously. He was taking my show and tell a little too casually. A normal person found it odd when you told them you were a dragon, and even odder when you showed them. Maybe Savannah was more like New York City than I thought, with a thriving subculture of freaks just like me. Maybe he had secrets, too.

"I just told you I'm a dragon's child, and all you can say is 'I'm cool with it'? Why aren't you running for the hills?"

"My granny is from the Ozarks. There ain't nothing stranger than some of her friends. Trust me, I've seen some weird shit growing up under her roof. Besides, I know you, Katie Bishop. I figure you would have killed me by now if you were evil." He went quiet and glanced at me timidly. "Can I touch it?"

"No one's killing anyone," I smirked. Nervously, I turned around again and let him run his hand over the back of my shirt. I could feel it move under the fabric, responding to his unfamiliar touch. "Careful," I warned, sensing its desire to come out and investigate the alien fingers.

He stepped back abruptly at my warning and sat back down, continuing to nod his head in that thoughtful way one does when contemplating a dilemma. "I've seen a few things in my day. This is low country, after all. Lots of root folks and such around here. I think you're gonna fit right in."

"Wait a minute, Sea Bass. No one's fitting in anywhere. The only reason I showed you is because you're one of my best friends, and I trust you." I was beginning to regret the decision. But the truth was zmaj were famous for protecting their villages. I'd learned very quickly that the people I cared about the most were just as important to my dragon—the equivalent of our village. It was only a matter of time before it showed itself to Sea Bass, so I thought it best to make an introduction first. "It's very protective. When it comes out it can be pretty fierce."

He blanched. "You mean it can—"

"That's right." I'd never thought of myself as a shifter, but I guess in a way I was. "I turn into it sometimes." This seemed to fluster him all over again, so I quickly added, "But only if there's a threat."

"Well," he laughed nervously, "I'll be sure to never threaten you then."

"It's not just threats against me, Sea Bass. Whether you like it or not, the dragon will probably try to protect you, too."

2

Employee number two was sweeping the floor when I entered the shop the next morning. She was called Mouse because her brown eyes were large and round, blending with her irises seamlessly. She also had tiny ears that projected from the sides of her head. The fact that she was barely five feet tall contributed to the illusion. A cute thing, but kind of mean. I made the mistake of calling her adorable a few days after she started working for me, and she flattened me with the saddest look I'd ever seen on a human face. Then she sneered and told me to shove it up my ass before stalking out of the shop. I think she spent her entire life fending off the idea that she was childlike, which fostered a deep resentment for being talked to like one. It took me two days to convince her to come back to work.

"Morning, boss." She glanced at the circles under my eyes. "Still having them dreams?"

"That obvious, huh?"

"I can get you something for that," she offered seriously. "I got a guy."

Mouse was a twelfth-generation Savannah native with blood going back to some of the earliest slaves brought into the Port of

Savannah in the eighteenth century. She knew every inch of the town and had a supplier for just about anything you needed— legal or not. Pharmaceuticals, psychedelics, herbal concoctions not for the faint of heart; if it altered you, she could get her hands on it. Lucky for me she didn't partake in any of it. I had one golden rule in my establishment—be sober and clean when you walked through that door. We were working on people's skin. One slip up could mean the difference between a happy customer and a lawsuit.

"I'll pass. But thanks, Mouse."

Sea Bass came strolling in right behind me, sunglasses shielding his eyes. Mouse snorted at him as he headed for the coffee machine. "Ain't made none," she said, taking a little too much pleasure in his obvious discomfort. By the way she kept glancing back and forth between us, I assumed she was waiting for me to read him the riot act.

"I already know what he was up to last night," I replied to her look. "He showed up at my place around three a.m. for a little babysitting."

Her brow arched. "Well, ain't you a knight in shining armor, Sea Bass. Better not let Maggie get wind of you spending the night with the boss."

"He didn't spend the night," I corrected. "We had a little talk about how I didn't need any babysitting, and I sent him on his way. Isn't that right, Sea Bass?" I gave him a warning look, making it clear that he needed to keep his loose lips shut. Eventually I'd probably have to share my secret with Mouse, too, but we weren't chummy enough for my dragon to feel protective of her just yet. Thank God for that.

"Yep. No impropriety last night. Except for them underwear you was traipsing around in, and that skimpy tank top you had on." A cocky grin climbed up the right side of his face as he poured a scoop of coffee grounds into a filter.

"Yeah, in your dreams," Mouse sneered. "Boss is way out of

your league. For the life of me, I don't know what women see in you. Big ol' dumb-ass."

Sea Bass darted across the room and threw her over his shoulder, knowing damn well it would piss her off. Just another reminder of how small she was. He howled when she bit into the flesh of his back and sent her crashing to the floor.

"Goddamn Neanderthal!" she spat at him.

"Well, you asked for it. Do that again and I'll—"

"For the love of God!" I stood between them and pointed to their stations. "Set up. We've got customers coming in." Sometimes I wondered if they'd come from the same womb, genetically wired to fight like siblings. They'd known each other since they were kids, and I'd hired Mouse on Sea Bass's recommendation.

MagicInk had been open for barely four months. With enough money scraped together over the two years before moving down here, I was able to open the shop on a shoestring. I'd signed a lease on an old building that used to house a butcher shop. If you sniffed hard enough, I swear you could still detect the smell of meat embedded in the walls and old plank floors. With a few chairs and massage tables and the bare minimum in machinery and supplies, I had enough to open the doors in a less than ideal part of town. But people were finding us. In fact, the dive quality of our humble establishment seemed to add credibility for those who lived the ink culture. Tourists and suburban kids looking to piss off their parents usually headed for the other side of town.

"Anyone heard from Abel?" I asked, referring to the absent fourth member of our team. Abel was the shop apprentice. Forty-six and looking for a career change, he'd spent the first twenty-two years of his professional life as a police officer for the Chatham County PD but was forced into early retirement due to a medical condition that meant a life behind a desk. It was the perfect opportunity to finally pursue his artistic talents. That, and a recent divorce that freed him to do whatever the hell he wanted. A clean slate. No more wife telling him what was or wasn't a respectable job, although his grown children reminded him frequently that he'd lost his ever-loving mind.

The door opened before anyone could answer, and in walked my missing apprentice. "Sorry, Katie. Traffic is a bitch this morning. I need coffee. Bad." He headed for the coffeemaker but stopped and shuddered when he saw it still dripping into the pot. "That's just fucking great," he grumbled.

Abel was a man of average height, but he was thick like a wrestler with a bald head covered in ink. Until his recent exit from the police department, the tattoos had been hidden by a full head of hair, and the scattering of marks on his arms had been tolerated by the department. Now that he was free to do whatever he wanted with his skin he was working on a full sleeve on each side.

Two months earlier he walked into the shop and grabbed the APPRENTICE WANTED sign right out of the window. It felt kind of strange considering someone almost twice my age for a payless job that usually attracted youngsters. To be honest, I looked for every reason not to take him on, figuring he'd end up quitting once the novelty wore off. But he was convincing. Not willing to take no for an answer, he dropped to his skivvies to show me his art, explaining that while he hadn't actually applied any of them to his own skin, he'd designed every last one. He was the real deal. A walking showcase of his artistic talent.

"Rough morning?" I asked.

"Yeah, you could say that. My kid decided to call me this morning to let me know she's pregnant and quitting school. She's been messing around with some married guy." He shook his head and tugged a deep breath through his nose. "I wanna kill that—"

"Nope. No, you don't," Sea Bass said, shaking his head. "In my experience, these things have a way of working themselves out. You ain't gonna do your kid any good in jail."

I glanced at him, surprised. "In your experience? Since you've never been married I can only assume that *she* was?"

"A lot of little Sea Basses swimming around out there," Mouse chimed in. "That pecker is gonna get you killed someday."

Abel gave him a dirty look and then turned to me. "What's on the calendar this morning?"

"Sugar is scheduled for ten," I said. "She wants that matching wing."

Lady Sugar was the reigning queen of the neighborhood. A performer at one of Savannah's more colorful clubs, she was a real legend in town. Of mixed parentage, she had cinnamon skin and striking hazel eyes that got your attention the minute she fixed them on you. She also happened to be the first customer who'd ever set foot in MagicInk. A picture of her Medusa tattoo was painted above the shop name on the window.

Mouse grinned at Sea Bass. "Enjoy."

"Oh, I will," he replied. "Her ass is a lot cleaner than most of the others that walk through that door." Sugar was getting the matching butterfly wing on her right cheek. The left one had taken a good four hours to complete, so Sea Bass was about to have a long day staring at the lady's behind. "Unless you'd like to do it."

"You know she won't let anyone but you touch her skin," Mouse snorted. "She's the only woman lusting after you that Maggie won't try to kill."

Right on schedule, Lady Sugar waltzed through the front door. She was dressed in a unisex pantsuit that looked like it just stepped out of the seventies, with a pair of stacked shoes reminiscent of Saturday Night Fever. No wig today, just a scarf wrapped over her head of black hair and a face full of makeup.

"Hey, Sugar. You doing all right this morning?" In just six months I'd started picking up a bit of a southern accent. It surprised me every time I opened my mouth.

"Right as rain, baby. You?"

"Shop's still open, and I'm eating," I said. "Could be a lot worse."

"I hear that. Best to be poor before you strike it rich. Makes it that much sweeter when you hit the lottery." She tossed her purse on a chair. "And I intend to win that damn Mega Millions someday."

Sea Bass greeted his client with a cup of our world-class coffee and patted the table. "Ready for a little pain, Sugar?"

"Well, honey, you know what they say about pleasure and pain. You just take your sweet time and make sure them wings match. I wanna be flying off this table by my ass when it's done."

He laughed and headed for the autoclave to retrieve his sterilized equipment, while Sugar dropped her pants without warning and climbed onto the table facedown. On his way back, Sea Bass stopped and looked toward the window. I followed his eyes and watched a man on the sidewalk stare at the shop sign painted on the glass. He kept shaking his head and talking to himself as if debating whether he should enter.

Mouse walked over to the front door and cracked it open. "You want to come inside and decide if you want that tattoo? It's all right if you change your mind, but at least you won't wear out the sidewalk any more than you already have."

With a disoriented expression, he took the offer and came inside the shop. His eyes went from Mouse to Sea Bass. Then he glanced at Abel. "I know you. You're a cop."

"Not anymore," Abel said. "How do we know each other?"

The man shook his head as his eyebrows drew together in a confused knot. "What? I don't know you."

Sugar pushed up on her elbows and examined the stranger. "Honey, you okay? You acting a little strange."

He looked at her, half-naked on the table, his eyes flying wide as he stumbled backward. The entire room seemed to lunge for the teetering stranger, but before he hit the ground he regained his footing and adjusted his displaced belt that had slipped lower on his hips.

"Good morning," he said in a smooth voice unlike the one

he'd entered with, seeming to have his reset button pushed. "My name is Victor Tuse. I'd like a tattoo, please."

"Okay, this man just ain't right," Sugar muttered, glancing at me as if to say, *You got no business putting ink on a man who ain't right.*

I hated to walk away from a paying customer, but I also happened to agree with Sugar. "You sure about that, mister?" I asked, giving him an out. "Because a minute ago you didn't seem too sure about putting a permanent piece of art on your skin."

"My apologies for coming across a little uncertain." He glanced at Sugar, who was giving him the stink eye. "I've been a little under the weather this morning, but my decision to get a tattoo has been solidified for some time now. In fact, it's already been started, as you'll see for yourself. Unfortunately, the artist only applied part of the outline in the first session before dying in an unfortunate accident. So you see, you'd simply be completing it."

"*Solidified*," Sugar repeated under her breath.

Victor Tuse pulled a folded piece of paper from the pocket of his shirt. He unfolded the drawing that looked to be as long and wide as the 8 x 11-inch paper it was drawn on, and handed it to me. "I'd like this tattooed in the center of my back. The size and color are very precise. It must be applied exactly as it appears on that paper. No deviations."

I nearly dropped the paper when I looked at it. The design was no small task, intricate and detailed, and large enough to keep him on the table all day. The image was outlined in black lines filled with vibrant shades of red and blue, just as it had been in my dream. It was the exact tattoo that had kept me awake at night, the one on the back of a dead man who seemed to wake up just before I did.

Victor Tuse was staring at me intently when I looked back up at him, a smile forming on his face.

16

"Where did you get this?" I asked, handing the drawing back to him.

He ignored my hand, seeming surprised by the question. "I drew it. It came to me in a dream."

I took a step closer and tracked his eyes. "That's interesting, Mr. Tuse. It came to me in a dream, too." My eyes burned as the dragon stirred.

"What?" Sea Bass said. "That's the one you been dream—"

I silenced him with my raised hand. Up to this point, my life had been pretty mundane since coming to Savannah. It was only a matter of time before the strange caught up to me, followed that trail of breadcrumbs I'd left on my way down from New York. "Okay. Have a seat." I motioned to a station. "Fifteen hundred." That would get rid of him.

"Fine," he agreed without flinching.

"Well, damn!" exclaimed Sea Bass.

"Mouse? You don't have any clients until later this afternoon, do you?" I asked without taking my eyes off the stranger. I didn't want any part of that tattoo. In fact, the sight of it made me feel a little sick to my stomach, just like it had in my dream. We'd oblige a paying customer, but someone else had to do it.

Her face lit up at the thought of all that money. "My pleasure, Mr. Tuse. Just give me a few minutes to make a transfer and we'll get started."

Tuse's smile vanished. "No. Miss Bishop must do it."

Mouse's subdued excitement deflated instantly. It wasn't personal, but I could see the disappointment on her face. She needed that money. We all needed that money.

"How do you know my name?"

His grin hitched as his mind went to work. "I've inquired about your work, Miss Bishop. You are the owner, correct?"

"Fine," I said without answering his question. "I'll do it." I agreed against the instincts in my gut telling me to show Victor Tuse to the door.

He removed his shirt and lay on the table with his arms folded under his chin. I examined his bare skin. "I'm guessing you don't have any other tattoos hidden under your clothes, do you? This will be your first?"

"Yes," he replied. "Remember, Miss Bishop, no deviations."

———

IT TOOK NEARLY six hours to complete, but I refused to schedule a second session to finish the tattoo. I cleaned Victor Tuse's reddened skin and applied a clear bandage. During the hours under the needle he barely flinched, even when I came close to the bone. I'd offered him a mirror to have a look before I covered it, but he refused and told me he knew it was perfect. When it was time to pay up, I almost felt guilty about accepting his fifteen hundred dollars, seeing how the price was meant to scare him off and not actually gouge him. But I had a feeling he could afford it, and in some way I'd earned my inflated pay.

"It's been a pleasure doing business with you, Miss Bishop." He shook my hand and headed for the door, but before walking through it he said, "You've earned a new customer. I'll be back for more, no doubt."

As soon as he was out of sight Mouse, Sea Bass, and Abel gathered around me and waited for an explanation about my earlier comment, the one about a complete stranger's drawing coming to me in a dream. And I'm sure they were all wondering if I'd lost my marbles—and my integrity—by quoting the guy fifteen hundred dollars for a four-hundred-dollar tattoo. Sea Bass would understand, but Mouse and Abel weren't privy to my secret.

I was about to fabricate a story when the front door opened. A tall man in his mid to late forties, wearing a pricey looking suit and a pair of black snakeskin boots walked into the shop, filling the space with an undeniable presence that commanded the attention of everyone in the room. He wore no tie with his gray shirt and smelled of cigars mixed with a hint of aftershave. Without a greeting, he removed his jacket and tossed it on a chair, taking a seat and crossing his boot over his knee. Then he exhaled a deep breath while combing his long fingers over the top of his head and asked, "Which one of you just gave Victor Tuse that tattoo?"

A short laugh burst from my mouth. Considering all the absurd shit I'd dealt with over the past twenty-four hours, my patience and manners were worn clean through. "Who the hell are you?"

His sharp eyes did a walk around the room before settling back on mine. "Well, I guess that would be you," he said with a touch of contempt in his voice. "I'm the man who's gonna fix the shitstorm you just started."

3

Finley Cooper was his name. Mr. Cooper walked into my shop and proceeded to grill me about the customer who'd just paid fifteen hundred green American dollars for a tattoo. Or rather, he proceeded to educated me.

"Call me Fin," he said. "The only person who called me Finley was my Aunt Rebecca, and she's been dead for over twenty years."

"Mr. Cooper," I began, "why don't you start by telling us who you really are and what you want."

"He's the fat cat who owns a good chunk of this town." We all looked up as Sugar came strolling back through the front door. "Isn't that right, Fin?"

"Sugar," Fin acknowledged with a drawl, uncrossing his legs but remaining in his seat. "How long's it been?"

Her eyes rolled over his torso. "Oh, at least two days. Wasn't that you up in the club the other night?"

Without waiting for his response, she came closer and fiddled with a stray strand of black hair resting on the side of my face. "Sugar just wanted to check up on you to make sure that strange man you was tending to earlier didn't do something unsavory.

But I see everyone is in one piece." She glanced at Sea Bass, giving him a soft stare and a half pucker. "Can't have no harm come to my boy." Sea Bass flushed and turned his eyes back on Cooper.

"You were telling us why you're here," I prompted.

"Sugar's right. I own a good part of this town."

Abel chimed in. "You're a real upstanding citizen, aren't you Mr. Cooper? How long's it been since the CCPD paid you a visit?"

"Moonlighting, Officer Ferguson? I thought the Chatham County Police Department frowned on that sort of thing." He glanced around the shop again, taking in the walls and all the hard work we'd done to convert an old butcher shop into a respectable tattoo parlor. "Why, I believe I own this very building. I see you've managed to cover up all the old bloodstains nicely."

"So, you're my landlord," I said. Until now the face behind that check I wrote every month was the woman at the property management company. I never imagined my landlord as a Southern gentleman with a strange but undeniable charisma. But even a snake is capable of charming its next meal, and my instincts told me to never turn my back on a man like Finley Cooper.

"That is correct. It's Miss Bishop, right? I do hope you're getting your money's worth, seeing how the rent I'm charging you is reasonably low."

Since he'd finally had the courtesy to stop by and introduce himself—after four months—I figured I'd take advantage of the opportunity. "Since you asked, Mr. Cooper, I've got a list of things that need fixing. I'll give it to you on your way out."

He was standing now, staring out the window with his hands clasped behind his back. We all waited for his next move, but he just stood there silently gazing up and down the street like he was waiting for someone to come walking down the sidewalk. When he finally turned around to look at me, his face had gone from relaxed to grave. "Miss Bishop, why are you in my town?"

I wasn't sure if I'd heard him right. "Why? Do I need permission to enter the city?" The look on his face was beginning to make me uncomfortable, and his questions were no longer amusing. As long as I paid my rent in full and on time, he had no right to walk in here and give me the third degree. "Why don't you just get to the point, Mr. Cooper, and tell me why *you're* here."

"The point, Miss Bishop, is that you just waltzed into my city and tore down a wall that has taken hundreds of years to build." His chiseled jaw tensed as he drew a breath through his nose. "In fact, I believe you just opened the gates of hell."

I shook my head and blinked. One crazy a day was all I could tolerate. Victor Tuse had already satisfied that quota. "Mr. Coop—"

He raised his hand to quiet me and for reasons I can't explain, it worked. Everyone in the room shut up, including Sugar, and that was no easy task. He walked over to my station and picked up one of the irons I'd used to tattoo Victor Tuse. "Is this the one you used?" he asked, staring at the tip. When I didn't answer, he looked up at me and snarled, "I asked you a question!"

His tone jolted me. "Yes!"

The iron broke as he violently hurled it against the wall. Abel lunged for him but caught himself before he did something stupid like assault a man as powerful as Finley Cooper. "I think you owe Katie an apology," he said, clenching his fists but minding his place in a town owned by those with the oldest bloodlines and the deepest pockets.

Cooper collected himself, brushing his disturbed hair back into place with his fingers. A shuddering breath rushed from his nose as he began to explain his bad behavior. "Miss Bishop, you've been duped."

My butt found the nearest seat. "What do you mean by

that?" I had a sickening feeling I was about to learn why I felt as if I'd earned that fifteen hundred dollars. Something wasn't right about any of this. I knew it the moment I touched the ink to Tuse's skin. The lines seemed to come alive, pulling my hand along as I traced the image. Not to mention the significant fact that I'd seen the tattoo in my dreams.

"Can we have a little privacy?" he asked, glancing at all the faces hanging on his words. "What I have to say isn't for public consumption." Sea Bass made a noise in the back of his throat, catching my attention and giving me a cautious look. "Trust me, son. It's best that you don't hear this." Cooper glanced at Sugar for an extended moment.

"Come on now," Sugar said. "Let's all get out of here and give the man some private time with Katie."

It was Tuesday—the shop's early day—so we were about to close anyway. "It's all right. I can close up myself." I stood back up and motioned toward the door. "Everyone can leave." Abel gave me a look, and I knew he'd be out there somewhere watching us through the window. It was the cop in him.

When the shop was empty, Cooper went to the door and turned the lock before flipping the sign to CLOSED. "Wouldn't want a customer to come barging in on us, now would we?"

"That depends on what you're planning to say—or do."

He scoffed. "Don't tell me you're afraid of me, Miss Bishop. I can assure you I mean you no harm." His eyes went to the broken tool lying on the floor. "Please forgive my outburst. It's just that the idea of what's been done brought out the anger in me. Something I rarely allow to happen. I'm sure you'd agree that a temper tantrum usually serves for nothing more than subsequent embarrassment. Something I'm experiencing as we speak."

"And what has been done?" I asked "I don't even know you, Mr. Cooper. What could I have possibly done to offend you?"

"The tattoo," he began. "Victor Tuse is not who or what you think he is."

23

I'd never seen him before. Some of our clients were referrals, but most were complete strangers when they walked through that door. "I don't know anything about most of my clients when they come into the shop for the first time. All I know is the man's name."

"Miss Bishop, are you familiar with root magic?"

I'd always known it as African folk magic. "You mean Hoodoo?"

"Hoodoo, folk magic, conjure." He looked at me and smirked. "Call it whatever you like. It all comes from the root. But the kind of magic I'm talking about makes all those look like cheap fortune teller tricks."

"I'm a busy woman, Mr. Cooper. Get to the point."

"The point, Miss Bishop, is that you just opened the door for that devil to walk right out of his prison. I'm a member of a society that makes sure that door remains closed and locked tight. I'm the very reason you get to sleep at night."

"Really. Do you have a secret handshake, too?"

"We've been watching this one for some time now," he went on, ignoring my sarcasm. "Smart son of a bitch. He's been through a couple of tattoo artists, but none of them have succeeded."

"Mr. Cooper—"

"Please, call me Fin."

"Then I guess you'll have to call me Katie."

"Of course, Miss Bishop."

I shook my head at his odd demeanor, a holdout from a more genteel time. "Whatever, *Fin*."

"For lack of a true name, let's just stick to calling him Victor Tuse, for now. He's a spirit who has lost his way. Of course, the poor soul who walked into your shop was actually a victim himself, seeing how the spirit randomly chose him as its unfortunate host."

"You're telling me that the man who walked in here this morning is possessed?"

"That's exactly what I'm saying. Victor Tuse—the host's real name—has been taken over by the spirit. Well, he wasn't fully possessed when he walked in here this morning, but thanks to you he is now." He glanced at the mini-fridge in the back of the room. "You don't by chance have anything stronger than coffee in this place, do you?"

"Sorry. We apply permanent ink to people's skin. Alcohol in here would be a bad idea, and illegal."

"Well, this is Savannah. Folks around here tend to greet by asking what you'd like to drink. But I guess you're right." He reached for his jacket on the chair and pulled a flask from the pocket. "Lucky for us, I brought my own."

He wiped the opening of the flask with his handkerchief and offered it to me. "No, thank you." Normally I would have welcomed a stiff drink after closing, but something told me to stay as lucid as possible for our conversation.

"Suit yourself." He took a deep swig and stuffed it in the pocket of his pants. "Now for the good part." He motioned to the couple of flimsy chairs near the door, in the spot masquerading as a waiting area. "You might need to sit down for this."

I ignored his suggestion and remained standing. If I had anything to say about it, our conversation would be a short one. After all, I had some sleep to catch up on, and that damned tattoo had drained me to the point where I thought I might actually get some for the first time in days.

"As you wish." He pulled the flask back out and took another drink, this time keeping it in his right hand. "There are two spirits. Two halves of a very unpleasant deity who has gone bad. Individually their power is impressive but limited. But should they manage to find their way back together—" He hesitated as if trying to find the right words. "Well, we're talking about war,

Miss Bishop. You just met one of those spirits. The Crossroads Society has been in place for hundreds of years in order to, among other things, keep that reunion from happening."

"To save the world from unspeakable evil?" I snorted.

The faint smile on his face slipped away. "You think this is a game, Miss Bishop? You don't believe in forces that are beyond what you can see or touch?"

"Well—" I began.

"I have news for you. That seemingly innocuous tattoo is a doorway. A thought form that the spirit uses to manifest into the tangible. All it needs is a host and an unsuspecting accomplice to render it into life. If the second spirit finds its way to that same host, well, I think I've made it clear what will happen."

Was that what my own tattoo was doing? Using me as its host? I had to keep in mind that he didn't know me, or the secret that lived on my own back. But my tattoo wasn't something someone inked into my skin—I was born with it. It wasn't until two years ago that I found out that the blackouts I'd experienced off and on since I turned sixteen weren't from too much drinking. It was the dragon inside of me emerging during precarious situations. The truth came out the day something very much like what Fin Cooper was describing went after my best friend. The beast came out and killed the threat. A few days later we discovered I was a dragon's child, the daughter of a zmaj.

"And where is this second spirit?" I asked.

"That's a discussion for another day," Cooper replied, eyeing me thoughtfully. "A discussion we'll be having soon enough."

"God, I thought I left this shit behind me," I muttered a little louder than I should have.

"What was that?" he asked, eyeing me suspiciously. "If we are to win the fight," he continued when I didn't answer, "you need to be up front with me about why you came to Savannah."

"What difference does it make?"

"The difference is that we need to know why it chose you, Miss Bishop. And why you're not dead."

My mouth dropped open. "Dead?"

"That's right. I mentioned that there were others who were unsuccessful in applying the tattoo. Two others, to be precise. They both died before the outline was even completed. You must have wondered why he came in with an unfinished tattoo, yes?"

Victor Tuse had mentioned the previous artist's unfortunate "accident" before finishing the job. "It's unusual," I agreed. "But it's not the first time I finished someone else's work."

"You see, the spirit has a little problem. No self-control, which is a dangerous thing for something so ancient and powerful. Pardon my vulgar analogy, but I liken his inability to allow the artist to finish that tattoo with the act of premature ejaculation. He simply gets too excited and ends up killing the artist before the deed is done."

"But I'm not dead." For a moment I wondered if it chose me because we were alike, nothing but hosts for our beasts. The idea made me uncomfortable. All this time I thought it served me, but now I wondered if I hadn't been serving the dragon all along. Would it kill me someday when my usefulness was gone? Then I thought about my paternity—my father the zmaj. I was adopted too young to remember anything about my birth parents, but I did meet a woman once who claimed to be my aunt. She had a similar tattoo, so there were others out there like me. We were different though. Not some random hosts for the demon spirits Fin Cooper was describing. Deep down I knew that.

"No, you're not dead, Miss Bishop. The spirit chose you for a reason and decided you were worth keeping alive." His eyes walked over me, sending a warning to my brain to be cautious of the predator in the room. A smart woman kept her eyes on a man like Fin Cooper. "You'd be a valuable member of the society. In fact, I'm extending a formal invitation."

"Clubs aren't really my thing, Mr. Cooper. And I've got my

hands full running a business. Leave your number and I'll be sure to call if Victor Tuse shows up again."

"I don't think you understand, Miss Bishop." He seemed irritated by my snub, unwilling to take no for an answer. "Now that you've created it, you're going to help us kill it. You owe us that much."

Before I could object, he grabbed his jacket and headed for the door, leaving me speechless by his audacity.

"By the way," I managed to say as he opened the door to leave. "I'll be deducting the cost of that equipment you broke from my next rent check."

FINLEY COOPER HADN'T BEEN GONE for more than five minutes when Abel knocked on the locked front door. I knew he'd been watching us through the window, and having obviously dealt with Cooper before I'm sure he was just waiting for his cue to come storming in if the man tried anything inappropriate.

"So, what's the story with Cooper?" I asked after letting him in and relocking the door. "You don't seem to like him very much."

"Meh, he's not as bad as some of the other big wigs around these parts, but he's had his share of run-ins with the local authorities." He rubbed his fingers together in front of me. "Money speaks louder than the law around here. Sugar can give you more juice on him than I can though. Owns a few clubs over by the river."

I heard the lock disengage on the door and in walked Sea Bass and Sugar.

"Jeez. Anyone else out there watching me and Cooper?"

"You better be glad you got good people looking out for you," Sugar said. "Fin's got him a reputation with the ladies, and it ain't all good. A pretty girl like you got no business in a room with a wolf. I don't care how good he looks or how fat his wallet is."

"He minded his manners," I said. "Had some interesting things to say." I glanced at Sea Bass to let him know we needed to talk.

"Mm-hmm, I bet he did," Sugar said, catching the look I was giving Sea Bass. "You got you a secret, Katie B? It's all right. You'll be telling me when you're ready. Just be careful with that man. He got a pipeline to some strange shit. I'd tell you he be crazy, but Sugar knows crazy and Fin Cooper is sane as they come."

"Strange shit?" I snorted. "You ought to see what I left behind in New York."

She sashayed over and straightened the twisted strap of my tank top. "I don't want to alarm you, baby, but things down here is a little different than up there in New York City. Some people down here be touched."

Abel scoffed. "They're touched, all right."

"You ain't helping, Abel," Sugar scolded.

"Then stop playing with the woman's head."

Sugar turned to Abel and expanded her chest. "*Playin'?* Who the hell you say be playin'?"

"You," Abel replied, unintimidated by her six-foot-three frame.

"Honey, you mess with them folks over at the Crossroads Society and you'll see who be playin'."

I stepped between them. "All right, you two! I'm locking up. Everyone out."

4

M y limbs stretched across the bed, taking up the full length of the mattress. For the first time in days I slept through the night without a single interruption. No trips to the bathroom, no dreams of tattoos, no waking up from all the noise in my head.

I climbed out of bed and slipped on a pair of shorts and flip-flops before heading to the kitchen to make coffee. It was Wednesday, which meant I was about to suffer a very long day. Wednesday was two-for-one day, but only on small pieces that cost a hundred dollars or less. We were a young shop still finding our feet in the community, and "two-for" day attracted a lot of new clients. Tattoos tended to be addictive. Those little hearts and butterflies usually progressed to bigger and bolder statements, and bigger cash flow for the shop. You know what they say: it takes money to make money. Promo day was a necessary evil.

Something soft brushed against my leg. I bent down and picked up my hungry feline—Jet. I called him that because of his jet-black fur and his ability to make it from point A to point B in less than a second.

"You hungry, baby?"

I fed him while the coffee brewed. Then I made myself a blueberry spirulina shake. I was on this new eating kick, trying to adapt a heathier lifestyle by cutting out junk and all the other food that made life worth living. Since Elliot left I'd gained around seven pounds. Stress eating from the separation, and the anxiety over the ever-looming threat that my business would fail and I'd end up in a cubicle slaving away for someone else's business. But MagicInk wasn't doing so bad. I wasn't buying lobster and champagne just yet, but I could afford a bottle of wine and a few shrimp every now and then.

While I pondered the day over my delicious algae shake, someone knocked on the door. I glanced at the clock on the stove panel. "Who in the—" It was way too early for Sea Bass to be dropping by, and no one else in their right mind would be knocking on my door at 6:52 a.m.

I got up and peeked through the front window. A car was pulling away with a sign decaled on the passenger side. It was one of those messenger services. I opened the front door and looked down at my coco fiber mat with the words WELCOME HOM printed in bold black letters. The letter E was missing, marking it down to a more affordable price in the clearance bin at the store. In the center of the mat was an envelope.

"What's that?" Sea Bass asked as he walked up the sidewalk.

I did a double take. With the exception of late nights at Mojo's that spilled into the early hours of the morning, Sea Bass never started a day before nine a.m. I knew this because he barely made it to the shop by nine-thirty and tried his best to hold off customers until at least ten.

"Am I seeing things, boy?"

He held his arms out to his sides, palms up. "What? Was I wrong about that look you gave me last night?"

I'd given him a visual cue, but I didn't expect the miracle of having him join me for breakfast in order to have that discussion.

"Well, will wonders never cease. I was thinking more along the lines of a drink after work, but sooner is probably better."

I picked up the envelope and motioned him in. "Care for an algae shake?" I offered, grabbing my glass of green slush and waving it in his face.

"What in God's name is that?"

"Spirulina, which technically isn't really algae—I think."

He shuddered at the green sludge, careening around the glass to grab a banana from the counter. "Okay, what exactly is going on between you and that dickhead, Fin Cooper?"

"So you know him?"

"I know who he is, and that's about as close as I want to get to them folks." He glanced at the envelope still wedged between my fingers. "You gonna open that? You got some kind of secret admirer leaving you love notes on your doorstep?" He grinned and stuffed half the banana in his mouth.

"I guess I need to, don't I?" I really didn't care for surprises. I'd had my share of them, and there was a fifty-fifty chance of a bad outcome every time. I ripped open the envelope flap and pulled out an ivory linen card with gold embossed writing on the front. "It's an invitation."

"To what?" He snatched the card from my hand.

The Crossroads Society of Savannah, Georgia
requests the company of Miss Katie Bishop
at the 2017 Annual Crossroads Society Ball
Saturday, July 29, 2017, 8:00 PM
Black Tie

"WELL, AIN'T THAT HOITY-TOITY," he said, handing it back. "I'll probably die before ever getting an invite to that kind of party."

I scanned the invitation. "There's no address listed."

"You're not seriously thinking about going, are you?"

"It's this weekend. Kind of short notice. It's not like I have a ball gown just hanging in my closet. And if you haven't noticed, I'm not exactly the 'ball' type." It suddenly occurred to me that Finley Cooper knew where I lived. That meant he was either spying on me or had someone else do it for him. "How the hell does he know where I live?"

"Uh, sunshine, you and I need to have that little talk now about Finley Cooper."

We took our coffee and went out to the patio to discuss what Cooper had told me about Victor Tuse. Since I'd already come out of the closet to Sea Bass and he'd obviously seen a lot of crazy shit in his day, Finley Cooper's story would probably read like non-fiction.

"According to Cooper," I began, "Victor Tuse is a host for some spirit the Crossroads Society had been guarding for a while. Like a couple of centuries," I smirked. The story was absurd, but Cooper was convincing. Why would he lie? "Apparently, I facilitated its escape from prison when I put that tattoo on Tuse's back."

I'd expected the synopsis to make him laugh and tell me how gullible I was, but instead he blanched and stood up abruptly. "You are *not* going to that ball, Katie."

"And I'm sure you're going to tell me why. Not that I've even decided yet."

"Oh, I'm not even gonna try," he said with a straight face. "My granny is."

TWO-FOR-ONE DAY OR NOT, the look on Sea Bass's face convinced me that he wasn't just being an alarmist. Finley Cooper's words had genuinely spooked him, and I knew enough about auguries and omens to know that the look on his face was a sign of something that needed immediate attention. My first scheduled appointment wasn't until noon, and Sea Bass rescheduled his morning client. Mouse would have to deal with the walk-ins for an hour or two while we went to see Granny McCabe.

I balked when he headed for his motorcycle. "I'm not getting on that thing. No offense, but I've seen you drive it. That thing's dangerous." He rode a vintage Triumph Bonneville that had seen better days. From the way he talked about it, a six-month project had turned into six years, and it was still barely legal to be driven on the road. "We're taking my car."

"Damn, Katie, you gonna make me show up at my granny's house in that?"

My ancient Honda Accord was no classic, but it passed inspection and ran just fine. "I can meet you there, if you'd prefer?" He relented and followed me to my car.

We drove across town and pulled into Davina McCabe's tiny driveway. She lived in an old green bungalow near Daffin Park with a postage stamp-sized front yard and a short wrought-iron gate wrapped around the front of the house.

Sea Bass knocked his knuckles against the pink door as he pushed it open. Granny was expecting us.

"Sebastian. Get over here, boy." She pushed herself up from the sofa and wrapped her frail arms around his shoulders as he bent down to accommodate her petite frame. Granny couldn't have been a day less than eighty, but she moved like a woman ten years younger.

After the reception of her grandson, she turned to me and grinned on one side of her face. I wasn't sure if it was from paralysis or slyness. She stood still as a stone for a minute, taking me in as if she were reading my aura. "So, this is the young lady you were telling me about."

"Katie's my boss, Grams."

Davina raised her brow and smiled with an even grin this time. "Well, she's a lot more than that." Before I could open my mouth to question the comment, she turned and headed for the archway. "I'll go fix up a tray."

"You don't have to do that, Mrs. McCabe," I said, fearing the hospitality might tax the older woman.

"Of course, I do," she replied without turning around. "And please, call me Davina."

"Grams likes to entertain," he said. "I swear that woman ain't never gonna slow down."

"Grams?" I repeated with a quiet chuckle. "That's sweet." I never knew my birth grandparents, and the parents of my adopted mother and father both died before I came along.

On the way over, Sea Bass had given me a primer on his grandmother's history. Davina McCabe came from mountain folk. The Ozarks, to be more specific. When she was fifteen, she married a man working for the Civilian Conservation Corps who was twelve years her senior from Charlotte, North Carolina. By the time she was seventeen she was pregnant and living in Savannah.

Glancing around the room, I could tell she was a woman who appreciated the history of objects. The shelves were filled with old things from the past like Staffordshire figurines and old books. The house was small but the large windows let in a lot of light, making the room feel bright and airy. It had a lot of charm: arched doorways, old pine floors that looked original to the house, architectural details that people spent an arm and a leg trying to replicate. Sea Bass's mother grew up in this house, and he himself had spent a good chunk of his childhood under this roof.

"Now I feel like a proper hostess." Davina came back into the room carrying a large tray. Sea Bass shot up to take it from her hands and placed it in the center of the coffee table. "Why didn't you call me, Grams? One of these days you're gonna fall and break a hip. Then what are you gonna do?"

"Boy thinks I'm old," she said. "Well, I guess I am, but don't tell anyone." The tray contained a pitcher of sweet tea, a few glasses, a plate of shortbread biscuits, and a pile of napkins to catch the butter from those biscuits. She bent down and poured some tea into a glass and handed it to me.

"Sea—Sebastian said you're originally from the Ozark Mountains?" I asked, noting her lack of the stereotypical dialect you'd expect from mountain folks. "I mean no offense, Davina, but you sound more like a native Southerner than someone who was raised in the Ozarks."

"Well, I've been a Southerner about five times longer. I was only fifteen when I climbed down from the mountain." She laughed quietly. "You should hear me when I get a couple glasses of wine in me. That mountain starts to spill out of my mouth like water."

Even with the easy conversation and the polite tray of Southern hospitality, her eyes kept tracking mine. She was watching me like a hawk. The talk in the room went quiet, and all I could hear was Sea Bass chewing on his biscuit and chasing it with a swig of tea.

"Such a pretty thing," she continued. "What is your heritage, Katie?"

"Well," I took a deep breath to ready myself for the foray into my complicated pedigree.

"Katie's adopted," Sea Bass blurted out, somehow thinking I needed assistance.

I gave him a deadpan look. "It's true. I was adopted when I was a baby. My mother was—possibly still is—from Slovenia."

"And your father?"

"I—I don't actually know anything about him," I lied.

She swallowed a sip of tea and paused. "Sebastian tells me you've been invited to the Crossroads Society's annual ball." She glanced at her grandson who was helping himself to a fourth biscuit. "He didn't bother to mention that you're a shifter."

I stopped breathing, partly because I had no idea how to

respond, and partly because I'd just thought of myself as a shifter for the first time two days earlier. Sea Bass shook his head when I glared at him, confirming that he hadn't opened his mouth and divulged my secret.

"You're wondering how I know that." I detected a twinkle in her eyes and a deeper wrinkling of the paper-thin skin underneath them as she scrutinized my face. "You have the black hair of a raven, and the bluest eyes I've ever seen. Unnaturally blue." She leaned closer, and I realized she was trying to get a better view of them. "But I can also see the green stirring in them. I bet the beast is just itching to come out right now, isn't it? I bet it's just dying to sniff the intruder in the room."

I jerked back into my chair and accidently spilled some of my tea on the floor. "I'm sorry!" I automatically set the glass down and reached for the stack of napkins on the tray as if the old woman hadn't just blown my secret right out of the water.

She grabbed my wrist without taking her eyes off mine. "Let it be, girl. We have more important things to tend to."

Sea Bass looked like a shell-shocked soldier wounded in a muddy trench. He snapped out of it and gawked at Davina's wrinkled hand wrapped tightly around my arm. "Grams! What the heck are you doing?"

She ignored her grandson and gazed deeper into my burning eyes, daring my dragon to show itself. I tried to pull my arm away but her hand felt like a metal vise, pinning me to the table. The chair was shaking beneath me, but I realized it was me doing all that vibrating and shuddering with a thousand pounds of adrenaline racing through my veins. She was right—my dragon was fighting to emerge.

"*Stop!*" I roared before it was too late.

Davina grinned widely and let go of my hand, settling back into the sofa as she sipped her glass of tea. "Well, that was a disappointment, Miss Bishop. We're going to have to do something about that."

I was speechless. Literally lost for words. I kept glancing at Sea Bass for some sort of explanation as to why he'd brought me here. Was this all planned? How was it even possible that she knew?

He just shook his head and continued to gawk, tongue-tied and incredulous as he looked back and forth between us. He was afraid of his elderly grandmother and I could see why. "I love you, Grams," he eventually managed to get out, "but right now you're scaring the hell out of me."

"I apologize for my lack of discretion," she said, glancing at her grandson. With a reassuring smile she patted his knee. "Sweetheart, if this is all too much to handle, you can wait in the other room while Katie and I talk."

"He stays," I insisted, uneasy about being left alone in the room with his granny.

Like a child being directed by a parent, he sat on the sofa and said nothing while the two of us decided his next move.

She nodded. "Fair enough." Then she replenished my spilled glass of tea and handed it to me, squaring her shoulders as she inhaled deeply. "Shall we start over?" she asked brightly. "I always find awkward situations much easier to tolerate with a fresh start. Wouldn't you agree?"

I said nothing as she proceeded to reintroduce herself.

"It's a pleasure to meet you, Miss Bishop," She extended her deceptively frail-looking hand, and I took it. "My name is Davina McCabe and I'd like to welcome you to the Crossroads Society."

5

———

Davina McCabe said little more than Finley Cooper about the history and mission of the Crossroads Society. She just smiled sympathetically and handed me the card for a boutique where I could find the perfect dress for Saturday night, assuring me that the bill for the gown was on them. Sure, I'd take a free party dress. God knows I didn't have the money to pay for one.

Poor Sea Bass. That boy just didn't know what to make of his sweet little granny transforming into a badass before his very eyes. Savannah was no more mundane than Manhattan when it came to the underworld society living right alongside the everyday Dick and Janes, and I imagined he'd been living his whole life under the same roof with one of its grande dames. I guess I'd find out Saturday night who was in that exclusive club and what side they were on—good or bad. Then I'd decide if the Crossroads Society was worth affiliating with.

"Jesus, Katie." He shook his head and got out of my car, looking apologetic as we headed for the back door of the shop. "I didn't know about any of that back there." It was the first conversation we'd had since leaving Davina's house. He'd gotten into the car and sat for the next twenty minutes in complete silence while we drove back. "I mean, I knew Grams was a little eccentric and I've seen her do some strange things, but I ain't never seen her act like that. And I had no idea she was a member of the society. I need to have a conversation with Mom." His foot caught on some imaginary obstacle, and I could tell by the pallor of his face that the thought had just occurred to him that his mother might turn out to be something of a stranger, too. "Shit, Katie. What if my mother—"

"Take a breath, Sea Bass. Want me to get you a paper bag?" I teased. "You told me she was different."

"Yeah, but I ain't never seen her manhandle one of my friends like that."

I tried to recall what it felt like when I found out what my father was, but this wasn't the same situation, because of what *I* was. I'd always felt different. Oddly, the truth was a relief, because it validated what I'd been feeling all my life and confirmed that I wasn't crazy. Poor Sea Bass had been blindsided—or was he? "Are you being completely up front with me?" I asked.

He looked incredulous. "About what?"

"Seriously? It never occurred to you that all the odd people and strange things your granny exposed you to was unusual?" I had to remember he was a guy. No offense to men, but women are a hell of a lot more intuitive about matters that can't be seen with their own two eyes. A sixth sense about certain things. A cheating man only stays hidden because his wife pretends not to see, chooses self-inflicted ignorance over the uncomfortable truth.

After pondering the question, he shook his head. "You're right, Katie. I guess it ain't normal to have a granny who entertains crows and sparrows—in the living room, or sells little bags of . . . whatever from the back door of her kitchen. I used to see strangers sitting at the dining room table, but when I turned back around there was nothing but a bunch of squirrels sitting in them chairs."

My brow cocked. "Now that *is* unusual."

I upset his carefully molded hair with my fingers, shaking the top of his head roughly like he was a little boy. "Jesus, Sea Bass," I said, pulling my hand away. "How much gel you got in there?"

"Cut it out, Katie." He smoothed his disturbed hair back into a neatly coifed mound. "Maggie's meeting me for lunch."

"Lunch?" I said. "We just got here."

We walked into the shop, and sure enough Maggie was sitting in one of the recliners with her left leg stretched out and Abel hunched over it. "Tell me you are not doing what I think you are," I said. He turned and looked up, giving me a clear view of a wolf baring its teeth. To my recollection, he didn't have his license yet. "Abel! You trying to get me shut down?"

"Relax, Katie," Maggie said. "Mouse did it. Abel's just getting ready to wrap me up."

Abel looked wounded. "I'm a former officer of the law. Do you think I'm that stupid?"

Maggie stood up, revealing her tall frame in all its inked glory. Her legs were fairly conservative, with only a few tattoos on one thigh and one on the ankle of her other leg. It was her right side that impressed the most, with a full sleeve running from just under her ear all the way down over her shoulder and arm, ending in a dainty black filigree on the back of her hand. Her fiery red hair curled over her shoulder and landed midway down her torso, complimenting her vivid green eyes. Maggie was a walking statement that wouldn't be ignored.

"Hey baby." Sea Bass walked over to examine her new tattoo. "That's a real nice one."

"Damn right it is," Mouse proudly proclaimed.

I headed for the front desk and started looking through the phone numbers in the customer database. I considered myself a pretty edgy woman, perfectly capable of pulling off a look, but balls and galas were outside my wheelhouse. My visit to—I looked at the card Davina had given me—L'Elite would require a little backup.

Maggie chomped down on the piece of gum in her mouth and grinned at Sea Bass. "How's Grams? I hear you and Katie paid her a visit this morning."

His smile went south, the bright expression he always got the minute Maggie stepped before his eyes dimming at the thought of what had happened an hour earlier.

"Why don't you two get out of here and get some lunch," I suggested, knowing he wouldn't press his luck after my comment a few minutes earlier.

Abel finished wrapping Maggie's leg before they left, and I found the phone number I was looking for. Then I called L'Elite and made an appointment for the next morning. The woman on the other end of the line practically snickered when I told her I needed something by Saturday. *This isn't Macy's*, she'd snipped. But then her attitude adjusted when I gave her my name. *Yes, Miss Bishop, nine a.m. will be fine.*

I ended the call, feeling both snide and a little uneasy with all the special treatment I was getting. Something in my gut told me I'd eventually pay for it. But right now all I wanted to do was get a damn dress and get this ball over with. If attending wasn't such a strategic move on my part, I would have tossed the invitation in the trash. But I was curious about Fin Cooper's story, and Davina McCabe had just cemented my decision to go.

L'ELITE WAS LOCATED in a part of town you'd expect for a shop with a name like that. I waited on a bench a few doors down for my shopping date to show up. At five minutes till nine, Sugar came flouncing down the sidewalk wearing an orange and pink paisley dress with a skirt that barely made it halfway down her long thighs, and sleeves that flared from her elbows down to her wrists. The dress was coordinated with a pair of mid-calf stiletto boots in a shade of orange that matched the dress perfectly.

"I like your hair," I complimented when she stopped in front of me. She was a blonde today—lavender blonde. Had the whole Nancy Sinatra thing down cold. "You're going to give the ladies at L'Elite a heart attack when you walk through that door."

"Shit, baby, them bitches know who Lady Sugar is."

She led the way and pushed open the front door of the exclusive boutique. A man came out of the back room and smiled pleasantly at me. His eyes swung around to Sugar and seemed to take a minute to reconcile the creature standing in front of him. When he did, his skin paled.

"Well, what do you know?" Sugar planted her hand on her hip and grinned at the stunned man. "How's your mama and them, Javier?"

His mouth opened but he seemed lost for words. A moment later a woman came through the same doorway and did a damn good job of ignoring the giant orange Creamsicle in the room. "Miss Bishop?" she asked.

"That would be me."

"I'm Sarah Winfield. I'll be assisting you today." She shook my hand and studied my form discreetly. Most people wouldn't have noticed her wandering eyes assessing me like some charitable project, but I caught every glance.

She turned to Sugar with a forced smile. "And you are?"

"I'm Miss Bishop's personal stylist," Sugar announced, extending her hand with a large mood ring on her middle finger. "Sugar, but you can call me Miss Mobley."

The woman hesitated but eventually took Sugar's long outstretched fingers, barely shaking it before pulling away, resisting the urge to excuse herself to wash it. Her distaste was palpable.

"Finley Cooper sent me," I said, providing a reprieve from all the bigotry monopolizing the room. "I need something to wear to the Crossroads Society ball this weekend."

She eyed the tattoo peeking over my shoulder and continuing down my arm. "Were you thinking strapless? Or perhaps something a little less revealing?"

My bigot radar was through the roof. *Smug, insufferable bit—*

"Miss Bishop would prefer strapless," Sugar interjected before I could. "With a body like that, wouldn't you?"

Sarah Winfield ignored Sugar and marched over to a rack against the far wall. "It'll be a stretch to have it fitted in time for Saturday, but I think we can manage seeing how you're a friend of Mr. Cooper's."

"We're not friends," I said, not knowing why I bothered.

She smirked knowingly, as if I'd just stated the obvious. "But he is paying for the dress, yes?"

"He better be," Sugar muttered, diving into the dresses and shuffling through them like it was the clearance rack at Walmart.

Sarah's eyes went wide. "Please don't touch the dresses." She stepped between Sugar and the rack and then pointed to a seating area near the front door. "If you wouldn't mind waiting over there."

"Sugar would mind." Her head bobbed from side to side as she shot Sarah Winfield a warning look.

"It's okay, Sugar," I said, defusing the ticking bomb before it went off. "I'm not deciding on anything without your approval, but let's give Miss Winfield a little room to do her job."

Sugar brushed the bangs from her eyes and reluctantly headed for one of the upholstered chairs. "You got any coffee up in here? Any cap-o-chino or express-o?" she mocked. She glanced at Javier, who still seemed to be in a bit of shock at seeing her in his place of business. My gut told me Javier led a pretty colorful life outside the walls of L'Elite, and at the moment he was terrified that Sugar might say something that would sully his employer's opinion of him.

"Would you get Miss Mobley a refreshment, Javier?" Winfield said.

The man disappeared to the back to get the coffee. He reemerged a minute later carrying a tray with a carafe and a small pitcher of cream. As he set it down on the table next to Sugar, he gave her a pleading look for mercy. Sugar just grinned, holding the poor man's balls hostage.

Sarah carefully sorted through the dresses, stopping on a blue gown that shimmered like a million sapphires being tossed into the sky as she swung it around for dramatic effect. It was a floor-length, strapless gown of sequins with a thigh-high cut on one side. "This one would go beautifully with your eyes," she said. "I must say, Miss Bishop, they're quite extraordinary. Are they real?"

I'd been told more than once that my eyes were a reflection of Elizabeth Taylor's, and my jet-black hair only enhanced that comparison. "They're all mine," I answered. "The hair is mine too, just in case you were wondering if I used Black #1."

"Touché," Sugar said over the rim of her cup.

"That was a compliment, Miss Bishop." She continued searching the rack and pulled out a red dress with a plunging neckline and long sleeves. "This one would complement your hair nicely." She grabbed a third option that was somewhere in the middle. Pink with shoulder straps, a sweetheart neckline, and a wide tulle skirt. "The dressing room is this way."

I figured I'd get the non-contender out of the way first. There was no way I was wearing the pink contraption out in public, and I was surprised Sugar even allowed it in the dressing room. The tulle shirt had matching tulle sleeves that partially concealed the tattoos running down my arm, and the only ink in full view was the dragon peeking out around my neck. If I wore my hair down it would hide most of it.

Sarah Winfield brightened up when I stepped out from the dressing room, I suspected because she'd done a fair job of hiding my marks. "Now that is lovely, Miss Bishop."

"Oh, hell no!" Sugar spat. "This ain't no damn prom." She got up from her chair and marched over to me, spinning me around to get a closer look at the hot mess of pink I was wearing. "And this ain't no damn silk anyway. What is this?" she asked, feeling the tulle skirt. "Nylon or polyester?"

I thought Sarah Winfield was going to combust before our very eyes. "That *is* silk, Miss Mobley. Where do you think you are? Dressbarn?"

Sugar ignored the comment. "You got two real nice dresses in that room, Katie. Go on in there and show this imposter what a real woman looks like."

Winfield held her tongue, but I could see her trembling from the outrage of having to swallow it and abide by the mantra of *the customer is always right*. Pissing off a customer referred by a top client was tantamount to professional suicide.

Being my favorite, I decided to try the blue dress on next. As I was unzipping the back, I noticed a tag pinned to the inside. I assumed Miss Winfield had forgotten to remove it before leaving the dressing room, because a place like this usually didn't bother letting the customer know the price of a gown until after they'd fallen in love with it. The tag contained details about the fabric and the designer—and the price of thirty-six hundred dollars. I nearly choked. Maybe it was a rental that I'd be expected to dry clean and return after the ball.

"Do you need help with the zipper?" Winfield offered.

"I'm fine." I struggled with it but preferred to slip into the dress without the judgmental saleswoman eyeing the full tattoo on my back. It was fitted but offered some relief where the split began on the upper part of my thigh. When I stepped outside the dressing room everyone gasped. Sugar slowly nodded her head and release her breath like a proud mama, while Miss Winfield eyed my exposed tattoos in horror.

Sugar picked up on it and set the record straight. "This woman is showing you exactly who she is and doing it proudly."

A garble of gibberish slipped from Winfield's mouth as she clearly tried to respond intelligently. "Well, there are ways to express yourself without offending anyone."

"*Offending* anyone," Sugar repeated, flabbergasted by the ignorance—and stupidity—of Sara Winfield. "What the hell do you think she should wear? A potato sack?" She waved her hand around me. "Because that's the only thing that's gonna cover up all this art. And art ain't meant to be censored."

"Let me remind both of you that the Crossroads Society is paying for this dress. They patronize this shop for more than just the designs and quality—they also expect a certain level of discretion."

"Oh, I don't think so," Sugar said, eyeing Winfield like she wanted to boot the woman in the ass. "Let me explain something to you, lady. Miss Bishop will be back on Friday afternoon to pick up that little blue dress she'll be wearing to the ball, after you've taken the time to alter it, of course. You may not agree with her style, but I don't think she much cares for yours either." Sugar glance at me standing like a statue in front of the octagon of mirrors. "Do you, Katie?"

"Not particularly."

She turned back to Sarah Winfield. "Now show me the damn shoes."

I picked out a pair of matching blue satin Manolo Blahniks. Sugar had argued for the Louboutin pumps covered with hematite stones encased in silver, but I couldn't stomach the idea of drawing any more attention to myself than the dress—and tattoos—already would.

We left L'Elite with my shoes and headed for the cars parked a few blocks away. Sarah Winfield—with her hefty commission—escorted us to the door and assured me the dress would be ready by six p.m. Friday evening. Under normal circumstances alterations usually took weeks, but it was clear that the Crossroads Society pulled some heavy strings in Savannah and didn't wait for anyone. The question was—why? If Sugar knew she sure wasn't talking, but I also knew she wouldn't let me walk straight into danger without a warning. She made it clear I needed to direct all questions about the society to Finely Cooper himself.

We reached the lot where we'd parked. Sugar climbed into her ancient Cadillac Eldorado—that by the grace of God was still running—and rolled down her window as I walked away. "You need some help with your makeup Saturday night?"

"Makeup I can handle. But I can use some help with my hair," I quickly added when I saw the disappointment on her face. "Come by my place around five o'clock. We can get drunk before I leave."

She laughed and accepted my invitation. "You know, Katie, you just walked out of that shop with about four thousand dollars' worth of freebies."

"Five thousand," I corrected, still wondering if it all needed to be returned Monday morning.

She grinned but quickly sobered up as she cranked the sleepy engine a couple of times. It moaned a bit but eventually turned over. "That's a hell of a gift from a stranger," she said as she shifted into drive and started to pull away. "You might want to think on that."

6

For three days, I thought about what Sugar had said to me. Why would a group of strangers invest enough money to buy a fairly decent used car into a stranger just to get her to attend a ball? I figured this Victor Tuse guy with the killer tattoo had to be legit, and tonight I was about to get a little more insight into why the spirit chose me—and let me live—to break the binds of his prison.

I came home the night before to find another note on my doorstep, informing me that a car would be sent to pick me up at seven-thirty. That cleared up the problem of locating the ball, seeing how the invitation didn't give an address.

Prompt as ever, Sugar knocked on my door at five o'clock sharp. Today she was a brunette stuck in the eighties, wearing ten pound earrings and a vintage Madonna T-shirt. She took one look at my dull and fatigued eyes and shook her head. "Oh no, baby," she said, heading for the kitchen. "You got to be razor sharp tonight." She filled the kettle with water and pulled a paper bag out of her purse. "I was afraid of this. You been gnawing on worry all week, haven't you?" When the water was near a boil, she filled a mug and dumped a teabag of herbs into it. "Drink this."

"What is it?" I asked, wary about consuming an unknown substance just before I had to slip on a thirty-six-hundred-dollar dress and pretend I knew how to act in one. I was nervous enough. The last thing I needed was to be altered in any way.

She tapped her fingernails on the countertop, waiting for me to comply. "Sugar knows her herbs, baby. There's all kinds of root folks around here and my mama raised her a good one."

I brought the cup to my lips tentatively. "I didn't know you were into that kind of stuff."

"Honey, you got to be a survivor when the good Lord gives you something different. Them herbs is backup. You about to walk into the lion's den, and the last thing you need is to go in there looking like their next meal. Now drink it up."

I drank the tea, and within a few minutes I had my energy back and a bright set of blue eyes. It seemed counterproductive to mix up a batch of margaritas, but Sugar assured me that one little drink wouldn't hurt, and would in fact enhance the concoction of herbs.

"So what do you know about the people I'll be rubbing elbows with tonight?" I asked as we sipped our drinks on the patio. She'd been intentionally holding back information since the day Finley Cooper walked into my shop. "Don't you think I should be prepared before walking in there tonight?"

She took a steady breath, staring at the line of trees in the backyard. "You about to meet some pretty powerful folks, Katie. Kind of people whose ancestors built this city. Kind of people you don't want on your bad side." Her glass landed on the table as she turned to look at me. "Whatever you do tonight, don't you let them smell your fear. I don't care if you got to swallow down ten bourbons to keep you cocky, you shove that fear down deep."

"Good to know," I said, heading to the kitchen for another drink.

"Hell no, girl!" Sugar followed me and peeled my fingers off the pitcher. "I said one. Ain't nothing good gonna come from getting you smashed before you even get there."

"You haven't seen me drink, Sugar."

"May *be*, but them herbs might think otherwise." She grabbed me by the arm and pulled me toward the bedroom. "Let's get that hair up so we can make your face."

"It might be better if I wear it down. I don't want to *offend* Savannah's finest before I have a chance to introduce myself."

She dropped my arm and braced her hands on her hips, straightening her posture for what I assumed was about to be a good tongue lashing. "You got all this"—she waved her hand up and down my body—"and you think the first thing they gonna see is that ink on your skin? If I had your looks I'd be running down Bull Street naked."

My brow raised. "I bet you've actually done that, haven't you?"

"Goddamn right." Her righteous look lost its grit. "You got to know who you are, Katie B, and like it. Can't worry about what anyone else wants you to be." Her eyes softened and I could see a lifetime of lessons learned stirring behind them. "Now what's it gonna be?"

She followed me into the bedroom as I sat in a chair and handed her my brush. "Put it up. Turn me into a siren, Sugar."

A DARK GRAY Bentley Mulsanne pulled up to my curb at exactly seven-thirty. I had to look twice through the window to make sure it was stopping at my house and not just taking a shortcut back to West Charlton Street.

Sugar walked me out and eyed the car. "Mm-hmm. That's what I thought. Them fat cats are already showing you some real ass-kissing, besides that dress you got on." She glanced at my sparkling blue gown and then licked her palm to smooth the sides of my chignon.

"That's kind of gross, Sugar."

Ignoring my protest, she finished grooming me. "I'll call you in the morning to make sure them lions didn't eat you."

The driver got out and opened the back door for me. I stepped inside, feeling a little bit like that sacrificial lamb Sugar inadvertently suggested. I had to keep in mind that the people I was about to meet needed me for some yet to be revealed reason, and if they turned out to be more foe than friend, my dragon would step up and put an end to it. The part that worried me the most was the emergence of *said* dragon unexpectedly, without any real provocation. I had no intention of revealing what I was unless it was absolutely necessary.

The seats were covered in the finest leather I'd ever had the pleasure of wearing or sitting on. It wasn't until I noticed my house disappearing from view that I realized the car was moving. "Damn," I muttered. "This must be what the Concorde feels like."

"Did you say something, Miss Bishop?"

"Nope. Just taking it all in."

The driver smiled at me through the rearview mirror and suggested I look inside the cabinet between the seats. I pushed the button at the top and the cover descended into a makeshift bar, revealing chilled flutes with a bottle of champagne between them. "Make yourself comfortable, Miss Bishop."

I could drink hard liquor and red wine all night, but hell hath no fury on a mixture of champagne with any other kind of alcohol, at least in my experience. "Where are we going?" I asked. As I spoke the black shades on the side windows automatically closed, blocking my view of the outside. "What is this?"

"No need for alarm, Miss Bishop. The location of the ball must be kept private for security purposes. We'll arrive shortly."

Since I had no intention of jumping from a moving Bentley

and I had a feeling the doors would be locked even if I tried, I settled back in the luxurious seats and calmed my overactive imagination. *Don't you let them smell your fear.* Sugar's sage advice kept repeating in my head.

The car shifted right, and through the front window I could see a large house in the distance. As we approached, I could hear the tires transition from the asphalt pavement of the main road onto something that sounded more like cobblestone. We came to a stop and the black shades receded from the windows, giving me a view of the elaborate double staircase leading up to the front door. Standing on those steps was Finley Cooper, wearing a midnight blue tuxedo with black satin lapels and bow tie.

"Miss Bishop," Cooper greeted as the driver opened the door to help me out. My leg exited first, the fabric sliding away from my skin all the way up to the top of my thigh. I was so nervous I'd forgotten about the exaggerated split up the side of the dress. When I glanced up both men were staring at my leg. The driver quickly recovered and got on with the task of helping me out of the Bentley, but Cooper didn't flinch. If I didn't know better, I'd swear he wanted me to see him eyeing my thigh. He was a good-looking man but a little old for me. Too much of a daddy figure. "That's a beautiful dress you're wearing. I trust you found Miss Winfield to be accommodating?"

"If it were up to her I'd be wearing a paper sack."

His eyes ran over my bare shoulders, my tattoos. "Yes, well, given the circumstances of our acquaintance, your brand of beauty seems fitting." He held his arm out to escort me up the steps. "Shall we?"

We walked through the large double doors and the room seemed to pause for all eyes to catch a fleeting glance at the new arrival. A moment later the murmuring in the room resumed. The house was spectacular: mile-high rooms with molded ceilings, dark pine floors covered with Persian rugs, floor-to-ceiling columns separating the rooms. From what I could see, there wasn't a room without a chandelier or a wall without a fine paint-ing. Some of the walls themselves were the canvas. And then there were the colors. The rooms were painted in the most beau-tiful shades of soft blues, greens, and creams. The quintessential palette for such a grand home.

"This isn't your house by any chance, is it?" I asked. That Bentley out there was proof of his ability to swing a pad like this.

He laughed quietly. "I'm afraid this is too much house for me, Miss Bishop. But it is beautiful, isn't it?"

I nodded and continued to look around. For a ball, the crowd was surprisingly small. Maybe forty or fifty people dressed to the nines. "I thought there'd be more people here tonight," I commented.

"The Crossroads Society is an intimate group. We usually open the ball up to outsiders, but in light of recent events we decided to make it members only this year."

"I'm not a member, Mr. Cooper."

"Not yet, but I think after tonight you might reconsider that invitation."

I was about to delve deeper into that foregone conclusion of his when someone touched my shoulder.

"Miss Bishop. I am delighted that you decided to attend." Davina McCabe was standing behind me when I turned around. She'd gone from a frail old woman to a sharply dressed Southern socialite wearing a flaming red sheath dress that trailed on the floor behind her. Her hair was different, too. Gone was the granny bun, replaced with a sleek chin-length bob. "How's that grandson of mine? Has he recovered?"

"I think he'll live. And please call me Katie."

She glanced at Cooper, and I got the feeling she was wondering how much I knew.

He took my arm and walked me into the great room. From there he proceeded to introduce me around to just about everyone in the place. Most of them were complete strangers, but I did recognize a few people from the local news.

"Let me introduce you to Agnes Freemont." He led me to a woman standing with her back to us. She turned around and I immediately recognized her from a local bakery a few blocks south of the shop.

"I know you," I said. "You work at Le Petit Gateau bakery, right?"

She shot me a wide smile. "Actually, I own it."

"Ah, of course. I own—"

"MagicInk," she said, finishing my sentence. "I know who you are, Miss Bishop." She motioned around the room. "We all know who you are."

The voice seemed slightly aggressive, but her face remained friendly and welcoming. When her impenetrable stare began to make me uncomfortable, I pulled my eyes away and looked at Cooper. "Is there a bar in here, or do I have to wait for one of those waiters with white gloves to come around with a tray loaded with glasses of wine and champagne?"

Cooper let out a hearty laugh. "I think I can scrounge us up a couple of proper drinks—and some of those fancy appetizers if you'd like. What'll you have?"

"I know we're in mint julep country," I said, "but I could sure go for a glass of single malt, if it's not too much trouble."

"You do realize a mint julep is nothing more than bourbon with a splash of sugar and mint?" He leaned closer to whisper. "Between you and me, Miss Bishop, I don't think anyone here actually knows how to make one."

"What a relief," I said. "Sugar and alcohol should rarely meet, but I do like a margarita now and then. I'll stick to scotch tonight. Preferably an Islay. Neat."

"You are a surprise, Miss Bishop." He grinned and glanced at my neck in that way a man does, lacking discretion. "A delightful one."

While Cooper went to fetch my drink, I quickly moved around the room to get away from Agnes Freemont. I must have looked like a real wallflower, because a man came up to me and asked if I'd like to join him and his friends across the room. He pointed to a group of two women and three men huddled in a tight circle of conversation. A few of them kept glancing over at us, I supposed, to see if the bait worked. "Why not," I said, wondering if we were ever going to get on with the real reason for me being here.

"I'm David, by the way." He placed his hand at the small of my back to move me along. "David Hayes." That's a beautiful dress you're wearing," he added.

"Thank you. I'm Katie Bishop."

He chuckled "Of course you are."

I stopped midway across the room, forcing him to turn around and look at me. "Why is it that everyone here seems to know that?"

"Well," he said, taking my arm and compelling me to keep moving, "it's not every day that we meet someone who has the ability to break a two-hundred-year-old ward. Not to mention survive doing it."

We reached his friends and I was greeted with five sets of staring eyes and stone-cold expressions. I recognized one of the men from a story in the local paper. He was a politician, although I couldn't remember what kind. An alderman or a commissioner. Before David could introduce me—as if necessary—one of the women spoke up. "Are you planning to join our little hunting team?" she asked with a sly grin, like the question was a formality and I'd already been inducted.

"I see you've already been introduced to some of our members," Cooper said, handing me my drink and glaring at the six people who were suddenly losing their cocky smiles. "I hope they haven't scared you away with their overenthusiasm to bring you into our exclusive little club." The look he gave them was sobering.

"Not at all," I said. "We were discussing hunting."

His brow went up. "Oh? Well, let's get you introduced to a few more folks. We'll have plenty to discuss shortly, and I'd hate for you to get the wrong idea because of something said over a few too many bourbons."

I took a hefty swig of my scotch, the finest I'd ever tasted, and instantly felt softened from the sensation of the warm peat rushing down my throat. A few more would have me relaxed just fine. My eyes wandered around the perimeter of the room and landed on a young woman standing at the window. With black hair reaching down to her waist and skin as white as snow, she reminded me of a porcelain doll. I sensed she was uncomfortable in a room with so many people milling around, and her reluctance to mingle with the rest of the guests made her seem awkward and out of place in this grand house.

"I want to meet her," I said, pointing to the ghostly girl.

Cooper followed my finger and smiled when he saw its target. He took my arm and led me across the room. The girl startled a bit when he spoke, breaking her distracted gaze out the window. "Emmaline," he murmured, "I'd like you to meet someone." The gentle manner in which he touched her arm did not go unnoticed. Her haunted eyes looked at his first and then turned to mine. She stared at me for a moment, and then her breath hitched as a discreet smile formed on her face.

"Katie," I said, extending my hand. The seemingly shy woman reached out and embraced me in a hug, her hand gently covering my exposed tattoo.

"I see you," she whispered into my ear before releasing me and settling back into the demure girl with the sad hazel eyes.

"Emmaline's family has strong roots in our organization. Isn't that right?"

She seemed to shrink deeper into the fabric of her black dress, which covered most of her skin. The only exposed parts were her hands, neck, and face. "Yes, Fin. We go very . . . deep."

I couldn't take my eyes off her. She emitted the strangest aura, and the feeling of familiarity like we'd met before. But I could never forget that face. If we'd met I would have remembered.

The sound of music suddenly floated through the air, travelling through a tall double archway leading into the next room. The room with the dancefloor, I assumed. Cooper hijacked the conversation, breaking the spell between Emmaline and me. "I'd ask you to dance, Miss Bishop, but our host is making her entrance.

The room fell silent as all eyes shifted toward the grand staircase leading to the second floor. A woman in her late forties or early fifties, dressed in a metallic pantsuit that looked like it had just come off a Paris runway slowly descended the steps, surveying the room until her eyes landed on mine. Without blinking, she kept them fixed on me with hawk-like focus. She made her way down with a leisurely glide and headed straight for us, glancing for a moment at Emmaline before focusing back on me. "This is her?" she asked while her eyes tracked back and forth between mine, then trailed down my face to my neck and shoulders.

"Katie Bishop," Cooper introduced, "I'd like you to meet Mrs. Whitman."

"Lillian," she added. Her smile widened but her face seemed tense, like she was conflicted between welcoming me and wanting to slap me. "You're a very odd woman, Miss Bishop." She turned to the crowd that had gathered around the three of us, swinging her eyes around the circle at their faces. "Leave," she ordered in a calm but firm tone. A hushed gasp filled the room but no one argued, clearly knowing who was in charge.

I glanced at Fin, shocked by the sudden dismissal. The ball was over before it even had a chance to get started. Was it all a guise just to get me here . . . the extravagant dress, the Bentley?

They could have saved a lot of money by just inviting me over for a drink and handing me the address.

"Don't you worry, Miss Bishop," Cooper said. "These folks are used to having their fun and revelry interrupted. They'll just take it somewhere else. And knowing Lillian, she'll make up for it with some over the top dinner party in the future."

The crowd seemed unfazed and began funneling toward the entrance. "Council can stay," Lillian added.

When the room thinned out and all that was left was a handful of people—the ones Lillian referred to as "the Council," I was relieved that Emmaline was one of them. She was the only one in the room I felt comfortable with and I had no idea why. But I planned to find out.

"Now," Lillian continued, looking at me, "let's have a little talk and see if we can make a deal."

7

The eight of us adjourned to a room with a stately oval table and thousands of books lining two walls of floor-to-ceiling shelves. The library, obviously.

"Would anyone like to refresh their drink before we begin?" Lillian asked.

I held up my glass. "Please." Something told me I was going to need it, although it was probably wiser to stay sober for the discussion.

Cooper got up and left the room. He returned a minute later with a bottle of scotch in one hand and bourbon in the other. He set the scotch on the table in front of me and took the bourbon with him as he took a seat and turned the discussion over to Lillian Whitman.

"I trust some of you have already met Miss Bishop." she said. "For those of you who haven't, there she is. We'll get around to introductions in a minute." All eyes around the table turned to look at me. "Miss Bishop is the woman responsible for setting the spirit free." Those friendly eyes weren't so friendly anymore, except for Cooper's and Emmaline's, which looked more sympathetic than accusatory. "Of course, it was unintentional." She looked at me for an unnerving few seconds, as if waiting for me to dispute that. "Isn't that right, Miss Bishop?"

I glared back at her. "I don't like games, Mrs. Whitman. You're going to have to tell me a little more than Mr. Cooper did if you want answers." I grabbed the bottle and filled my glass while I waited for her to enlighten me.

"Fair enough." She opened her mouth but hesitated. "Why don't we do away with the formality? Call me Lillian. May I call you Katie?"

I nodded once in concession. "You can start, Lillian, by telling me what this is all about."

She got up and walked across the library to an imposing kneehole desk that matched the grandeur of the room. She grabbed a large book lying on top of it and carried it back to the table. "*This* is what this is all about." With a forceful shove, she sent the book sliding across the table.

Before it slammed into my lap, I caught it and turned it right side up. The book looked old, with no title and a large unfamiliar symbol on the cover. "What am I looking at?" I asked.

"It's a replica," she said. "The original is very old and I wouldn't recommend touching it."

"Okay," I snorted, flipping through the first few pages of the book. I noted the lack of front matter, but I doubted whoever authored the original was concerned with publishing rights. The pages were parchment, obviously imitation because who wrote on sheepskin these days? On the first page that wasn't blank was a drawing of an animal, some kind of cat. On closer inspection, I noticed the eyes were very human-like, intelligent as they seemed to look directly at me from the parchment. I found it difficult to look away or turn to the next page.

"What am I looking at?"

"It's a grimoire," Cooper interjected. "And not a friendly one."

I knew enough about magic to know that a grimoire was

nothing to mess with—a book of spells and incantations. I tried to read the caption around the drawing. "What language is this?"

Lillian smiled weakly. "That's a very good question. It seems to be some sort of a hybrid language." She went on to explain that the grimoire had been discovered in the slave quarters of a plantation near the Savannah River. What made it so unique was that the language appeared to be some sort of Goidelic language mixed with several African languages. The only link between those languages was the fact that Scots migrated to Georgia to protect the coast in the mid-1700s. A decade later, the Atlantic slave trade at the Port of Savannah was in full swing. The two cultures could have easily clashed—or aligned—to create the grimoire.

"You mean you don't know what it says?"

"No," she replied. "But we do know that the book is danger-ous. There are two spirits trapped inside by some pretty powerful magic. Does the name Legvu mean anything to you?"

I'd never heard it before. "No. Should it?"

"Not necessarily, but I promise you'll never forget it after today. Legvu is a god. A rogue god who tends to be a little unpre-dictable. A trickster and a master of languages, hence the convo-luted mix of Goidelic and African. Broken into two separate spirits to dilute his strength, and held that way by a powerful incantation that can only be broken by deciphering the spell. So you see, Katie, no living person knows what those words mean, and that's exactly how it needs to stay." She paused and consid-ered what she was about to tell me next. "Based on oral history, we know Legvu came to Savannah on one of the slave ships. We believe he hitched a ride on a young woman who was with child. When the child was born, Legvu immediately took control of it. Grew from a babe into an old man in a day. As you can imagine, his master was suspicious. But it was what they found in his possession that set their plan into motion."

"Legvu was carrying a bag of bones." Fin said, hijacking the story. "The bones of Adro. Half man, half god of pure evil. Most people would call it myth, but lucky for us our forefathers knew better."

"That's an interesting story," I noted. "You Savannahians are full of them."

"I would say that's true, Katie," Lillian said. "But unfortunately, the story is real. The ancestors—we'll just leave it at that—obliged the master and broke Legvu into the two spirits and imprisoned them in the grimoire. If those spirits escape and find their way back to one another, they'll be a force of evil in their own right. Throw in those bones and—" She shook her head, stopping short of describing the destruction that would fall on the city. "And now one of them has managed to break free and manifest into an unsuspecting host."

"What happened to the bones?" I asked.

"The bones are at rest," Lillian continued. "That's the one good thing that has come out of all this. We know that Legvu buried them at a crossroads, but they've never been found, which is for the best. Best to leave them buried."

I nodded. "So that's where the society got its name."

"Well, partly," she explained. "You see, Katie, Savannah itself is an intersection where the supernatural roads meet. The society has grown into more than just the keepers of that grimoire. Our mission is to steward the well-being of the entire city. As a major crossroads, you can imagine the kind of things that try to upset the balance of good and evil in this place, yes?"

I looked at the benign faces around the table and thought, *God help Savannah*, if this was its front line.

Lillian got back down to business. "The book has already killed several people who've had the balls to handle it."

With an involuntary jerk, I let go of the page I was touching and pushed my chair away from the table.

Cooper laughed. "It won't bite, Miss Bishop. As Lillian said, it's a replica."

I pulled myself together and looked at all the faces around the table. Emmaline was staring at me, silently forming words that I couldn't hear, her fingers twisting nervously around the crushed velvet sleeve covering her arm. And then she croaked out, "Look at the next page."

Lillian's eyes shot to Emmaline. "Quiet, girl!" Emmaline shrunk deeper into her chair like a drying sponge. Realizing who she'd just yelled at, Lillian lowered her tone. "I'm not angry with you, Emmaline, but please let me handle this."

The words had been said, and there was no way I wasn't turning that page. I flipped to the next one and looked at the incomprehensible text. My eyes were immediately drawn to the picture on the opposite page. It was the same symbol I remembered so vividly from my dreams—the one I'd tattooed on Victor Tuse's back. The air left my lungs as the sound of my beating heart filled my ears, my reaction visceral. As soon as I laid eyes on it I felt sick, knew the gravity of what I'd done.

Miss Bishop, you've been duped. Fin Cooper's words made sense now. I was an unwilling accomplice in freeing something demonic. "Where's the original book?" I asked.

By now Lillian's face had gone stone cold. "It's in a vault under our feet. About a hundred feet below the foundation of this house, to be exact. It's been locked away for more than two hundred and fifty years. None of its evil has ever been able to manifest. Until now."

Cooper got up and headed over to the desk and rummaged through the top drawer. He found the cigars he was looking for and dropped down into the swivel chair. He bit off the tip and propped his feet up on the desk. "Anyone mind?" he asked before lighting it. With no objections, he lit the cigar and puffed it briefly before continuing. "As I mentioned the day we met, Miss Bishop, there are two. Two evil spirits locked away under this house. Of course, now there's only one trapped inside that book.

The other one is running around Savannah doing God knows what."

"Where are my manners?" Lillian said out of the blue, as if we'd just been discussing garden parties instead of demonic possession. "I believe you've already met Emmaline, but I don't believe you've met the rest of the Council. Or have you?" I shook my head. "Well then, let's have a proper introduction." She nodded to the man with the cropped salt and pepper hair and dark skin sitting to my right.

"Dr. Greene," he said, extending his hand. "I treat a lot of the bad tickers in this town." Noting my confusion, he clarified. "Cardiologist. I'll be seeing Fin in my office real soon if he doesn't lay off them cigars."

"Now you could have objected, Moses," Cooper countered, taking the hint and extinguishing his Cuban smoke.

Like participants at a seminar, everyone around the table took their turn introducing themselves. There was Alma Turner who taught fifth grade at a private girl's school, and Pete Harper who spent his days operating a sanitation truck through the neighborhoods of Savannah. Finally, there was José, a flamboyant hairstylist from an upscale salon that catered to some of Savannah's wealthier citizens. No last name—just José. He made a point of letting me know his services weren't cheap, but he did offer discounts to Council members. He glanced at my head and offered to touch up my protruding roots for free. Funny, considering my hair color was natural.

"Everyone at this table is a direct descendent of the original custodians of the grimoire," Lillian explained. "Except for you, that is." Then she glanced at the youngest member—Emmaline. "If one of us dies, our children are elevated to the Council seat."

Once the formalities were out of the way, she got right to the point. "The question that has us all so perplexed, Katie, is why the spirit chose you?"

I shrugged. "From what Mr. Cooper told me I wasn't the first one it chose."

"Now that is true, Miss—" he stopped and sighed. "Can we please dispense with the surnames? I'll call you Katie if you can manage to call me Fin." I nodded in agreement as he continued. "Maybe it didn't seek you out. Maybe it just got lucky. Third time's a charm."

Emmaline had that same pained look on her face as earlier. Like she was bursting to say something. *I see you*, she'd whispered in my ear when we met earlier that night. Under the circumstances, maybe it was best to just come out with my secret. They'd probably think I was crazy anyway. Might buy me a ticket out of this place so I could get back to my life.

"I don't think it just got lucky. I think it was drawn to me, and I know why it couldn't kill me." I took a deep breath in preparation for my big reveal. "Dr. Greene, can you help me with my zipper?" I asked as I stood up and turned my back to the table. He stood up next to me, nervously glancing around the table before complying with the strange and inappropriate request.

"It's all right, Moses," Lillian assured. "Help the girl with her zipper." He reached for the slider at the top and began to pull it down the back of my dress.

"I'm a—"

"She's a creature!" Emmaline blurted out before I could explain.

I gawked at the shy specter of a girl, staring back at me with wide eyes. I figured she knew there was something off about me, but how did she see all that? Then I remembered the way her hand nearly caressed my tattoo. "How did you know?" I asked.

A flood of murmuring traveled around the table. Seeing my shocked expression, Lillian clarified what I should have recognized from the moment I saw the girl. After all, my best friend back in

New York was a pretty powerful one. "Emmaline is a witch. A real one," she added. "Not one of those new age proprietors over there on River Street. She's a priestess of one of Savannah's oldest and finest covens—Blackthorn Grove. Don't be cross with her, Katie. We all knew there was something special about you."

Emmaline seemed to shy away from the accolades. A very modest witch, I noted.

Fin got up from the desk and headed back to his seat at the table. "Well, I wasn't expecting that. I thought maybe you were a witch yourself." I let the sides of the dress fall away from my back. "That's a fine tattoo," he said. "But there isn't a self-respecting tattoo artist in the city who doesn't practice what he or she preaches. What makes yours different? And what's this creature Emmaline is referring to?"

"Take a closer look." I could feel the dragon begin to stir and lift away from my skin before settling back down into a flat canvas of inanimate ink.

"A dragon!" Emmaline gasped.

Fin shook his head. "No wonder the damn thing couldn't kill you."

Dr. Greene hesitated when I asked him to zip my dress back up. "It's okay, Doctor. It won't bite." He carefully complied and then retook his seat. "You see, it's not just a tattoo—it *is* a dragon. It lives on my back. I think Victor Tuse walked into my shop because we have something in common."

After a few moments of quiet gawking, Lillian broke the silence. "All the more reason to bring you on board. The services of a magical creature could be quite useful to the society." She stood up and extended her hand across the table. "Welcome to the club, Miss Bishop."

I glanced at her outstretched palm but didn't take it, fearing the binding contract it might create. "I haven't agreed to anything. I'm not one of your descendants, so what do you need me for? The spirit is out. That tattoo is already on Victor Tuse's back, so the deed is done."

Fin spoke up. "Because the other one hasn't managed to escape—yet. If the first spirit was able to snake its way out of that book, the other one could very well find a way out, too. We'll do our damnedest to keep that from happening, but if it does my guess is it'll make a beeline straight for you." His expression went lax with a surrendered look in his eyes, one I hadn't seen on his face before. He always seemed so controlled, shrewd. "We're not completely confident we can recapture that AWOL spirit you aided and abetted the other day, let alone both halves if that grimoire buried below this house breaks wide open. But our chances are substantially more optimistic if we don't have to face Legvu in his true form, which is what will happen if spirit number two gets you to apply that final tattoo. We can help each other, Katie."

"If the other half breaks free it won't matter," José mused as he examined his manicured fingernails. "We'll all be toast."

"He's right," Lillian agreed. "If the other one escapes we'll be looking at Armageddon. It's going to take some serious magic to put that genie back in the bottle, but we're working on a solution to that little dilemma."

I stated the obvious. "I'll just say no next time Victor Tuse walks into my shop asking for a tattoo. Got a big sign right against the wall stating my right to refuse service to anyone."

"Katie," Fin began, condescendence lacing his words, "you do realize the second spirit will probably need an immediate host while it looks for its other half. Probably accost the first unfortunate soul who passes by. It won't be Victor Tuse walking into your shop next time."

"Then I'll just keep an eye out for the tattoo itself. If a stranger walks into my shop with a drawing of it, I'll refuse service."

Lillian looked confused "And how will you recognize the

tattoo?" she asked. "Do you plan to turn away every new customer who walks through your doors? That little business of yours won't survive that kind of weeding out. Not to mention the fact that it can take anyone as a host, including an existing customer. Hell, it might take up residence in one of your own employees."

I glanced back and forth between her and Fin, realizing they didn't know my connection to Victor Tuse's tattoo. "Because I dreamed about that tattoo before Victor Tuse walked into my shop, and I'd bet money that I'm going to dream about the next one before it walks through my door, too"

Fin stood up abruptly, nearly knocking his chair backward in the process. "You failed to mention that pertinent little fact."

"Didn't I?" I guess it never came up during our introduction. At the time I just wanted him out of my shop.

"Then I guess there's no doubt the spirit sought you out," he said. "The damn thing has been in your head, Katie." When I didn't react the way he'd obviously expected, with fear and pleading for the society's help, he shook his head. "You still don't get it, do you? Without our help, you're a dead woman. The spirits will use you as long as you cooperate, but once they realize you're on to them, they'll find a way to kill you."

"What makes you think they can?" I asked. "You said yourself that the one running loose right now killed the first two artists who tried to finish the tattoo on Tuse's back. I believe you likened its lack of self-control to a sexual act that I'd prefer not to repeat in front of all these strangers. But I'm still alive."

A humorless smile crept up his face. "I believe you just proved to the spirit that you're worth keeping around a little longer. The others were too weak. But don't confuse your useful-ness with the ability to match its strength. You are just a pawn, Katie Bishop. A toy it will tire of as soon as it gets what it wants." He sat back down and took a deep breath. "I guess this is the part where we bargain."

From what I'd been told, Fin was a shrewd businessman who owned a good part of this town. The word "bargain" coming from his mouth automatically put me on guard. I did my best to keep from looking nervous or weak, because that's what men like Finley Cooper preyed upon. One poorly executed decision could mean a lifetime of servitude.

"I'm listening."

He made himself more comfortable by pushing his chair back and raising his feet up on the edge of the sturdy walnut table, to the disapproval of his host. He glanced at Lillian but kept them there. We may have been in the grande dame's house, but it was obvious who called the shots.

"We'd like to offer some incentive for your participation in the society. Something that might make it easier for you to pull the trigger on your decision to join our club." He hesitated and looked at Dr. Greene sitting next to me, nowhere near the large desk. "Doctor," he continued, "would you mind going over to that desk and getting me another one of them cigars?" His eyes remained fixed on his prey until Greene sheepishly complied. The doctor got up hesitantly and went to the desk. He pulled a cigar and lighter from the drawer, then grabbed the ashtray and cutter as an afterthought before headed over to Fin. Fin punctuated his authority by waiting for Dr. Greene to cut and light the tip. "Why thank you, Doctor."

Greene retook his seat with his eyes fixed downward on his twitching right hand, and Fin proceeded to lay a deal on the table. "We're prepared to offer you protection from the spirit. Now we can't guarantee that it won't find a way to kill you, but we can make it a hell of a lot more difficult than just slipping into your house or place of business and slitting that pretty little throat of yours."

I scoffed. "That's reassuring, but I'll need a little more incentive than that."

"Has it ever occurred to you to ask what kind of magic is

powerful enough to trap those things in that book?" he asked. "That spell binds them with their own magic. Puts the bone to them. Sometimes I wonder if that cryptic language in the grimoire means anything at all. A smokescreen to confuse and hide the simplicity of a simple bone incantation. Damn things can't fight their own magic any more than you or I can cut out our own heart. It's just the way things work, Miss Bishop."

We were back to surnames again. I suspected it was just another mind game he was playing with me. "Your point?"

"My point is that sometimes the simplest solution is the best solution. Don't overcomplicate what we're offering. Joining the Crossroads Society is a no-brainer. Can't hurt, and it just might keep you alive."

"Are you offering to sprinkle me with bones to keep the bad spirits away?"

"Something like that. Although I offer no guarantee that it'll work," he said with amusement. "But I can offer you some incentive. Sweeten the deal." He removed his shoes from the table and yanked his bow tie from his neck, extinguishing the obnoxious cigar before continuing. "If you become a member of the society and help us hunt down the spirit, I'll hand you the deed to that building you work out of."

I could feel my jaw slacken, but I immediately tightened it back up so he couldn't see how easily he'd enticed me. "Let me get this straight. All I have to do is join the society and help you recapture the spirit, and you'll give me the building?" It was in my best interest to cooperate anyway. "All of it?"

"That's right, Miss Bishop. Free and clear."

8

The way they were rubbing the bridge of my nose and limiting the natural sunlight that was so vital to my cheery mood, my sunglasses were beginning to irritate more than help. I never understood the appeal of wearing them other than for fashion. Some of my friends would rather forego shoes than leave the house without their shades.

I'd only had a few drinks the night before but my head was saying otherwise, and those shades did help to cut the glare that was sending spikes of pain between my eyes. I suspected it was the pre-party margaritas I'd indulged in prior. As much as I liked a good margarita, tequila and I did not mix. Not to mention the additional drinks I had when I got home, replaying Fin Cooper's offer in my head repeatedly to make sure I'd understood it right. But I wasn't holding my breath, considering I'd failed to get that generous offer in writing.

"Morning, little Miss Sunshine." Sugar was already at the shop, holding out a cup of coffee to me as I walked inside. "I figured you could use this after a night with all them alcoholics over there at the society. It's from a little place around the corner."

"You know I have a coffeemaker, Sugar."

She grinned as I took the cup and raised it to my lips. "Oh, I know what kind of stuff comes outta that contraption, but I figured you was gonna appreciate a little extra octane this morning."

I took a big swallow and nearly spit it on the floor. "Shit, Sugar! What the hell is that? Tar?"

"That's some Cuban coffee, baby. A whole lot of caffeine and a whole lot of sugar. Exactly what you need after a night with them society folks."

I unceremoniously dropped the cup on the counter. "Jesus! That stuff will give you a heart attack."

She took a seat in one of the chairs and scrutinized me while I milled around the front desk. "Well?" she eventually said. "You gonna just stand there toying with my head, or are you gonna tell me what happened last night?" By the way her legs were crossed and that foot of hers was swinging back and forth, I knew she was losing patience with my lack of disclosure.

"Damn, woman. If I wanted the third degree every time I went out, I'd get myself a husband."

Her eyebrows flew up toward the ceiling. "Now, I wouldn't recommend that."

Mouse came through the front door, slumped over and dragging her feet. She was definitely not a morning person, which was why I preferred to take the early walk-ins myself. Nine a.m. clients who specifically requested her services did so at their own peril. "Morning," she mumbled as she shuffled past me and headed for the coffee machine.

"Got you a cup of the good stuff on the counter, Mouse," Sugar said. "Might want to throw it in the microwave first to heat it up."

She grabbed the Cuban coffee I'd discarded on the counter and took a swig of the lukewarm crude oil. Without flinching, she finished it off and dumped her backpack on the floor. "Thanks, Sugar."

"You knew, didn't you?" I asked, referring to the livelihood of the Crossroads Society.

"Honey, you got to be a little more specific than that," she replied evasively. After a minute of silence and feeling the seething accusations coming from my eyes, she finally relented. "You asking if I know what they got hidden under that house?"

It dawned on me that it was possible she knew all about the grimoire, but the part about the evil spirit I'd let loose would be a revelation. If I told her about that, I'd have to tell her my secret, too. Then again, she'd become one of my closest friends, and if Fin and his people trusted her with their secrets, mine would be safe too. It also meant that the odds were pretty good that she'd believe me, seeing how malicious spirits were a main concern of the society's charter.

I thought it wise to vet her a little further before giving up everybody's secrets. "What do you know about grimoires?"

She glanced at Mouse and gave me a warning look. "Not here, baby," she whispered.

"Mouse," I said, eyeing the clock on the wall, "Sugar and I are going over to Lou's to get some breakfast. You want me to bring you anything?" Mouse shook her head. "Sea Bass and Abel should be dragging their asses in here any minute now. They're already late."

Sugar and I headed to the diner across the street to have a quick come-to-Jesus about what was going on in this town. I also planned to find out if Fin had inadvertently left out any important details that might inspire me to go back to Lillian Whitman's house to turn in my membership card.

We crossed the street and headed into the diner. Lou's buttermilk biscuits were second to none. The hash browns were just as good, nice and crispy on both sides. But it was the atmosphere I liked the most. No pretense and no bullshit. If you didn't know what you wanted when you got up to the counter, Lou or Mae would decide for you. And if you didn't like it they'd move you to the back of the line until you made up your mind. I learned that the hard way the first time I walked in and hemmed and hawed over the menu. And God help you if you caused a ruckus in their fine establishment.

Sugar ordered two fried eggs and a side of bacon, and I decided on the egg and cheese biscuit. We sat at the end booth where the sun shining through the front window had a little mercy, with my hangover and all. "Like a little egg with that hot sauce?" I asked as Sugar practically poured half the bottle on top of her sunny-side-up eggs. Then she shook enough pepper on them to make it look like an army of ants was travelling over her plate.

"Don't you mind my food, baby." She glanced up at me through her long lashes and grinned. "How do you think I stay so spicy?" Taking a heaping bite, she continued around a mouthful of food. "All right, now. You better ask me them questions you got on your mind before I finish this plate."

After considering my options, I just came out with it. "How do you know about the book—the grimoire? And why didn't you bother to mention it to me yesterday, or the day before that, or—"

"All right, you've made that point of yours." She chewed thoughtfully as the wheels turned in her head. "You got to understand something, Katie. Folks around here ain't all what they seem." She took another bite of eggs and quickly swallowed before leaning into the table. "*I* ain't what I seem," she muttered. The butt of her clenched palms landed on the table with her fork held tight. "Lord Jesus! What the hell is wrong with me?"

Now, Sugar wasn't a particularly religious person, so the mention of Jesus was a sign I'd hit upon a sticky subject requiring her to have a little faith in me. I leaned in with my brow pulled into an exaggerated knot. "You mean you weren't born looking like this?" In all the months she'd been patronizing my shop and breaking bread with me, we'd never actually had that conversation. But everyone knew who Lady Sugar was.

"Don't you go there, Katie B," she warned.

I smiled and ended her misery, because clearly we both had some sharing to do. "Look, Sugar, you need to tell me if you know about that book and all the evil things trapped inside of it." I guess she knew now, didn't she?

"Well, what in Hades do you think?" she hissed. "Of course I know. But it wasn't my business to tell." Her frustration leveled off. "But now that Fin has taken care of that little detail, maybe you can tell me why the Crossroads Society has taken such a shine to you. That Victor Tuse clown has something to do with it." It wasn't a question. She'd smelled the connection the second Fin came in asking about that tattoo.

"You still haven't told me what your connection is to the society," I said. "Exactly *how* do you know about the grimoire?"

She pushed her plate away and squinted her eyes at me. "I consider myself a pretty savvy judge of character. And since you're a member of the club now." She stopped and cocked her head. "You are a member now, right?"

"I agreed to work with them, but now I'm wondering if I'm being played."

She sat deeper into the booth and rested her arm over the top of the worn yellow vinyl. "Well baby, if you're being played, so am I."

I gaped at her in disbelief. "You're a member?" Council members were direct descendants of the original keepers of the grimoire, but I got the distinct impression that all general members had some kind of unique connection to it—or special talent.

"Do I look like the kind of girl who joins them silly little clubs?" she asked.

Yeah. Stupid question. Sugar would no more join the Crossroads Society than the local garden club. "I guess that would be a *no*?"

"Mm-hmm. I knew you had some sense in that pretty little head of yours." She sipped her coffee, keeping up the suspense for another minute or two before explaining her connection to Fin Cooper and Lillian Whitman. "Ever hear of hoodoo?" she asked. I slowly nodded. "Then you know what a conjurer is?"

I didn't see that coming. "You?"

"I dabble a bit, but my mama," she shook her head, "now she's the real conjure woman in the family. Her mama was one of the best in the South. My whole family goes way back with them society folks."

"You still haven't told me how you know so much about them. If you're not a member, how do you know so much about their business?"

"I guess you could call me and my kin honorary members, except we don't have to go to all them boring meetings unless we need a cure for insomnia." She relaxed deeper into the booth before revealing the final piece of the puzzle. "You know them slave quarters where that book was found? Well, guess whose ancestors lived in that little room? Hell, Mama and me are on speed dial for just about any news comes out of that motley crew. Now why don't you tell me why the most exclusive club in Savannah just made *you* a card-carrying member? I'm gonna find out anyway when I talk to Fin. Might as well hear it from you."

It took less than six months for my crazy past to catch up with me. Did I really think I could leave it all behind, raise a nice little family of baby dragons under the guise of being as normal as the Joneses?

"Come on now, baby. Tell Sugar your big secret. You a witch or one of them faery folks? Ain't nothing surprises me in this town. I seen it all."

In quid pro quo fashion, I obliged. "Ever heard of a shifter?"

Based on the indifferent look she was giving me, I assumed the answer was yes. "I'm kind of like one of those."

She just sat there staring at me, squinting her eyes and pursing her lips. Just as I was starting to regret telling her, she relieved the uncomfortable tension strangling the confines of our booth. "I see," she said. "I knew there was something funky going on with you. Ain't no one that gorgeous without a little extra specialness in their blood."

I smirked. "Yeah, well, that 'extra specialness' put a target on my back. Apparently one of the spirits previously trapped in that book has chosen me as its accomplice. Victor Tuse is just an innocent host, and that tattoo it tricked me into applying to Tuse's back was its ticket to manifesting into the poor man's body. Now I guess it's just waiting for its other half to break free, and according to Lillian and Fin we're all going to war if that happens."

Sugar looked like she'd just seen Christ himself walk across the table. "Well, *fuck* me!" Just as quickly, her astonishment turned to anger. "Wait a damn minute! You telling me one of them things is free? Well, why the hell haven't the members been notified?"

I was about to tell her to direct that question to Fin when a loud rumbling noise distracted the entire diner. "What the hell is that?" I scooted against the window and watched the bikes roll past the shops lining the street. The noise from the engines hurt my ears as three choppers pulled into the parking spaces across the street—in front of my shop.

"Uh-uh. Hell no," Sugar said, shaking her head and climbing out of the booth. "Them fools ain't parking there."

Sugar was no shrinking violet, but taking on a pack of bikers wearing club jackets was a bad idea. I stumbled out of the booth and chased her toward the door. "Sugar, don't! They're going into the shop."

They're going into the shop!

I hadn't seen Sea Bass or Abel arrive yet, so that only left Mouse to deal with the three intimidating men. Maybe my tardy employees had come through the back entrance. Without bothering to look both ways I ran across the street, with Sugar running after me in her platform shoes. She was in a seventies mood today.

"Hold up, Katie!" she yelled. "These shoes ain't made for running!"

I ignored her and pushed the front door open. Two of the bikers turned to see who'd just come barreling through the front door, ogling me once they got a good look. Sugar came through a few seconds later. One of them made a remark under his breath as he stared at the confusing figure in front of him. Of all days for Sugar to go wigless with a face full of makeup and a purse dangling off her forearm.

"Can I help you gentlemen?" That was a stretch. I was relieved to see Abel and Sea Bass in the room. They'd come in through the back door as I'd hoped.

Sea Bass looked up. "Morning, Katie. These guys want tattoos."

"Well, obviously," I mumbled under my breath. The one who was too preoccupied with the drawing Mouse was sketching finally looked up. His hair was almost as black as mine, reaching down past his huge shoulders before stopping halfway down his back. Along with his pale skin and intense eyes, he looked gothic. He assessed me for a minute before turning back to Mouse. "All three of you want tattoos?" I asked.

"Is that a problem?" the guy working with Mouse asked without looking back up. His voice was bottomless, as baritone as I'd ever heard.

"Not if you make an appointment." I walked over to the computer and checked the schedule. "We only have one open slot today," I lied, feeling an overwhelming and unexplainable need to get rid of them.

"You can do mine today." He stood up, revealing his true size. The guy had to be at least six and a half feet tall, with a modest two tattoos on each of his biceps, not the full sleeve you'd expect from his type. There was a smaller one on the inside of his forearm.

Mouse handed me the drawing. It was a detailed image of a red-tailed hawk with its wings in mid-flight. "I've got a client coming in at eleven," she said. "I told him the boss might have some time to do it though." I don't know why but I found myself stuck in place, unable to respond as if she'd lost her freaking mind. She picked up on my strange reaction. "That's okay, isn't it? I checked your schedule first."

He looked at me with his brooding eyes a little bit longer than he needed to, realizing that I was the boss—a mere female. Then he glanced at Sea Bass. "I want him to do it."

"Oh no, he didn't," Sugar muttered just loud enough for me to hear.

Sea Bass shook his head. "Sorry, dude. I got a client coming in any minute now. Katie's the best in the shop. Believe me, you want her to do your tattoo."

He turned to his friends to have one of those silent conversations that everyone in the room seemed to be having. After concluding that conversation, he turned back to insult me directly. "Any other shops around here?"

I huffed, incredulous at his audacity, like he'd just walked into a bar and asked the bartender where he could get a good drink. "Sure," I said with a whole lot of sincerity. "There's the bakery across the street and a real good auto repair shop about a block north of here." I mused further as he crossed his arms and leaned his ass against the table behind him. "Oh, and there's a great thrift shop right over there." I pointed through the window. "We're just loaded with shops around here. I guess that means you boys aren't locals?"

The perpetual scowl on his face softened into a more amused

grin. "Got a little attitude, don't you?" He lifted away from the table, closing the gap between us. "I like attitude." Then he looked at Sea Bass again. "When can you fit me in?"

Feeling the passive aggressive vibes between me and the giant biker, Sea Bass hesitated as if waiting for permission. "Go on," I said to him. "Check your schedule." I backed off and got busy fiddling around the front desk.

"I can do it Tuesday at two."

"And we can fit your friends in on Wednesday," I added.

The guy nodded and gave Sea Bass his name and number before leaving the shop with the others.

Sugar stared out the window as they walked toward their Harleys. "Dicks! Coming in here like they own the place." She had her eyes on the tall blond one with the lanky limbs. "I do kinda like that little blond boy though."

"Yep," I agreed. "Real dicks." I joined her at the window and watched them pull their helmets on and straddle their bikes. The engines revved with the same annoying decibels as when they arrived.

"Ain't there some kind of ordinance against all that?" she asked. "All them pipes sticking out all over the place."

I walked over to the computer and looked at his name on the appointment list. "Jackson Hunter," I muttered. As soon as I heard the bikes roar down the street I locked myself in the bathroom and gripped the side of the sink, staring in the mirror at the deep green fighting to take over the blue of my eyes. My dragon was wide awake, and if I hadn't been able to control it so well we would have had a real problem a few minutes earlier. My pulse was racing so fast I nearly dropped down on the toilet seat to steady myself. But the worst effect Jackson Hunter had on me was the heat throbbing between my thighs, traveling like a thermal snake all the way up to my navel. "*Fuck.*"

9

Everyone deserved a sanctuary like MacPherson's Pub. Cheap drinks, no tourists, and plenty of discretion made it the perfect place to unwind—and get Jackson Hunter out of my head. Like Sugar said, he was a real dick, and a brooding one at that. But you know what they say about attraction. I'd spent the entire afternoon trying to shake his voice from my head, but that deep baritone and those penetrating green eyes wouldn't go away. Thank God it was Sunday so I only had to make it through a little more than seven hours of clients. At six o'clock I finally flipped the CLOSED sign on the door and headed over for a drink.

Like most Sunday nights, the crowd was small. Most of the regulars were at home by now, recuperating from the weekend before going back to work Monday morning. Lucky for me the shop was closed on Mondays.

MacPherson's wasn't very big, which meant the busiest nights were standing room only. The place consisted of a bar with a dozen stools, a smaller room for the pool table, and a single unisex bathroom which I'm fairly certain was breaking some kind of city code. But the Irish cops who patronized the place seemed to turn a blind eye. The bar actually had a second bathroom, but the one marked LADIES had an Out of Order sign hanging on the door ever since I first set foot in the place.

"What can I get you, Katie?" Fiona asked as I grabbed a stool at the bar. I'd been coming here since the first week I moved to Savannah, and the bartender knew me by name. She also knew I ordered a Guinness about ninety-nine percent of the time.

"The usual," I said. Thinking about it for a second, I stopped her as she held a glass under the tap. "You know what? I think I'll have some scotch tonight." She grabbed the cheap but drinkable Dewar's blend. I shook my head and pointed to the bottle of Talisker, feeling generous with myself and spoiled from the night before. Tomorrow morning I'd regret spending that much money on a half inch of liquor. "I'll take that Guinness, too."

She placed the two glasses in front of me and leaned her elbows onto the padded edge of the bar, pushing her breasts over the edge of her scant tank top. Her grandfather owned the bar. She had a beautiful head of auburn hair the first time Elliot and I found the place, but since then she'd decided to shave it off and get a tattoo of the horned god on top of her head.

"Rough weekend?" she mumbled around the tiny red straw she was chewing on. Fiona liked boys and girls, especially girls with ink. We'd come to an understanding early on in our relationship that while I was flattered by the attention, I liked boys exclusively—and at the time I was taken. I guess now that I was single again it didn't hurt to keep throwing suggestions my way.

"Rough?" I replied. "Goddamn freak show is what it's been."

She gave me an exaggerated look of sympathy. "Look on the bright side, sweetie. Tomorrow is Monday." She straightened up and dipped her fingers into the foam of my beer, flicking it at me playfully as she walked toward the guy sitting a few seats down.

I swiveled around on my stool and eased my elbows back against the bar. Although I could drink most of these guys under the table, that small glass of liquor had me feeling a little loose.

Maybe it was all the stress. There was a guy at the pool table who kept glancing between me and the ball at the tip of his cue. I smiled back at him, swinging my leg and sipping the foam off my beer. Anything to keep Jackson Hunter's voice out of my head.

Something kept clicking, like a tiny little horse galloping in place on top of the bar. I turned back around and glanced at the guy a few stools down and noticed his fingernails tapping on the wood. He stopped when he caught my eye. He had a blazing red mohawk and a set of piercing blue eyes that rivaled mine. I looked away and stared at his reflection in the mirror behind the bar. A moment later he was doing the same. There was something creepy about people staring at each other through a mirror, like their souls were being projected, bouncing off the glass into the other person's mind. My eyes casually rolled around the bar and back toward his legs when I heard his knee bouncing with that same impatient rhythm. The guy looked jacked up on speed or Red Bull.

"Can I get you another one of those?"

I turned toward the voice and looked at a different guy offering to buy me a drink. "Sure." I motioned to the stool next to mine. "Fiona, I'll have another Talisker, please."

"You've got good taste," he said, referring to the pricy drink I'd just added to his tab. He nodded to Fiona and held up two fingers. She came back with two glasses of scotch and smirked at me.

"Are those both for me?" I asked.

"One is for me, but I'd be happy to buy you the whole bottle if you'd like."

I gave him a genuine smile. "I'll put you out of your misery and stick to Guinness for the rest of the night."

"Clark," he said, extending his hand as he sat down, "Kent."

"Ah-ha." I took it and ran my eyes over his T-shirt and jeans. "Clark Kent?" I repeated, working very hard to suppress a cocky reply.

He polished off the expensive scotch in a single swig. "You do realize what a waste that was? You should save the chugging for the beer."

"Ah! Nonsense! Another?"

I shook my head. "I'm off tomorrow, but when you hunt evil spirits you never really have a day off. You know what I mean?"

He held his arms out. "Hey, I'm Clark Kent."

My eyes widened. "I see your point."

We chatted politely for the next half hour, discussing our pretend lives and preparing for the inevitable segue into going back to his place. He was my escape from that voice filling my head. The one that would be back on Tuesday at two o'clock.

Fiona shot me a look as I got up to leave with Clark Kent. He took my hand, the envy of the guys at the pool table, and led me out the door.

TURNING OVER ON THE BED, I studied the blond head of hair on the pillow next to me. He had unusually long eyelashes for a guy, the kind women painstakingly glued on or paid good money for every few months at the lash salon.

I pulled on one of them gently. "What are you doing?" he asked in a gravelly voice.

"Just checking for glue."

He laughed with his eyes still closed. "You staying tonight? I can finally cook you breakfast in the morning."

I sighed, uncomfortable with the conversation that was about to follow. "Uh-uh. I have to go." Staying till morning would break my number one rule. I threw the sheet off my legs and swung them over the side of the bed. My skirt and underwear were on the floor next to the door. "Where's my shirt?"

He sat up and looked under the blanket that was tossed at the foot of the bed. My tank top was crumpled under it. "Here you go, your highness."

As I pulled my top over my shoulders, he ran his hand over the lower half of my tattoo. I grabbed it as he cupped my waist and pressed my palm against his. "Clark Kent?" He used a different name—usually a famous literary character—every time we had one of our little role-playing sessions. His real name was Christopher Sullivan. He was an Assistant District Attorney for the Chatham County DA's office. We'd met right after Elliot left —at MacPherson's—and he'd become a dependable diversion ever since. But the whole dating thing just didn't work for us, and we mutually agreed that we were much better off as casual lovers. Fiona knew exactly what was going on the second he walked through the front door of the bar.

"Katie—"

"Christopher," I pleaded, "you know as well as I do what this is. We'll be on each other's last nerve before the week is up." With the rest of my wrinkled clothes gathered, I got dressed and headed for the door.

"So, are you just going to call me next time you feel like getting laid?" he asked, trying his best to make me feel guilty for saving us both a lot of grief. Even though I knew leaving was the right thing to do and I couldn't wait to get out of that house, it still pained me every time he did this. But he'd thank me for it tomorrow.

"Yes," I whispered before walking out the door.

SEA BASS WAS WAITING on my doorstep when I got home. "Where the hell have you been?"

"What? Are you my father now?" I walked past him and opened the door while he stood there gawking at me like I had three heads. "Well? You coming in or not?"

He was good at making himself at home, heading straight for the refrigerator to search the shelf for a cold beer. Then he pulled out a container of leftover pasta and sat himself at the kitchen island.

"You sure I can't cook up something fresh for you, Sea Bass?" I asked with the appropriate amount of sarcasm.

"Aw, no thanks Katie, this is good." He jammed his fork into the Tupperware and twisted it with a heaping ball of linguine before stuffing it in his mouth. "You want some?" he mumbled around the food, shoving the container toward me.

I shook my head and grabbed a bottle of red wine from the counter. After pouring a glass, I questioned why he was in my kitchen eating my food and drinking my beer at close to midnight. "So why are you here, Sea Bass?"

"Fin Cooper's been trying to reach you all night. Hell, Grams called me three times already to help him find you. Said it's an emergency."

I grabbed my purse and pulled out my phone. The battery was dead—again. "Did she say what it was about?"

"Nope. Just said it was real important and you needed to call Fin ASAP. You had me a little worried when you weren't answering, Katie, considering all the strange shit going on around here lately." He pulled out his phone and scrolled to Fin's number before handing it to me. "Grams gave me his number. You better call him."

"It's a little late. Maybe I should wait until morning."

His brow went up as he cocked his head. "Ah, I wouldn't do that. Grams said it was an emergency, and I ain't never heard that word come out that woman's mouth before."

I took the phone and stepped out on the patio. It barely rang once before Fin picked up. "Miss Bishop?" he asked before I could announce myself. I guess there wasn't anyone else he was expecting a call from this late on a Sunday night.

"Yeah, it's me, Fin. Sea Bass said you've been trying to reach me all night. What's so important it couldn't wait till morning?" I could hear a heavy sigh release on the other end of the phone, making the hairs on my arm stand up. "You're making me real uncomfortable, Fin."

"Your instincts are strong. That's a real good thing, Miss Bishop. It's best that you meet me at Lillian's house. The sooner the better."

"You don't mean right now?" I asked, hoping he meant first thing in the morning.

"That would be preferable. And wise."

I DROVE through the majestic tunnel of live oaks lining the road, covered with a thick veil of cascading Spanish moss. Lillian Whitman's house and home of the Crossroads Society was just ahead. The location had been kept secret the first time I was here, seeing how such a dangerous artifact was buried in the bowels of its foundation. But since I was now a member of the society and I refused his offer of an escort in the Bentley, Fin relented and gave me the address.

He was waiting on the steps when I pulled up in front of the house. "That was fast, Miss Bishop. What kind of GPS you got in that thing?"

I pointed to my head and walked past him toward the open front door. "I'm good with directions and I'm tired. Let's just get this urgent business over with so I can go back home and get some sleep."

"It's nice to see you again, Miss Bishop." Lillian Whitman greeted me in the hall and I automatically extended my hand. "Nonsense," she said as she cupped my shoulders and kissed me lightly on the cheek. "Members are practically family."

Instead of the library, she led the way to one of the great rooms with spectacular high ceilings and tall windows that I imagined let in a tsunami of light during the day. One wall was covered with old portraits in gilded frames. "Are these your people?" I asked, motioning to the wall.

"I like to think that some of them are," she said. "The rest are unfortunate contradictions to my very long and wise pedigree." I realized she was waiting for Fin and me to make ourselves comfortable. Once we sat down, she took her own seat on the sofa next to me. She immediately stood back up. "I must be losing my mind," she said as she walked over to the bureau. "You having bourbon, Fin?" She poured his drink without paying any mind to his response. "How about you, Miss Bishop? What's your pleasure?"

What the hell. It was my day off already. "Scotch, neat." It wasn't every day that I had the opportunity to sample a bottle that probably cost more than my rent. I thanked her for my drink and waited for one of them to tell me what was so important to drag me all the way over here at nearly one a.m.

Fin got right to the point. "Victor Tuse is dead."

It took a moment to reconcile what he'd said, but when I did the first thought that came to mind was, *Great. Problem solved.* Then reality set in. "I don't suppose this means that the spirit is dead, too?"

"Hardly." Fin stood up and started traipsing around the room. I was beginning to see a pattern with him. A nervous habit. The man rarely sat still for more than a few minutes at a time. "I'm afraid he's on the hunt for a new host."

"Can he do that?" I asked.

Fin stifled a laugh. "A two-hundred-year-old spirit can do just about anything it wants, Miss Bishop. Hell, it can take up residence in a dog if it wants to." He polished off his drink and set the glass on the fireplace mantel before describing all the gory details of Tuse's death. "I'm sure the spirit can body hop all it wants, but seeing how it managed to fully manifest into this one, it had no choice but to kill its host. The man was found nearly petrified, dried up like an old piece of leather. The spirit even took the tattoo."

"The tattoo?" I had a visual of the poor man's dead body, his back skinned.

"Sucked the life right out of that man like a spider consuming a trapped bug," Lillian interjected. "I suspect it just sucked up the tattoo right along with all the entrails."

Fin took his seat again. "I personally examined the remains, at the discretion of the Chatham County Medical Examiner who also happens to be a member. A faded outline of the tattoo was still visible on Victor Tuse's back, but the spirit had clearly taken the rest."

"So what do we do now?" I asked.

"This is new territory for all of us," Fin replied. "So for now, Miss Bishop, we wait."

FIN AND LILLIAN had some misguided notion that they could talk me into staying at the society, at least until the new host surfaced. But I made it clear I had a life—and a dragon on my back for protection. They dropped the argument when I agreed to keep my phone sufficiently charged so I could suffer a daily call from Fin to make sure I was still alive, while they came up with a plan for capturing the spirit.

I pulled into my driveway and noticed my neighbor's living room light was on. I feared what would happen if the spirit's latest host decided to show up on my doorstep. My dragon would have a field day with that, and so would my neighbors if they heard a commotion and looked outside.

Either my imagination was getting the best of me, or there was someone standing under the streetlight a couple of houses down. It was a woman. I could just make out her long hair and a pair of glasses with oversized frames. I'd say it was just someone from the neighborhood walking her dog at two-thirty in the morning—the very reason I didn't have one—but there was no dog on a leash or running loose on the lawn. And then there was the creepy fact that she was staring at me.

Fumbling nervously with the handle, I dropped my keys between the seat and the door. I reached down to grab them and by the time I looked back up she was gone. The lines of my tattoo stirred on my back. Not the usual restless movement I felt when the creature wanted to come out; something much deeper.

I sat back against the seat and let the growl snaking up my throat calm to a low rumble that eventually receded. But there was no time to reflect on what just happened. I needed to get inside the house before she—or it—came back.

Surveying my surroundings, I hurried toward the front door. If it hadn't been for the moonlight shining down on my doorstep, I probably would have stepped right over the line of dust scattered across the threshold. I bent down and pinched some of it between my fingers, clumsily fiddling with the key in my left hand, missing the keyhole three times before finally getting the door open. As soon as I was inside and the door was locked, I examined the grit between my fingers, a mix of fine and coarse rust colored material. I suspected it was red brick dust, and I knew enough about hoodoo to know it was used for protection by root folks.

The light in my kitchen was on. My memory told me I'd turned off all the lights when Sea Bass and I left earlier that night, but it wouldn't be the first time I'd left one of them on. I went to the living room window and peeked through the blinds, praying I wouldn't see that woman staring back at me. She wasn't out there, but as I turned away from the window I spotted something in the corner. I grabbed a paper towel and reached for the strange object that in the dim light looked like a shriveled or petrified squid.

"What in the hell?" I muttered as I carried it at arm's length to the bright light of the kitchen to get a better look. It was some kind of dried root.

I ran to the bedroom and found another one in the corner. By the time I went through every room of the house, I'd found a total of six, one in each room. Someone was either trying to protect me or harm me.

10

M y day off felt like a blip in time. I spent it staring at that pile of shriveled roots on my kitchen counter, but it flew by because I was dreading going to the shop the next day. The next day was Tuesday, the day Jackson Hunter was coming in for that hawk tattoo. Based on its size and intricacy it would take several hours, and I prayed Sea Bass could get it done before we closed so Mr. Hunter wouldn't be back for a second session. There was something about that biker that set off a chain of events in my head and groin that scared the living hell out of me. Only one other guy had ever done that to me—Constantine, a satyr back in New York who'd managed to reduce me to a sloppy cliché with a permanent hard-on for the sound of his voice. That tumultuous affair was one I preferred not to repeat.

I was the last one in, having overslept due to less than two hours of sleep. Mouse was working on some guy's arm, while Sea Bass conferred with a young woman who barely looked legal and was having second thoughts about getting her first tattoo.

"What's your policy if I don't like it?" the girl asked.

LUANNE BENNETT

Sea Bass refrained from rolling his eyes. "Well, once it's done, it's done. Can't take it back."

She closed her eyes and nodded once, clearly conflicted with a choice that was permanent, or expensive and painful to rectify later.

"Look," he said, handing her the drawing he'd done of an infinity symbol with the word "peace" intertwined, "why don't you take the drawing and think about it for a few days. You can always come back later." He smiled to ease her angst. "You know what they say—measure twice, cut once."

Normally we wouldn't just hand over a custom stencil that took some time and skill to render, but infinity symbols were our bread and butter around here. Took about five seconds to print one off and change the word from "love" to "hope" to "peace", etc.

As I turned and headed for the coffee pot, I stumbled over something large and unyielding on the floor. I flew over it and landed on my elbow—aka funny bone. Nothing funny about it though. "*Fuck!*" I squealed, sitting on the hard floor waiting for the irritated nerve endings to stop throbbing with pain. Then I spotted the culprit.

Sea Bass came running. "Jeez, Katie! I'm sorry."

"Damn it, Sea Bass!" I got back on my feet and looked at the big white obstruction lying on the floor. "What's Marvin doing in here again?"

Marvin was his dog. He'd found the massive white German shepherd under his old truck a few winters back while he was visiting his uncle in Atlanta. They'd had a rare snowfall that year that rendered the ground white, and Sea Bass nearly ran the poor thing over because he couldn't see it against the snow. The dog slid out from under the truck just in time and jumped up on his window. Clearly dumped during the coldest part of the season, Sea Bass brought him home to Savannah and dubbed him Marvin.

"Maggie's picking him up around eleven. He needs a good bath and some manscaping."

"What's she going to do?" asked Abel "Wax the hair off the poor dog's balls?" He gave Marvin a sympathetic glance. "You could get arrested for that, you know. Animal cruelty, section 9-5034."

Sea Bass cringed. "Hell no. She's just giving him a good grooming." Among other things, Sea Bass's girlfriend listed dog grooming as one of her current occupations.

Marvin dragged himself off the floor and nudged my hand with his snout. His tail wagged apologetically as he waited for me to comply and pet his head. It wasn't his fault he was the size of a small pony. Besides, I owed that dog one. The first time Sea Bass brought him to the shop, he'd served as the perfect mediator when a couple of gang members walked in and started to lose their manners. That dog was a welcome guest in my home any day, but the health department wasn't as tolerant when it came to animals in a facility that required sterilization.

"Sorry, big boy," I said as I ran my hand over his head. "You're going to have to wait outside. Auntie Katie can't afford any violation fines right now." It was still early enough for the heat to be bearable. "Put him in the shade and make sure he's got water." Sea Bass led Marvin out the back door.

With a cup of coffee in my hand, I looked at the schedule. Jackson Hunter was still down for two o'clock. I had a client coming in at eleven to complete a large tattoo I'd been working on. I figured it would take at least a few more hours to finish, which would be the perfect distraction when that biker came in.

I'd barely had a chance to sit down and properly wake up when Sugar walked through the front door, brushing a thick section of long golden hair over her shoulder. She headed straight for me. "You okay, baby?" she asked.

I glanced from left to right. "Why? Shouldn't I be?"

"Well, I don't know," she replied. "You called me this morning."

She deadpanned me like I was being deliberately evasive. Then I realized she must have been waiting for my call since Sunday night, knowing all about Victor Tuse turning up dead and wondering why I didn't call her on my day off. I'm sure the society had some kind of phone tree for notifying members and other pertinent individuals. I guess Sugar was considered pertinent.

"I'm just fine," I reassured her, burying my face in a magazine on the counter. "Had a nice day off to think about all the bullshit going on in my world."

She pulled it out from under my eyes and tossed it on a chair. "Come on. Time is money, baby. You and me got to talk."

"I have a client coming in at eleven. I don't have time for this, Sugar."

"You got a whole hour and," she glanced at my phone on the counter, "seven minutes."

I relented and followed her across the street to Lou's for a cup of coffee and a quick chat. Besides, I had something to show her. "So I guess you know about Victor Tuse," I said.

"I know that man turned up like a prune left out in the hot Georgia sun for a few days," she confirmed. "I also know that thing inside of him is on the move." Her eyes shifted around the diner as if the spirit might be sitting at the next table. "Now you know I ain't afraid of much, Katie, but only a fool be turning his back on what's roaming free out there looking for a new body." Her expression showed a rare glimpse of fear. "You need protection, baby."

"Don't worry about me, Sugar. I wouldn't make a good host. I can't apply that tattoo on its back if it's living inside of me." I glanced nervously across the table. "You, on the other hand—" My shoulders shuddered. We'd never finished our conversation about my dragon the last time we sat in this booth, seeing how we were interrupted by the thunder of choppers rolling down the street. "Trust me, Sugar, I can take care of myself. I guess I need to show you what we were talking about the other day."

"I bet you got some real interesting skills, Katie B." Her mood lightened a little. Not much, but a little. "But you got to understand what you're dealing with here. This ain't no garden variety spirit gunning for you—more like a demon, with them bones and all."

I'd faced some pretty bad things over the past couple of years, but the look on Sugar's face had me wondering if I was underestimating the one I was facing now. "There's something else," I said. "I met Fin at Lillian's house Sunday night after he called to tell me about Tuse. When I came home I found this red powder sprinkled in a line across my front door. I think it was red brick dust. I guess you know what that is." Coming from a long line of conjure women, I figured red brick dust was hoodoo 101 for her. "Then I found these hidden around my house." I pulled a hand towel from my purse and unwrapped one of the strange looking roots. I hesitated to touch it or put it in my purse, but I needed to show it to Sugar. "I found six of them."

"Seven," she said. "You missed one. Probably the one in the kitchen pantry in the bag of flour."

An incredulous laugh blurted out of my mouth. "You?" She arched her brow and demurely sipped her coffee, looking everywhere but at me. "I don't believe this. You broke into my house and planted these creepy roots all over the place? I guess the brick dust came from you, too?"

"Angelica root," she clarified. "And yes to the dust. And by the way, you need to get you one of them metal rods for that patio door of yours. All it took was a little lift off the track to disengage that flimsy lock. Didn't your mama ever teach you anything?"

We sat silent for a minute, staring at each other over the table. She finally leaned across and crooked her finger at me. I met her halfway as she took my chin between her knuckle and thumb. Sugar rarely let down her sassy and fearless walls, never showed her vulnerable side. Always genuine, I never questioned her loyalty. "I'm just trying to protect the people I love," she said in a voice deeper and richer than the one I'd become accustomed to. "But the kind of safe you need ain't gonna come from a bag of dust or a few roots thrown around that house of yours."

I pulled away from her hand, feeling kind of awkward as my stomach heated up deep down inside. She smiled, recognizing the look on my face. Then she was back to the Sugar I knew so well. "There's somewhere I need to take you. That tinkering Sunday night was just enough to get you through that day off of yours, seeing how you was avoiding me all day yesterday."

"I wasn't avoiding you, Sugar. I just needed a break from everything. That's why it's called a day off."

"That's all right, baby. But I'm taking you to see the big guns tonight if I have to drag you there."

Before I could ask where she was planning to take me, I glanced around the room and saw a face staring over at us from a table on the far right side of the diner. I'd only made out the hair and glasses from a block away, but I'd bet my shop on it that the woman sitting at that table was the same one I saw standing under my streetlight yesterday morning. My breath hitched as I turned my eyes back to Sugar. "There's a woman sitting across the room—"

I guess the look on my face was enough to alarm Sugar, because she turned around to look before I could finish my sentence. Her eyes came back to meet mine. "What woman?"

She was gone when I looked back at the table. "Sugar, I swear there was a woman sitting right there." I pointed to the spot where she'd been sitting a few seconds earlier. "She was standing on the sidewalk when I came home from Lillian's house, just staring at me from under the streetlight at two-thirty in the morning. What kind of person does that?" I could tell by the way

Sugar was looking at me that we were having the same thought. "You don't think that woman could be the new host?" My eyes darted around the room as the lines on my back stirred.

She shuddered briskly. "I don't know, but you got to use your head, girl. And you ain't gonna just sit around like some fat beetle waiting to get sucked dry like Tuse. We're gonna get you good and jujued up tonight."

Sugar walked me back to the shop and I agreed to meet her after we closed. She warned that the night could get intense, and it might be wise to take the next day off. Not likely. I had a business to run and tomorrow was two-for-one day, which meant twelve hours of cute little hearts, roses, and significant other's names. Figuring it couldn't hurt though, I accepted her invitation. The fact that it was near impossible to put her off once she got something in her head didn't make refusing any easier.

I walked into the shop with about five minutes to spare before my client arrived. Becky was in her early forties and catching up on her bucket list. After years of that son of a bitch she was married to smacking her around, she was finally getting to that tattoo she always wanted. We'd been working on covering her back with a tattoo of Diana, Goddess of the Hunt, starting it on the day she finally got the courage to file for divorce. I guess she got tired of him telling her what she could eat, who she could see, and what she could and couldn't do with her own body.

Every few weeks she'd come in with enough money to have a small section completed. I would have done it for free if she'd let me. My contribution to women living with assholes everywhere. But I sensed that Becky took great pride in paying for something that went completely against the grain of her former life—and husband—even if it meant a sparsely filled refrigerator for a week. I applied a little extra each time she came in, free of charge.

"Ready to get this done?" I asked as she walked through the door with a wide grin on her face.

Becky laughed. "I'm going to wait until he signs those

divorce papers next week, and then before that damn ink dries I'm going to lift my shirt and show him what I think about his rules."

"Good for you, Becky. Just make sure your lawyer's in the room when you do it."

She laughed again. "That'll make his head explode, flashing my tits in front of another man."

She climbed on the table and we started the final phase of her tattoo. I took my time with it, wanting to make it perfect for her big reveal. I looked up every time the door open, waiting for that biker to come walking in.

By one-thirty the masterpiece I'd been working on for months was complete. So much for stretching it out to distract me. "It looks perfect, Becky."

She walked over to the full-length mirror and looked at it through the reflection of the smaller one in her hand. For a moment, I thought she was unsatisfied with the final work, the way her lower lip quivered and her brows pulled together. "This is it, isn't it, Katie? Like they say, one journey ends and another begins."

"I should tattoo that on your arm, Becky."

She left the shop and headed for her car. I couldn't help but wonder if she knew how lucky she was. A lot of women in her situation either never found the courage to leave, or left in a box. So far the verbal abuse had been worse than the physical, but it would have only been a matter of time before the bruises on her body progressed to broken bones.

I headed back to clean my station when Sea Bass came in through the back door, holding his phone and looking panicked. "Maggie had an accident." His eyes were wide and vacant, like he didn't know whether to bolt back out the door or prep for clients. "Tow truck's on the way."

"Jesus! Is she okay?" I asked, fearing the worst from the look on his face.

"Maggie is, but she thinks Marvin's leg is broken." He looked at me apologetically. "Katie, I gotta go."

Abel tossed his car keys to Sea Bass. "You're not getting that dog on the back of your bike. Just bring it back in one piece."

Bike—Biker. The words made my stomach do a heavy flop. "Don't you have a two o'clock?" I shamefully asked, suddenly realizing I might be doing hand to skin combat for the next few hours with Jackson Hunter. I glanced at Mouse, but she was barely halfway through her client's tattoo. Abel just stared back at me when I looked at him next, thinking the unthinkable.

"You're right," I said "I'll take care of it. Go on. Deal with Marvin."

Fifteen minutes after Sea Bass left, I heard the unmistakable growl of a Harley coming down the street. Jackson Hunter pulled into one of the parking spots in front of the shop. He took his time climbing off the bike and garnered looks from passersby when his spray of long black hair fell out of his helmet, a Gothic monolith descending on their town.

My heart started to race like it had on Sunday when he so easily insinuated that a woman wasn't qualified to apply ink to his precious skin. Not like some pitter-patter from a crush, but like I had a bad case of stage fright. How could a guy I didn't even like send my adrenaline rushing straight up my throat? Maybe it was just my instincts warning me of trouble. God knows I'd run up against his type a thousand times before in the bars on the lower side of Manhattan. I'd just never run up against one the size of a truck before, with piercing green eyes.

His head lowered automatically to clear the height of the front door like it was second nature. Then he glanced at Mouse and Abel before making his way around to me. "Where is he?" he asked. "Steel Head, Flounder, whatever his name is."

Mouse laughed without looking up from her client's arm.

I forced back a smile. "You mean Sea Bass?" He just kept staring at me with that deep gaze that said one of two things:

Yeah, who the fuck did you think I was talking about?, or *You're the loveliest thing I've ever seen.* I was pretty sure it was the former. "Family emergency," I said. It was true. Marvin was family. "I would have called you to cancel but he just left."

Why didn't I call him?

My stupidity astounded me. I had fifteen whole minutes to call Jackson Hunter to let him know he should reschedule. But no, I let him drive down here and walk into my shop just so we could have this painful little tête-à-tête.

He stood there showing no reaction to the news. Then he looked at my empty station. "Is that your chair?"

My mouth opened and closed. "Yeah, but—"

But what? My schedule was clear for the rest of the afternoon and he was a paying customer.

Without doing me the courtesy of asking, he walked over to my chair and sat down. A moment later I collected my scattered brain off the floor and got down to business. I guess Mr. Hunter decided to live dangerously by allowing a female to grace his skin with ink. "That was rude," I muttered to him as I met him at my station and started preparing a tray.

"Yeah, I can be a real asshole sometimes," he replied, straight-faced with absolutely no apology in the words.

Sometimes? I must have missed the other side of his personality. "You're lucky," I said. "I just happen to have time today."

His brooding eyes never left mine as our uncomfortable exchange continued. "Is that what I am? Lucky?" he asked.

God, he was infuriating. I went to the back to retrieve the sketch of the hawk Mouse had done on Sunday and held it out to him for final approval. "Do you want to make any changes?"

He glanced at the drawing. "I don't like it. I want you to draw me a new one."

"A new one?" I repeated.

"A new one," he repeated back a little slower. Aside from his mouth moving, his expression remained neutral.

"Are you toying with me, Mr. Hunter?" He slowly shook his head while his eyes took a walk over my face. "What's wrong with this one? You were happy about it a couple of days ago, and it's good." Normally I wouldn't question a client's wish to modify an image that was about to be permanently embedded in their skin, but this guy was just being the asshole he said he could be.

"Yeah, it's good," he said with a shrug. "But you didn't draw it."

Without further ado and because I could feel the skin on my face heating up, I headed for the back and started rendering a new sketch. The extra time it took would make it impossible to complete the tattoo in one sitting, and that meant I'd have to suffer through the pleasure of his company again. I'd done a lot of birds before, but I made damn sure the drawing I presented to Jackson Hunter was the crème de la crème of all hawks. I wanted that man out of my chair, and the sooner I got his approval, the sooner I could start the damn thing and send him back to where he came from.

"Does this work?" I handed him the drawing. "It's intricate and we close early today. You'll probably have to come back for another session."

He examined it for a good minute. "That's a good-looking hawk, Miss Bishop. Let's see if you can tattoo as well as you draw."

My last name coming out of his mouth sent my pulse racing. He'd actually taken the time to find out who I was. He must have sensed my reaction, because his eyes wandered down to my business cards on the tray.

"Yep," I grumbled, walking away to make the stencil. "You're gonna remember me, Jackson Hunter."

11

I felt guilty for about two seconds, pushing a little harder than I had to, making sure he felt every drop of ink that I embedded in his skin. After three hours of working in utter silence it was time to call it a day. The man in my chair had said about two words the entire time, choosing instead to stare at me while I worked. Every time I glanced up at him he was boring those green eyes into mine without the slightest bit of discretion.

Technically we were closed by the time I cleaned him up and wrapped the tattoo. It wasn't unusual to stay late after the doors were locked to complete work on a regular client, but Jackson Hunter hadn't earned that privilege and I had a date with Sugar at seven o'clock.

"Shouldn't take more than a couple of hours to complete." It would take a couple of weeks to heal before we could finish the rest of it. "You want to schedule another session now?"

He examined the partial tattoo under the plastic wrap. "I'll call you."

Sugar pulled up next to the Harley, eyeing it suspiciously as she passed it on the way to the entrance. Abel unlocked the door to let her in. The first words out of her mouth made me cringe. "Don't tell me you got yourself a new man, Katie B."

"He's a client," I said. "And he was just leaving." I took his money and pointed to the door with my eyes.

He smirked and turned to leave, but not before leaning over the counter to get within a few inches of my ear. "I knew your name before I walked through that door," he said. "Thank God for family emergencies."

There went my damn pulse again. He nodded to Sugar on his way out and climbed on his bike, staring at me through the window while he corralled his hair and pulled his helmet over his head. His bike engine revved as he sat there for a few more minutes. I waited for him to pull away and disappear down the road before slipping back into the bathroom for another one of those sink gripping sessions. *Jesus, Lord!* What the hell was wrong with me?

Sugar knocked on the door when I stayed in there a little longer than normal. "You okay in there, Katie?" The last thing I needed was for anyone to see my flushed face and shaking limbs from all that adrenaline pumping through me like a freight train.

"I'm fine, Sugar. Be right out."

I could hear her lean her ear up to the door. "That boy didn't do nothing to you, did he?"

Depends on what she meant by *nothing.* I opened the door and she nearly fell inside. "Of course not. And he's not a boy."

She glared at me, obviously picking up on my jacked nerves like a hound smelling a raccoon, but for some uncharacteristic reason she dropped the third degree. "You ready to go?" she asked.

"I guess. You plan on telling me where we're going?"

She countered. "You plan on telling me what just happened in that bathroom?"

Neither of us pursued the conversation any further. I locked the shop door behind her and Abel and climbed into the front seat of her boat-sized Eldorado. "I could just follow you," I said. "Save you the hassle of driving me back to my car."

"I don't think so, baby. I might be driving your ass home tonight and escorting you to work in the morning."

I was beginning to worry about where she was taking me and what she had planned when we got there. Sugar and I had gotten close, but I knew relatively little about what she did when she slipped into the underbelly of the city. The question was, was she planning on taking me with her into *said* underbelly tonight, and would I live to regret it?

We drove down a two-lane road for about a half hour, passing through stretches of Savannah's signature old oaks covered in Spanish moss before coming up on a few houses on the left-hand side. They were spaced a few acres apart, the last house being the one we were heading for. It was basically a box with weathered plank siding, a gabled roof, and a small front porch that favored the far-right column holding it up. There was a well-tended garden on the side of the house.

"What is this place?" I asked, refusing to get out of the car and test that porch unless she told me who or what was inside.

"Come on, Katie. You're about to meet my maker."

I hesitated with my hand on the door handle. "By 'maker' I hope you mean your mother."

She gripped her hips. "Well, what the hell do you think I am? A goddamn vampire? Of course I'm talking about my mama."

I steadied my nerves. "Why are we here?"

Sugar had revealed just the other day that her mama was a conjure woman, which had my blood pumping from all the images of what I might see behind that old door a half a dozen yards away. I assumed our visit was for official hoodoo business, Sugar's way of protecting me. But once I gave her a demonstration of what my dragon could do I'm sure it would ease her mind about my ability to take care of myself. But we were here, so I decided to humor her.

The light in the living room grew brighter as we approached the rickety steps leading up to the porch. "You sure it's safe for both of us to stand on it?"

"This old porch is strong as dynamite. Mama lets it sag like this to keep the solicitors away." With the heel of her shoe she pressed down on the first plank that was painted a shade darker than the rest of the decking. "See that?" she said as it bowed in the center and nearly split. "Mama did that one herself. Folks around here know better than to step on that one, but strangers think the whole damn porch is about to come down."

"Humph," I said, nodding. "Now I know where you get your brains from."

We stepped over the trick plank and Sugar turned the door-knob. "It's just me, Mama. I brought me a friend."

An elderly African American woman who could have just as easily been Sugar's grandmother came walking into the small but surprisingly roomy space, I suspected at the expense of the rest of the tiny house. She was wearing a yellow apron over a housedress covered in tiny little flowers, and her white hair worn closely to her scalp reminded me of a bouquet of baby's breath. Her eyes were hazel like Sugar's and twinkled like glossy gems as the light above our heads reflected off of them. She looked at Sugar and grinned from ear to ear, revealing a mouth full of dark spaces between the handful of teeth that were still intact. I glanced at Sugar, wondering just how old she was. I'd always guessed her to be in her late thirties, but the woman she called Mama couldn't have been a day younger than ninety.

"Where you been, Ray?" she asked in a lyrical voice that matched her wide grin. She moved surprisingly fast for her advanced age and gave Sugar a thorough hug. Then she felt the long strands of hair from the blond wig and nearly tugged it off Sugar's head. "What the hell you got here, boy?"

Sugar exhaled dramatically, ignoring her mama's comment.

"This is Katie Bishop, Mama. She's a friend of mine. This is my mama, Pearl May Mobley."

Are you supposed to extend your hand to a ninety-something Southern lady? Or is a hug more appropriate? She didn't wait for me to decide and gave me the same welcome she'd given Sugar. "It's a pleasure to meet you, Mrs. Mobley," I said as she stood back to get another look at me.

"Mrs. Mobley was my ma. You call me May," she said, patting the sides of my arms. Then she turned back to Sugar. "Where you been, son?"

"Now come on, Mama. I ride out here to see you every week."

"The hell you do!" Her quiet Southern charm was replaced with a cantankerous beast. "I ain't seen you in months, boy!"

Sugar looked at me and rolled her eyes. "Mama got a little issue with remembering certain things. But you ain't got no problem remembering the root, now do you, Mama?"

May suddenly shot me a look that made my heart skip a beat, ignoring Sugar's question about her diminishing memory. Her bright hazel eyes lost their shine as she regarded me with concern. "You got a whole mess of worry, girl. Got that trickster in your head." She walked a circle around me and then stood a foot away and looked me in the eye. "What's wrong with you?"

Sugar jumped in. "That's why we're here, Mama. Katie is working with Lillian and Fin."

May looked distraught, shaken from something I did or said since walking into her house. "The society?" she asked.

"One of them spirits found its way out of that book, and Katie here helped it manifest." Pearl May Mobley's suspicious gaze turned venomous, spiking my discomfort and fear of what the conjure woman standing in front of me might do next if Sugar didn't clarify that statement quickly. "Now hold on, Mama. It wasn't intentional."

"I know, I know, boy. I can see!" She turned back to me and

lifted her hands to cover my eyes. "That Legvu is a trickster. You got yourself a real gift, but the spirit got more. You got to learn to see him, else he'll come right up on you and put the *bone* to you." She removed her hands and pinned me with her eyes on the word *bone*.

"I figured maybe you could throw a little protection on her, Mama. At least till Fin and them society folks can figure out how to capture that thing. I already put a little angelica root around her house, but that ain't gonna last very long."

May was barely listening to Sugar. She just kept peering into my soul via my eyes. "Juju ain't got no power against them bones. You got to get them bones before they get you. You understand what I'm telling you, girl? Ain't no amount of angelica root or salt gonna keep it away."

Lillian Whitman had told me a story about bones. *Legvu had in his possession a bag of bones.* I gathered that the bones Pearl May Mobley was referring to were one and the same, the ones buried at a crossroads, which could be anywhere.

"It was nice to meet you, May. I'll remember what you told me." I looked at Sugar. "It's getting late. We should go."

We left May's house, careful to avoid the trick step. The sky was turning to dusk and Jet was probably standing over an empty bowl on the kitchen floor, waiting for his dinner. "I need to get home and feed Jet," I said, heading for the car.

"Being here in Mama's neck of the woods reminds me of something," Sugar said. "You better keep that cat inside. A black cat in hoodoo country ain't safe."

"I know. Already been warned." Jet found me right after we moved to Savannah. One morning he was just sitting on my patio, staring into the kitchen like he was waiting for me to let him in from his nightly carousing. When I opened the patio door, he waltzed in with his tail pointing to the ceiling. I knew all about the cruel practice of collecting black cat bones, a warning already given by a technician at the vet's office. Most people I talked to said the practice was dead, but I preferred to play it safe and keep Jet inside, and he'd been more than happy to comply.

We climbed into the Eldorado and headed back to the shop. "Ray?" I asked. "Is that the name on your birth certificate?"

"Raymond. Mama ain't never gonna accept who I am. I'm still Ray when I walk through that door."

I'd noticed the way May seemed to look right past the makeup and clothes, at the son she gave birth to. For a second I thought she was going to tear the wig right off Sugar's head. Maybe it was all a show of rebellion, a subtle demonstration of her refusal to acknowledge something she considered a choice. Then again, maybe she just lived in a bubble of denial when it came to her own offspring.

"Promise me something, Sugar." She glanced at me and then steered her eyes back to the road. "Take care of Jet if anything happens to me. Marvin doesn't get along with cats, and Mouse can barely take care of herself."

Sugar hit the brakes in the middle of the empty road and shifted the car into park. "What the hell kind of nonsense you talking about?"

"You're going to get us killed, Sugar." The road was clear for the moment, but it would only take an instant for a car to come barreling over the top of the hill and hit us in the middle of the dark road.

"Well, if you're already planning your funeral, what difference does it make?" She emptied the air from her lungs and reached over me to the glove compartment for a pack of cigarettes. She lit one and dangled it out the window in her left hand. "The Katie Bishop I know is a fighter. Who the hell are you?"

"I thought you quit."

"Oh, I did, but this is medicinal tobacco. You making me ill, woman." She took another drag and flicked the lit cigarette into the road. "We need us a strategy to catch that thing, and I think it's about time you showed me that creature of yours." She shifted the car back into drive and set off down the road, just as a pair of approaching headlights glowed in the rearview mirror.

She was right on both counts. It wasn't a question of *if* the spirit would come for me, but *when*. The other half of that demon was still trapped inside the grimoire, but if the first one got out, the second one would probably escape the same way. And since I seemed to be the only one who could aid and abet in manifesting them into the corporeal, it was just a matter of time before the second one paid me a visit. Right now, my biggest fear was that I'd have another one of those dreams, followed by a call from Fin warning me that the other one had escaped.

"Okay," I said matter-of-factly. "I'll show it to you." Next to Sea Bass, she was my closest friend in Savannah, so it was only a matter of time before the dragon came out in front of her anyway. It's funny how people always think they can handle seeing things that aren't normal. But the dragon on my back wasn't some unsightly birthmark or a missing toe. Might as well prepare her for it before we found ourselves in a dangerous situation and she got to meet it in person.

We drove into town and passed by MacPherson's Pub on the way to the shop, making me itch to pick up the phone and call Christopher for another little diversion. We'd been hooking up more than usual lately, which fueled his ideas about that relationship that would never happen. He'd eventually find himself a nice trophy wife that fit the mold of an assistant DA's spouse, so when he finally pulled the trigger on that political career he was always harping about he wouldn't have to explain all her tattoos, or the scant skirts paired with the occasional combat boots. If that didn't kill his public image, the dragon certainly would.

"Humph," Sugar said. "Looks like them biker boys is making themselves right at home."

As we came around the block in front of the bar, I saw what she was referring to. Jackson Hunter and four other men came out of MacPherson's and headed for the row of Harleys parked out front. Under the weight of that arm I'd just tattooed no more than three hours earlier was a redhead wearing a skimpy tank top and a pair of ultra-tight jeans rolled up above a pair of stiletto boots.

"Slow down," I said. She eyed me contemptuously. "Don't you look at me like that, Sugar."

"Like what? Like you done lost your ever-lovin' mind? Men like them ain't nothing but trouble, girl. Nothing but trouble."

"Look at that fake redhead," I said. "Wearing that trashy tank top."

I heard a snort come from the driver's seat. "Yeah, kinda like the one you got on." She slowed down like I asked—maybe a little too slow—but before I could get a good look at his face, she hit the pedal and left MacPherson's Pub in the dust.

I FILLED Jet's bowl with dry food and put a plate of canned food next to it. "You're hungry, aren't you, baby? Bad mommy for coming home so late."

Sugar decided to do a sweep of the house before we got down to the business of the dragon. "Place is clean," she announced. "No spirits stuffed in the closet."

"You really think you'd see it if it was?"

She dropped down on the couch and crossed her long legs. Then she draped her arms across the back and waited for the show to begin. Without further ado, I stripped off my self-described trashy tank top and stood there in my bra, feeling completely at ease standing half-naked in front of her. "Ready?"

"Ready as I'll ever be." She twirled her finger, gesturing for me to turn around. I turned to show her my back, where my dragon was sound asleep. "Well now, I have to admit, baby, that is a fine tattoo. Must have put you back about twenty hours of pain."

Like most people, she'd only seen the parts that peeked out around my clothes. I sighed and dropped down on the couch next to her. "See, that's just it. It didn't take twenty hours to complete. It didn't even take one."

She turned and looked at me like I was off my rocker. "What the *hell*?"

"It's like a birthmark. I was born with it."

She laughed in a short burst and shoved me playfully but firmly against my arm. "Stop messing with me—" Her cocky smile flattened as a low growl came out of my mouth and my eyes flashed a brilliant green. The shove didn't hurt, but the creature on my back didn't take kindly to anyone pushing me around, playful or not.

She bolted off the couch and gawked at me, her face sober from what she apparently wasn't prepared to see. I took advantage of the brief appearance and turned around to let her see the lines move before the dragon settled back down. I could feel it undulating under my skin, restless and waiting to emerge at the next sign of trouble.

She blinked a couple of times to shake off what she was seeing. But of course, she couldn't make it go away. "Now that there is some fucked-up shit," she said as I put my shirt back on and turned back around.

I was pretty useless the next day. Images of bones flying in and out of my head, Pearl May Mobley's frantic eyes staring back at mine, the look on Sugar's face when I came out to her the night before. Jackson Hunter walking out of MacPherson's with a woman under his arm was the real distraction though. It was bad enough that he and his meandering flock of bad boys were invading my shop, but now he was making himself comfortable at my bar, too? There were hundreds of bars in Savannah and he had to pick *my* bar?

Christopher had been more than happy to rearrange his plans for the evening in order to satisfy my desire to play, and if Jackson was there to witness it, all the better. Maybe that would end this unwanted obsession I had with a man who irritated the hell out of me.

In a skimpy little skirt and my signature tank top—you know, the trashy kind—I got out of my car and headed around the building. I'd driven up to MacPherson's from behind and parked in the rear lot. It was around ten p.m., and I'd intentionally gotten there a little earlier than Christopher planned to arrive so I could loosen up at the bar and have a little chat with Fiona.

I rounded the side of the building and halted the second I saw the row of Harleys parked near the front door.

"Okay. I can handle this," I told myself before marching up to the battered green door with the word BEWARE in small letters on the front. It was a joke that someone had painted on the door years ago, Fiona had told me, that became a permanent part of the bar's charm.

I reached for the handle to open it, but before I could take a step inside an empty beer bottle came flying straight at me. I instinctively ducked and watched it somersault through the air and shatter as it hit one of the bikes parked directly in front of the door. That was about the same time the noise from the brawl taking place inside hit my ears.

"Get the fuck out of the way!" someone yelled.

I flipped my back against the outside wall next to the door as three guys rolled out of the pub, fists flying as the smell of sweat, liquor, and blood all seemed to hit my nose at once. I was close enough to reach my hand out and touch them. The smart thing would have been to head back to my car, but instead I slipped right past the fight and into the pub. It was worse inside.

"Get out of here, Katie!" It was Fiona warning me to get back outside, but I froze when I caught Jackson Hunter in my peripheral vision about six feet away. He was in mid-punch when he spotted me. The guy at the other end of that punch took full advantage of the distraction. Jackson's face jolted from the sharp blow to his right cheekbone, a spray of blood releasing from his mouth and peppering the wall behind me.

It felt like the wind had been knocked out of me because it had been. My head hit the wall as two guys barreled into me on their way to killing each other. I shook off the throbbing pain at the back of my skull and scurried toward the entrance, sliding along the wall to clear the brawl that was still taking place outside the door. By the time I made it around the corner of the building, I was paralyzed with the overpowering sensation that I was no longer in charge of my own legs.

I swiped my hand over something wet on my forehead and looked at the bright red blood on the tips of my fingers—*his* blood.

"What the hell are you doing here?" Jackson Hunter came around the corner of the building and looked down at me with those perpetually angry eyes of his.

"What am I doing here?" I repeated, incredulous to the question. "This is *my* bar."

"Jesus," he said, shaking his head. "I've got enough shit to deal with. Now I have to keep you from getting your head smashed in by a bunch of jacked-up dicks in there."

My eyes were already starting to burn, and my skin was literally crawling from the beast trying to get out. His self-righteous expression began to fade, and I noticed a slight cock of his head as he watched what must have been a fascinating but terrifying transformation taking place in front of him.

"You *fucking guy*," I growled, stepping into the few feet separating us. With a right hook, I landed my fist on his good cheek. He stumbled back, reaching for the spot I'd just assaulted and glared at me.

I glanced down at my shaking hand—sore from the impact—and spotted the talons that were starting to protrude from the tips of my fingers, the skin around them thickening and covering with scales. But it was my razor-sharp vision and the hiss coming from my throat that told me I was about to be born into the dragon, and I liked it. For the first time since I knew what I was, I felt myself trapped somewhere between Katie and the beast, like I couldn't decide which one to be. It had always been me or the dragon, but tonight it felt like there was no separation between us. The dragon was just another limb being controlled by my brain. I was different tonight.

"In," I whispered, ordering the beast back inside. And you

know what? It listened. My talons began to recede and draw back inside the soft pale skin around my fingers. The scales vanished as quickly as they'd appeared, and the burning in my eyes lessened as the serpent green faded back to blue.

"Well, that's just fucking great," he scoffed, turning to walk back to the bar. "A *fucking* shifter."

My head snapped up in disbelief. "What did you just say?"

He turned back around and glared at me with contempt. "You shifter chicks are nothing but drama. I kind of like my balls intact though, so I'm just gonna leave."

By the time I came back to earth and processed what he'd just said, I heard his bike start up. He was halfway down the block by the time I came back around to the entrance. The owners of the other two bikes came through the front door and noticed their missing comrade.

"What did you do to the poor guy, tattoo girl?" the lanky blond asked, recognizing me from the shop. "Now we have to go chase him down before he does something stupid." He was bleeding from his hairline but appeared relatively sober for a guy who'd just participated in a nasty pub brawl.

I looked them both in the eyes but didn't care to engage them in conversation. Tipsy bikers mixed with pissed-off women usually ended up with someone getting their feelings hurt. And besides, what happened behind that building was no one's business. I just hoped Jackson felt the same way and knew how to keep his mouth shut.

Fiona was reorienting a few overturned chairs when I walked inside. Johnnie—cook and mediator of brawls—was having a come-to-Jesus with one of the drunk guys slumped in a chair next to the pool table. Disheveled with a few cuts and welts that would turn black and blue by morning, the other guilty participants were already calling it a night, leaving only me and the half-comatose guy in the chair.

"What the hell was that all about?" I asked Fiona when she came around the bar and started pouring me a glass of Talisker.

She set it down in front of me. "On the house. Compensation for pain and suffering for that knot on the back of your head. Please don't sue my granddaddy."

"I've had worse done to me," I said. "So, MacPherson's is a rowdy biker bar now?"

"They didn't start it." She flicked her head toward the guy being counseled by Johnnie. "Einstein over there thought it might be a good idea to piss off a bunch of bikers three times his size. Kept calling them Rapunzels."

"I guess he got what was coming to him," I said, feeling oddly protective of my new clients.

"Mike's just trashed. Decent guy, but he can't hold his liquor. He'll be in here Saturday night apologizing left and right. And then he'll get the bill for the damage." She grinned and set a bowl of peanuts on the bar. "In Jackson's defense, he did warn Mike half a dozen times to lay the fuck off."

Johnnie called across the room. "I'm heading out for a few minutes, Fiona. I need to get Mike home before he gets any foolish ideas about getting behind the wheel. Can you handle the place for a half hour?" He lifted the very drunk and bruised Mike out of the chair and headed for the door.

"A pub with a designated driver," I commented. "You are a pillar to your community, Fiona."

She grinned and waved Johnnie off with his lump of half-dead weight under his arm. "Mike is his cousin. Can't have your kin driving drunk."

I agreed and then got back to our discussion. "You know Jackson?"

"A little. They've been in here a few times over the past couple of weeks. Drove down from Atlanta about a month ago." She put down the bar rag and did that boob leaning thing she'd mastered.

"Why?" she grinned, sticking that red straw in her mouth again. "Do *you* know Jackson?"

"Did you notice that fresh ink on his arm?"

Her brow raised. "Your work?"

"Yes, ma'am."

Fiona bent down to grab something from under the bar and I found myself staring into the tattoo on the top of her head, the one of the horned god.

"Fiona," I casually asked, "have you ever heard of Blackthorn Grove?"

She stood back up and eyed me carefully before answering my question with another question. "What do *you* know about Blackthorn Grove?"

It was obvious she'd heard of it. Why else would she react in such a suspicious way? For various reasons, I chose not to mention the Crossroads Society. "Nothing. That's why I asked. I met one of their priestesses the other day and I was curious."

"Really," she said, diving back under the bar. "Which one?"

Which one?

"Emmaline—" I suddenly realized I didn't know her last name. Fin never mentioned it when he introduced her to me. "I don't know her last name."

Fiona shrugged. "I know who she is."

"Would it be out of line if I asked you to come home with me?" someone purred in my ear, grazing a pair of soft lips over my lobe.

I swiveled to my right and looked at Christopher. "You have awful timing, but I'm so glad you're here." We gazed at each other for a minute and I decided not to play the game tonight. I was too worked up after the events of the evening, and all I wanted to do was lose myself in him before Jackson Hunter had a chance to fill my head again. Jackson and I needed to have a conversation about what he saw and subsequently said to me in the rear parking lot, but right now there was nothing I could do about it.

LUANNE BENNETT

"I'm ready," I said with a double entendre. "Let's get the hell out of here."

Fiona glanced at Christopher and then back at me. "You two have fun now."

———

CHRISTOPHER SULLIVAN WAS one of those neat freaks who couldn't stand to see a dirty dish sitting in the sink or a stack of books that weren't squarely aligned on the coffee table. Women always said men like that made great husbands, but I kind of liked my men a little less fixated on perfection. I mean, if I misplaced a magazine would it send him off the deep end? What would a lazy Sunday afternoon lying on the couch with ice cream bowls and empty cups scattered around the room do to him?

I glanced at the newspaper on the edge of the entry table and the plastic sleeve it was delivered in crumpled on the floor. Before I could tease him about living dangerously, he grabbed me around the waist and pushed me against the wall, rattling the picture that was hanging to the left of my head. He kissed me deeply, and Jackson Hunter was no more. His fingers found the hem of my skirt and worked it higher as he ground his hips against mine.

"Christopher," I managed to say around his hungry mouth, "slow down."

I was all for abandoning thoughts and unleashing our pent-up sexual desire, but pacing ourselves had always been part of the game. Christopher was an expert at foreplay. He knew exactly what a girl needed, to the point of making me question just how many he'd slept with to get him to his level of expertise.

He pulled away and took a step back, his breath rapid with his brown eyes fixed on mine in a thoughtful way. "Too aggressive?" A faint grin edged up one side of his face as he cocked his head, a sharp cracking sound coming from his neck as he snapped it upright again. "Wine?"

"Got any scotch?"

"Anything for you, baby." He ran his thumb over the curve of my chin and peered into my eyes like he couldn't wait to devour me. "Neat or with ice?"

I huffed at the question. "Really, Christopher? Ice?" I'd never taken my scotch with anything other than a drop of water. Ice was sacrilege, and he knew it.

As he headed for the kitchen to grab the drinks I studied him, trying to figure out if it was a change in the way he styled his hair tonight or if he'd changed his cologne. Maybe it was just his eagerness to get down to business. It didn't take much to get Christopher going, but he was the one who usually had to be encouraged to speed it up—a girl's dream.

I sat on the sofa and looked around his impressive but sterile house. Everything in it was modern and new, mostly metal and glass, with only the leather and fabrics of the furniture to soften it up a bit. My place was full of eclectic things I'd collected from flea markets and garage sales. I liked my stuff nice and old, to have a history. My house was a little cluttered but clean, despite the dust on my blinds and boxes of old books that didn't fit on my packed shelves. The thought of having a real relationship with someone like Christopher was unrealistic, a recipe for a nightly argument. And don't get me started about his allergies to anything with fur.

My cat had seniority.

A glass appeared in front of my face as he reached over me from behind the sofa. "Thank you, Mr. Sullivan."

"You're welcome, Miss Bishop."

He sat on the sofa next to me minus his own glass. Christopher liked to drink. I wouldn't call him an alcoholic, but on our game nights he always had a glass in his hand. I think the buzz opened him up a little more and allowed him to be what he couldn't be in the halls of justice where he wore a mask of civility.

"Not thirsty tonight?" I asked, noticing his intense stare and a slight twitch in his right eye.

Without answering, he put his hand on my shoulder and moved it up the side of my neck, stroking the hollow between my clavicle bones with his thumb. His other hand landed on my thigh and quickly moved up my skirt. "Finish your drink," he ordered, his sternness all part of the game. I complied and polished off the scotch, relaxing from the smoky heat it created down the back of my throat. Taking my hand, he led me toward the kitchen.

"The kitchen," I said. "That's a new one."

He turned around and lifted me off the ground, moving me onto the kitchen island, shoving my skirt up to my hips in the process. He wedged my thighs open and pressed into me as far as the granite countertop would allow, gripping my breast aggressively with one hand while the other jabbed between my legs.

"Jesus, Chris, take it easy." Suddenly it came to me, the difference about him tonight. The eyes staring back at me were brown, but Christopher's eyes were blue.

I shoved him but he barely budged. "Stop it, Christopher. You're hurting me!"

Ignoring my protests, he buried his face in my neck and pulled his hand away from my breast, circling it around to my back. His other hand kept working deeper inside of me until his probing turned painful. I screamed and fought harder, but he was too strong. Suddenly both of his hands were on my shirt, tearing at the neckline until it was split down the center. He gripped me around the back of my ribcage and pulled me tighter against him, running his tongue and mouth over the skin above my right breast. And then I felt his teeth sink in, pulling at my flesh, sucking.

The counter trembled like a small earthquake was cracking

the foundation of the house. My eyes burned and I could feel my skin start to split, making way for what was fighting to come out of me. My hands were bound behind my back with one of his, but I could feel the tables turning as the talons of the beast broke through my fingertips and ripped through his constricting hand as if it were made of soft butter. It was like watching a movie through the eyes of the dragon as I took hold of Christopher's arms and began to pull. A growl came from his mouth, his teeth still buried in my flesh as I yanked his arms away, ripping them from his torso.

A glistening string of saliva mixed with blood stretched between us when he pulled his mouth away from my broken skin and leaned back to look at my face. "I wasn't going to kill you," he said with a shocked look in his eyes. "But I couldn't resist."

The horror of what was happening hit me in the gut. I was caught somewhere between the human and the beast, my repulsion dominated by a more powerful surge of excitement, triggering the urge to vomit and flick my tongue at his face at the same time.

I glanced at his limbs gripped in my claws and let them fall to the floor. He fell back against the kitchen wall, his mouth smeared with blood while his eyes tracked back and forth across my face. He laughed in a short burst, and then his mouth froze in a grimace as his skin started to shrink. Christopher was shriveling before my eyes.

"Katie," he whimpered, cocking his head in the direction of one of his severed arms, his expression locked in shock while he bled out on the kitchen floor.

I looked away as Christopher's eyes turned back to blue and pleaded with me. But it was too late. Mercifully, his eyes went dead as the spirit finished sucking the life out of him, then slipped from his body and floated up in an incorporeal mist that snaked across the ceiling and then began to disappear.

My vision blurred for a moment and then cleared as the

dragon receded, leaving me to deal with the pain and guilt of watching Christopher take his last breath. A wave of grief washed over me, and then panic set in. I stumbled across the room, relieved that the blinds were closed. Then I found my purse and pulled out my cell phone to call Fin Cooper.

13

I nearly jumped out of my skin when Fin knocked on the glass patio door with two men wearing jumpsuits and gloves. When I opened it, Fin took one look at my swollen eyes and released a shuddering breath. An hour had passed, allowing more than enough time for me to have a meltdown over what had happened. But my pragmatic side kicked in as I unlocked the door and motioned them in.

Fin glanced at the body. "I take it this was your doing, Miss Bishop?" He showed no repulsion or shock from the sight of the shriveled remains sprawled on the kitchen floor.

I nodded. "He attacked me. The dragon—"

He raised his hand to hush me. I'd changed into a T-shirt from Christopher's drawer, which only made me feel worse because the cotton still smelled like him under the scent of laundry detergent. "Self-defense," he said. "Unfortunately, the courts won't see it that way, seeing how the man has no arms or insides left."

"Who are these men?" I asked, watching them haul a large trunk through the door. "Are they planning to put him inside of that?"

"They're the cleaners, Miss Bishop. They'll be handling the body." He shook his head and headed for the kitchen. "It's best you don't know the details." After rummaging through one of the drawers, he pulled out a metal rod—a knife sharpener—and walked over to the shriveled body that resembled a deflated blow-up doll. Carefully, he lifted it on one side. "Gentlemen, turn him over." The two men wearing gloves flipped the body to exposed Christopher's back. Fin used the rod to move the shirt out of the way and exposed what he was looking for.

"My God!" I gasped, recognizing the faint outline of the tattoo I'd placed on Victor Tuse's back, and confirming what I already knew.

"Looks like the spirit found himself that new host." He stood back up and dropped the metal rod into the opened trunk and looked at me questioningly. "Miss Bishop, what is this man to you? Which leads to my next question: Why are you here?"

"We were friends. Christopher and I . . ."

"Had a romantic relationship?" he asked, finishing what I was having trouble saying.

I corrected him. "I wouldn't call it romance."

"If I may be blunt, Miss Bishop, and I believe under the circumstances bluntness is warranted. You and Mr. Sullivan were engaged in a purely sexual relationship?"

With a nod, I confirmed his statement. "How do you know his name? I didn't give it to you over the phone."

"Property records. Rule number one when cleaning up a murder scene—know whose house you're walking into. You just killed yourself an assistant DA for Chatham County. This little mess is gonna take some serious cleaning to keep you out of jail, Miss Bishop."

I nearly broke down again when he said the words *murder* and *jail*. If the police connected me to the crime, I was going to *prison*, which sounded a lot worse than *jail*. I'd probably get the death penalty because of the brutal nature of the crime. But then again, what sane person manages to deplete a body of its internal organs by sucking it dry? Maybe my defense team could argue insanity.

"Miss Bishop? *Miss Bishop?*" Fin repeated, interrupting my distracted thoughts. "Did you hear what I just asked you?"

"Sorry. What?"

"I asked if anyone saw you with Mr. Sullivan tonight?"

The nail had just been hammered into my coffin. Christopher showed up at MacPherson's after the place cleared out, and after Johnnie left to take his cousin home, but Fiona knew exactly who I left with.

"By the look on your face, I take it there were witnesses that saw you with him tonight?" he asked. "Where's your car?"

"Parked behind MacPherson's Pub. The bartender—" As soon as I said it, I feared for what he might do to protect his golden member of the Crossroads Society. I was the key to helping them find the rogue spirit. They needed me, and I had a feeling they'd go to extreme lengths to make sure I stayed out of jail.

"Fiona MacPherson?" he asked.

"She's a friend, Fin. I'll turn myself in before I let you hurt her."

"Don't you worry about Fiona. Nobody will be laying a hand on a MacPherson in this town." He refused to expand on that, just offering me his word that no harm would come to her. "Now I need you to tell me exactly what happened tonight."

I recounted the evening, starting with the bar fight at MacPherson's but leaving out any mention of Jackson by name. Last thing I needed to hear was that Jackson Hunter was somehow in bed with the society like everyone else seemed to be. I was beginning to wonder if the whole damn town was in cahoots with them, fattening me up as the sacrificial lamb to bait the spirit back into that book, perhaps with me right along with it.

"He bit me!" I spat. I pulled the neck of the oversized T-shirt down to where the bite mark should have been, but it was practically healed, leaving just a series of faded red spots.

"Your wounds heal quickly," he noted. "Must be the dragon's blood in you."

Come to think of it, they did. I fell from a zip line when I was twelve. I wasn't allowed on it, but like most kids I didn't listen very well. Hurt like hell. I remembered one of the other kids screaming like a banshee when she saw the tip of my arm bone telegraphing through my skin. By the time my mother got me to the hospital, the pain was gone and there was no sign of the injury. The X-rays were clean. In fact, I couldn't recall ever suffering a nasty cut or bruise that lasted more than an hour or two.

I looked at Fin suspiciously. "What exactly are we looking for, Fin? Are we hunting vampires?"

He glanced at the shriveled body as the two men bagged it and carried it toward the trunk. "Of course not. It wasn't after your blood, Miss Bishop—it was after your essence. It couldn't help itself. You're its liberator, kind of like a vampire's maker. Only unlike a vampire it doesn't have any loyalty. It just wants to be you."

I couldn't resist, it had said to me before vaporizing out of Christopher's body.

Fin got up and had a few words with the men. Then he motioned for me to follow him out the back door. "I think it's about time you considered moving into Lillian's house. You'll be safe there until we can figure out the best way to trap this thing."

"Do I look like I need protection, Fin? You saw what I did to —" I swallowed the erupting emotion creeping up my throat. That thing wasn't Christopher. The moment the spirit took control, Christopher was lost. "I'm not moving in with anyone."

"You should at least consider the well-being of the folks around you," he said. "You may be a creature of formidable means, Miss Bishop, but your friends and colleagues will not be as well-fortified if it comes for one of them. It's watching you, knows your people. This is just the beginning."

He was trying to manipulate me, but I knew my friends were at risk regardless of where I stayed. I figured the spirit had even more incentive to use the people I loved if I was locked away somewhere it couldn't get to me, so why not leave myself wide open so it wouldn't have to? Besides, with what happened here tonight, I think I'd just made my point about the futility of that strategy. "All the more reason I need to stay close to them, so don't waste your breath trying to convince me that moving into the big house will keep everyone safe, Fin. It won't."

He considered me for a few seconds before conceding. "We need to let these men finish doing their job." Like a proper gentleman, he pulled the sliding door back and waited for me to step outside.

I glanced at the front door. "The driveway is out front."

"That would be rule number two, Miss Bishop. Never announce yourself at a crime scene you're cleaning up. Wise, don't you think?"

FIN DROVE me back to my car parked behind MacPherson's. It was late, but the pub was still open. I remembered his comment earlier about no one laying a hand on a MacPherson and considered going back inside to find out why, but he was just sitting there in his big fancy car waiting for me to pull out and head home.

I finally relented and drove out of the lot. I rolled down my window to take advantage of the wind against my skin, seeing how it was the height of summer in Savannah and my air conditioner had only worked for about a week in May before it died. Halfway home I pulled off the road into the parking lot of a closed restaurant, dangling my arm out the window as Fin pulled in behind me.

He rolled up next to me from the opposite direction so our windows were side by side. The air conditioning escaped his window as it rolled down, snaking across my face to mercifully cool my hot skin. "A little hungry?" he asked.

"Go home, Fin. This little following act is kind of creepy."

"Miss Bishop, did you just call me a creep?"

"If the shoe fits," I snickered.

He glanced around the dark, empty lot and then back at me. "As you wish." Then he reached for the pack of cigarettes on his console and lit one. "One more thing before I send you on your way. After you've had a few hours to digest the gravity of it all, we'll need to get our ducks in a row about what happened here tonight. It'll take about half a day for Mr. Sullivan to be missed down there at the DA's office, so don't be surprised when you turn on the news. Folks around here like to hunt things, especially pillars of the community who go missing."

I stared straight ahead at the dark restaurant in front of me. "I guess so. Should I call you tomorrow?"

"I'll call you," he said, flicking the barely smoked cigarette to the pavement and rolling the window back up.

Before breaking down, I waited for him to pull away and disappear down the side street. My chest heaved as I sobbed and let it all out: the death of Christopher at my own hands, fear that the rest of the people I loved might be next, this ridiculous effect Jackson Hunter had on me. I even cried over the memory of Elliot packing up his car and heading off to L.A. Yeah, this Savannah thing was really working out. My life was a shitstorm since stepping foot on Georgia soil.

After about ten minutes of feeling sorry for myself, I was done with it. I pulled out of the parking lot and headed home, keeping an eye out for any other cars that showed up and persisted in my rearview mirror. Before pulling into my driveway,

I scanned the block for anything out of the ordinary, which was a loose term these days.

Jet met me in the hallway and did a figure eight around my legs. "Don't act like you're starving, mister." Before heading to MacPherson's that evening, I came home to feed the cat and change clothes. And if I walked into that kitchen I was pretty sure I'd find half a bowl of dry cat food left. I kicked off my shoes and went into the living room to turn on the TV, expecting to see coverage of a local assistant DA's murder, with my face plastered all over the screen as a person of interest. Everyone knew "person of interest" was code for suspect. But that was silly, wasn't it? It would take at least twenty-four hours before my face showed up on the screen.

The sudden urge to vomit had me running for the bathroom. Jet followed and stood up on his hind legs to see what was so interesting in the toilet bowl. "Go away, Jet." I pushed him away, because the bowl was only big enough for one head. Nothing came up because nothing had gone in my stomach since break-fast, and that was only a banana. I needed food.

I went back to the kitchen to search the refrigerator for left-overs and found some pizza from a couple of days earlier. Pizza was one of those foods that got better with age. Went great with a cup of coffee in the morning, especially when recuperating from a hangover. I leaned back against the counter and chewed it straight from the foil wrap, cold.

Something caught my eye outside on the patio. I tossed the slice on the counter and dropped down to the floor, crawling along the length of the island to the side that was closest to the glass door. "Shhh," I said, quieting Jet as he started meowing loudly, a reaction to me getting down on all fours. He walked past me and looked out at the patio before heading toward the living room. I could make out the tip of a shoe sticking up over the arm of the chair. "What the hell?" Someone was sitting in one of my chairs, with a foot up on the table.

I moved back around the island and stood up, waiting to see if the dragon felt the threat. It never even stirred. Concealing myself from view, I opened the cabinet door to my left to pull out the small wooden box shoved behind a row of canned beans. Inside was a 9mm Glock. I hadn't touched it since the day I got my permit, and I was hoping I'd never have to take it out of that box.

Before unlocking the safety and creeping toward the sliding glass door, I considered the option of cowering in the corner while I waited for the police to arrive. But considering I'd just killed a man a few hours earlier and hadn't had time to wash the DNA off my skin and clothes yet, I opted for handling the situation myself. I would just scare the intruder.

With both hands fighting to hold the gun steady and my heart about to come out of my chest, I stepped in front of the window and went to knock on the glass to get the intruder's undivided attention. A second before I knocked, I saw a spray of black hair cascade over the edge of the chair.

"Fuck!" I yelled. The sound was loud enough to travel through the glass. Jackson Hunter stumbled out of the chair when he saw the gun pointed at him through the door and swiftly stepped out of its sight. I really didn't know the man, so it was kind of stupid to unlock the only barrier between us. For God's sake, he was trespassing and making himself at home on my patio. What kind of savory person did that?

"What the fuck are you doing on my patio?" I demanded, sliding the door open with the gun still pointed in the general vicinity of where he'd just been standing. "And how do you know where I live? Jesus! I could have shot you!"

"You wanna put that thing down?" he said, coming up from the side and taking it from my trembling hands. He reengaged the safety and walked past me to the kitchen with it. "Where?" I pointed to the wooden box where he stowed it safely away before walking back outside. "You want to try that again and invite me inside?" he asked.

"Why? Are you a vampire?"

He laughed, but it wasn't funny. Instead I stepped outside. "You still haven't told me how you know where I live. And where's your bike?" It wasn't in the driveway. He motioned to the right side of the house. "Tell me you didn't drive up on my grass and park on the side of my house."

"Fine."

"Fine what?" I asked.

"I won't tell you. Actually, I drove up your neighbor's driveway and then over a few feet. What? You got about ten feet between houses around here." He glanced at the two chairs, inviting me to sit on my own patio.

"Hell no! You stand, because you're not staying."

"It's easy to find out where someone lives," he continued, showing no indication that he planned to get back on his Harley and drive off my property. "I don't know this neighborhood, and I kinda like my bike."

"Well, maybe you shouldn't leave it unattended while you nap on other people's patios." Thank God my neighbor was out of town. "You're going to resod my yard if you damaged it with your bike, and you can bet I'll be out here first thing in the morning to check."

If he could have had a more contemptuous look on his face, I would have stepped back inside and locked the door again. "Why do you always have that scowl on your face?" I asked, not really expecting an answer. "Did your best friend die or something?"

He glared at me for a few seconds. "Yeah. My best friend died. Now you're gonna tell me who sent you."

14

W e still hadn't addressed the elephant in the kitchen. Jackson Hunter stood on my patio, asking me some strange questions about a man named Kaleb, and we still hadn't brought up the fact that he'd called me a shifter earlier that night.

"Look," I said. "I'm tired. I'm hungry. And I'm about to walk back in that kitchen and put that gun to my head if this day doesn't end soon."

For the first time since we met, his face softened and looked remotely friendly. I don't know if it was his intense eyes, his long black hair that screamed Goth, or his unusually tall height; the man standing in front of me seemed downright dangerous. But despite the physical warning signs, there was something in his deep baritone voice that was soothing. If he could just say something nice for a change instead of always addressing me like I was intolerable, I might actually like him.

After a few minutes, he made a move to that chair he seemed to like so much. "Hey, hey, hey!" I blurted. "I didn't say you could make yourself comfortable."

He ignored the protest and sat, spreading his long legs wide as he eased back in the seat. "You got any beer?"

I laughed incredulously, an immediate response escaping me. Eventually I shrugged and said, "What the fuck. Sure." I went back inside and grabbed a bottle from the fridge. His brow furrowed as I handed him a bottle of light beer.

"Who's this Kaleb?" I asked, taking a seat on the other side of the table.

He eyed me like he couldn't decide if I was fucking with him or genuinely didn't recognize the name. Then he downed half the beer and told me to take off my shirt.

"What?" I snorted. "Boy, are you in for a letdown tonight." An uneasy feeling started to make its way up my throat as the snide grin left my face. He was about ten inches taller than me, and since my dragon was being unusually quiet on my back, I figured he'd have plenty of time to do some damage before it woke up and smelled the threat.

I shot out of my chair. "I think it's time for you to leave."

With the bottle midway to his mouth, he froze. He set it back on the table and shook his head, muttering something I couldn't understand. "Let me rephrase that. I need to make sure you're not one of Kaleb's disciples." He hesitated, waiting for my reaction, I assumed. When I didn't flinch, he continued to "rephrase" his request. "There's a mark between the shoulder blades. I need to know if I'm gonna find it on you before this conversation goes any further."

"And if you do?" Of course he wouldn't find anything other than the dragon tattoo on my back, but I was curious—and a little wary—about the capabilities of the man I was conversing with in the seclusion of my backyard.

"Then the conversation is over and I leave—town."

I humored him, if for no other reason than to hurry the conversation along and get to this Kaleb person. Then maybe we could call it a truce and have that other conversation we'd been avoiding, the one about how he knew what I was, and why it didn't send him running in the opposite direction instead straight to my house.

Jet strolled out through the open door and looked at the stranger sitting in the chair on his patio. His paw stopped in mid-step. Cautiously at first, he approached, but then picked up the pace and plowed into the side of Jackson's leg. I almost jumped out of my chair when Jackson bent down to pick him up. "Hey, guy. Who are you?" He deposited Jet in his lap.

I watched him stroke Jet's back and tail, clearly comfortable with felines. "That's Jet. You like cats?"

He shook his head. "Nah. Hate the damn things." He peered up from Jet, a smile on his face.

"Imagine that," I said, smirking. "A big manly-man like you liking cats."

He lifted Jet and put him back on the ground. "Cats are about the only thing that show you exactly who they are. I like dogs, but I don't trust them. Too eager to please before you've earned it."

"So you think you've earned it?" I asked. "My trust?"

"I'm still deciding if I trust *you*," he answered. "Based on that forthright attitude of yours, I'd say you're more of a cat than a dog." He took another swig of beer and nodded toward my shirt. "But I still need to see for myself before we take this conversation any further."

"Why, thank you," I said, flashing a sarcastic grin. "Now let me get this straight. You walked into my shop, showed up at my bar, and now you're sitting in my backyard, and I have to prove to you that I'm trustworthy?"

"It's a small world, but it seems a little too convenient that I was referred to a tattoo shop that just happens to be owned by a shifter."

"I don't call myself a shifter." I stood up and turned around, knowing damn well he wouldn't tell me anything unless I proved

I wasn't one of these disciples he'd referred to. "I'm obviously not taking off my shirt, but if it'll make you shut up and tell me what you want from me, you can look down the back." I never thought I'd hear myself say those words to a practical stranger.

He wasted no time taking advantage of the offer, pulling my T-shirt down just enough to get a good look at where my shoulder blades intersected. Then he pressed his hand on the spot through the fabric.

I whipped around and glared at him. "I didn't say you could touch me."

He threw his hands up in surrender. "It can take a while for the mark to surface. I'm just making sure it isn't under your skin." He ran his hand over the top of his head. "You sure are uptight." With a quizzical look, he cocked his head slightly right and opened his mouth to say something else.

"What?" I challenged. "Be very careful about what you say to me next, Jackson Hunter. I've had a very bad day, and I'm not interested in any more small talk. Are we clear?"

"Got it. No small talk." He sat back down and finished his beer. "Kaleb Matthew Daniels. He's the guy who wants me dead. Heads up a biker club out of Atlanta. The Sapanths."

"Ah. And somehow you got the idea I might be one of them? Are you crazy?" He shook his empty beer bottle. "Forget it," I said, refusing to get him another one. "Finish what you were saying."

"They're shifters, and they're dangerous. I've got a bounty on my head. Dead or alive."

I found myself glancing around the yard, an involuntary reaction to hearing that the man sitting across from me was wanted by a bunch of outlaw creatures. If they were half as dangerous as I was when the dragon came out, Jackson was looking at an early grave. "What did you do? Steal something from them?" He smirked and shook his head. "You did, didn't you? A lot of questions have been going through my mind since the day you walked into my shop, but I never took you for a thief."

He smiled genuinely for the first time since we met. "So you've been thinking about me ever since?"

Good one, Jackson Hunter.

"Well, yeah," was all I could think to say. It was true. I couldn't get his face out of my mind, or his lean muscled form with that conservative scattering of tattoos, or his bottomless voice that sent a warm snake up my middle every time I heard him speak. He was a rock star on a Harley. "But don't get the wrong idea."

He leaned onto his knees and nearly dropped me with his eyes. "I wouldn't dream of getting the wrong idea about you, Katie."

I shook it off, remembering that he was a thief. "So, what did you steal that has them so pissed off?" I glanced toward the side of my house where the Harley was parked. "You own that bike, right?"

"Let's just say I walked away with two of their most precious possessions: their secrets, and Kaleb's daughter. Well, his daughter's pride. But if you're a Sapanth, that's the equivalent of an entire bank account." He sighed heavily, like the thought of recounting it all over again was tedious. "Sapanths make a lot of money from marital arrangements—dowries. Only in their world the dowry comes from the guy, and that future son-in-law expects untouched property, if you know what I mean."

A thought suddenly smacked me in the head as I glanced at his feet and worked my way back up to his face. "Hold on. Is this your way of telling me you're a shifter, too?"

He shook his head. "Not even close. But I know that *they* are, and that was just fine as long as I was a lifetime member. Generally, if you make it to membership level, it's for life. They didn't appreciate me disappearing in the middle of the night."

"This woman was your girlfriend?"

"I wouldn't call her that. Kara just didn't like the idea of being owned by one man, and believe me, I wasn't the first guy she messed with. Unfortunately, my best friend Pete was the first. They killed him for that."

He got up and walked toward the door. "I'll have that second beer now." He came back out with two bottles and handed one to me. "I got out of there before they killed me, too. I knew some people down here, so here I am."

"And then you walked into my shop and decided to insult me with your chauvinistic charm," I added.

A sly grin slid up his face. "I couldn't guarantee I'd be able to maintain my manners with your hands all over me. You should thank me, Katie. I did you a favor." He took another swig and penetrated me with his eyes again. "Then I got a peek at those claws and green eyes tonight and figured you were one of Kaleb's girls, sent down from Atlanta to tie up loose ends. But now I got a feeling you're nothing like them, are you?"

"It depends on what they're like," I replied. It wasn't really a question though. He was musing about what I might actually be. And for some odd reason I wanted to show him.

"I want you to go somewhere with me tomorrow night," he said. "It'll be fun."

15

"Thanks, Mae." I took my breakfast to my usual booth, the one with a view of the shop. I'd barely slept after Jackson drove off the night before, the same way he came, across my grass and down my neighbor's driveway. I did check the grass when I got up. Except for a path of flattened blades that were already recovering under the morning sun, the lawn was fine. Had it been rainy and soggy the night before, he'd be getting a bill for the damage.

I had the whole day to think about where he was taking me after work. Even more distracting was the thought of what we might do when we got there. In fact, we came dangerously close to crossing that line just before he left in the early hours of the morning. Trying to ignore the attraction between us was futile.

"Shit," I sighed, my mind racing over the past twenty-four hours, and how any day now I'd turn on the TV and hear the news about the missing assistant DA who'd vanished into thin air. Fin Cooper was a powerful man in this town, and I prayed that power was enough to get me out of this mess. I'd killed a man. Self-defense or not, I had to live with the memory of Christopher's dying face looking back at me as the life left his eyes. My one chance was that they never found that body, because it was a hell of a lot harder to convict without one. But they still could if they built a case around an eyewitness placing me with Christopher the night he disappeared. Who would a jury believe—a respected member of the local community or an outsider covered with tattoos? The power of social prejudice was not in my favor.

And then there was the spirit responsible for all of it, still prowling out there like a loose cannon. If Fin didn't call by noon, I was calling him. We needed a plan and we needed it now.

My eyes wandered around the room. Every face looking back at me was a possible new host, and I refused to let it just walk up on me again. Christopher was practically hurling red flags at me last night, but I just shrugged it off as a mood until it was too late. That would be the last time I ignored my intuition, and don't think for a minute I didn't vet Jackson Hunter for signs of possession the second he looked at me through that glass door last night.

I took a bite of my biscuit and saw Mouse through the window opening the shop. Mouse always came in from the front of the building. Having no driver's license, she walked to work every day, which was no burden since she only lived a few blocks south of the shop. She probably would have walked even if she had a car.

My eyes panned back around the room. Lou had been operating the diner for close to forty years, serving breakfast and lunch. The place closed by three p.m. every day and reopened the next morning at six a.m. I suspected the menu hadn't changed much since opening day. Maybe a few new items added over the years for the lunch crowd, but breakfast was one of those meals that you really couldn't improve on. People who wanted eggs Benedict or croissants stuffed with chocolate didn't come to Lou's, nor did the folks who worried about fat and calories. Good old heart attack food came out of Lou's kitchen.

I finished my breakfast and headed across the street to the

shop, glancing at my phone as I dodged traffic. It was 9:43 a.m. I'd lost track of time, but under the circumstances it was warranted.

Sea Bass shot me a frustrated look when I walked through the front door, about the same time a blur of bright orange hair and freckles blew past me and nearly knocked over a tray of ink.

"Tommy!" someone yelled. "Get your ass over here and sit down."

It was Beth Hendricks, my 9:20 a.m. appointment. The boy careened back through the shop and slammed into her chest.

"This ain't no daycare, Beth," Sea Bass said. Beth Hendricks went to high school with Sea Bass. He knew her well, which excused the attitude I normally frowned upon when dealing with clients. But she'd been warned more than once not to bring her kids to the shop, because they were little hellions without a shred of manners or discipline. More for liability reasons than anything else. Nothing like a wild Indian crashing into you while you're applying a fine line of ink to a client's skin. At least she only brought one of them with her today.

"I'm sorry, Beth," I apologized. "I had a little family emergency." Mouse's ten o'clock client walked through the door and I shook my head. "Tommy can't be in here, Beth." I pointed to the sign on the wall that said NO SMALL CHILDREN IN THE SHOP. "It's not fair or safe for the other clients."

"Well, what am I supposed to do with him?" she asked.

"That ain't our problem, Beth," Sea Bass continued, taking a little more pleasure than necessary putting her in her place. "Jeez, it's not like you're coming to the ER." They were like a pair of bitchy old neighbors bickering over one's dog shitting in the other's yard.

"He's right," I agreed. "We'll have to reschedule when you can get someone to look after the kids."

She grabbed her redheaded hellion and stomped toward the

door. "Maybe I'll just go over to Tattoo Haven. I bet they're kid friendly over there."

Maybe. I'm sure they'd love to entertain that child of hers while she got her two-inch heart applied to her hip. Hell, an hour of daycare cost more than that, so technically she'd owe us more than double by the end of the session. "You do what you have to do, Beth," I said.

Mouse's client looked relieved. I went for the coffee pot to have my fourth cup of the morning, like I wasn't already buzzed enough to cause my own bull-in-a-china shop episode if I didn't slow down on the caffeine.

"You okay, Katie?" Sea Bass asked.

"Not really, but I'm working on it." He went back to prepping his station. "How's Marvin doing?" The vet had ruled out any broken bones, but the big guy had been badly bruised when he slammed against the window during the car crash. I guess doggie seat belts weren't such a joke after all.

"Milking it for all he can," he snorted. "That damn dog is smart. He walks just fine when he thinks no one's looking at him, but damn if he doesn't hold that paw up and dangle it in the air the minute one of us starts fawning over him."

"Yeah, real manipulators," Abel said. "Just like kids."

Sea Bass looked up at me. "You know, I never asked you how it went with that biker the other day. Did he break down and let an inferior girl do his tattoo?" Without looking up from the sketch she was preparing, Mouse picked up a pen and threw it at him. "Hey now, I'm just repeating the facts."

"He let me work on him." I left it at that. He was picking me up at home for our little outing that evening, so I opted for discretion until I determined just what was going on between us. For all I knew Jackson Hunter would turn out to be a real asshole, and after that tattoo was complete I might never lay eyes on him again.

IT WAS NEARLY one o'clock when Fin Cooper walked through the door. I was beginning to get antsy waiting for his call and planned to pick up the phone myself as soon as I finished with the client in my chair.

"You know, Fin, you could have just called," I said without taking my eyes off my client's arm.

"It's a fine day out there, Miss Bishop. I thought you and I might take advantage of one of our lovely squares and continue that little talk we were having last night." I glanced at Sea Bass and Abel who were both listening to our conversation, and then back at Fin. He got the message and shut up. "Maybe we can just grab some lunch."

"Give me a few minutes," I said.

Fin strolled over to the other side of the room and started up a conversation with Sea Bass. "How's that grandmother of yours, Sebastian?" He grabbed a magazine someone left on the counter and started flipping through it.

"All right, I guess. You've probably seen her more than I have lately though." He barely glanced at Fin. I think he was still a little wounded about finding out that Davina McCabe—his sweet little Grams—was a card-carrying member of the Cross-roads Society. She apparently had a gift for spotting people with unusual talents—me, for one—which made me suspect she had her own secret talents that made her invaluable to the society.

I finished wrapping up my client's arm. "Ready, Fin?" He dropped the magazine back on the counter and nodded to Sea Bass. "I'll be back in an hour," I said as we walked out the door and headed a few blocks toward the park.

"I do love to walk in this city," he said to fill the awkward gap of silence between us. "I've been meaning to get more exercise."

Fin didn't strike me as the type to spend his time in a gym. Despite his bad habit of smoking an occasional cigar or cigarette, he was lean and fit. I imagined he did have to work at it and probably had an arsenal of exercise equipment buried in his basement. "I bet you're one of those types who gets up at four a.m. to work out," I said.

He laughed. "Something like that."

"What are we doing, Fin?"

"Right now, Miss Bishop, we're just walking."

We walked through the entrance of the square and strolled down the cobblestone path, past the rows of monkey grass and the majestic trees. "Can we please stop pretending that I didn't kill a man last night?"

"A thing, Miss Bishop. You dispatched *a thing.* That was no longer a man lying on that floor."

"And yet Christopher Sullivan is dead. He was a good person, Fin. How do I live with what I did?"

"If that creature of yours didn't come out when it did last night, the society could very well be hunting you right now, Miss Bishop. I doubt the spirit intended to inhabit you, but it appears it came very close to losing control and doing just that." His eyes shifted toward me and I could hear his breath deepen and his voice drop an octave. "You are an irresistible woman, Miss Bishop. You must know that."

I slowed down and he turned to face me, making it impossible to move under his firm gaze. "Now I need to know that you're steady as a boat on smooth water. You see, Miss Bishop, your actions are the society's actions. Anything stupid that you might decide to do will have a direct impact on a whole lot of people. Do we understand each other?"

After a moment of digesting the threat he'd just politely delivered, I nodded.

His arm wrapped around my shoulders as he moved us along the sidewalk again. "Good. Now, about this man you were entertaining last night—right after you killed Sullivan."

"What?" I nudged his arm off my shoulder and shot him a

dirty look. "Are you spying on me now? Let's get something straight, Fin. We're in bed together—figuratively—but who I see and what I do in the privacy of my own home is my business. Off limits to you, Lillian, or anyone else at the society. If I find so much as a strange car parked on my block when I get home—" I shut my eyes for a second to rein in my anger. As much as I hated to admit it, I needed Fin Cooper. But I drew the line at my privacy. "If you want to know something about me, ask."

"I believe I just did."

"Don't play games with me, Fin. I don't like being followed or spied on. I'm loyal. If you're up front with me, I'll be up front with you—if it pertains to our common goal. Are we clear?"

A fleeting smile flashed across his face. "Well, Miss Bishop, I believe you just put me in my place." That smile faded a second later as he countered. "As long as it doesn't threaten my freedom in any way, I'll be respectful of your privacy. But if it does—"

"Don't worry. I'm not interested in a life behind bars any more than you are."

He nodded in concession and we continued with our stroll. "So where do we go from here?" I asked. "How do we catch this thing?"

"Now that is a good question," he replied. "But I think we may have come up with something that just might work. Are you available this evening, Miss Bishop?"

The question caught me off guard because I wasn't sure if he was talking business or pleasure. "No. I have plans." I left it at that. No need to expound on what those plans were, especially since he'd already overstepped his bounds. And a little knock on the door of my intuition told me his interest wasn't purely professional.

"Very well. But I must insist that you make yourself available tomorrow night. Lillian is throwing a little dinner party for a few members to discuss a strategy for hunting down the spirit. I'm sure everybody will be obliged to delay in order to accommodate your schedule, Miss Bishop. Besides, parties are always better on a Friday night." He waited for an argument. When he didn't get one he continued. "I'll send my car around to your house around say . . . seven-thirty?"

I LEFT the shop in Sea Bass's hands and went home a couple hours early to feed Jet and take a shower before Jackson showed up for our mysterious night out. All he'd said was to dress comfortably because we'd be outside. Not ready to call this a date, I slipped on a casual sundress and a pair of sandals that had no connotations attached.

Around nine o'clock I started to get a little annoyed. He never specified a time he'd pick me up, but common sense said that anything later than eight o'clock on a weeknight was unreasonable. I fiddled around my clean kitchen, wiping the counters and glancing at the clock on the stove every few minutes. An hour later I finally conceded that I'd been stood up.

"Asshole!" I spat, sending Jet flying out of the room. I didn't even have his phone number to call him and give him an earful, and I had a good mind to drive down to the shop to get it off the computer.

I changed into a pair of shorts and a T-shirt and climbed on the couch with a glass of wine. It was ten-thirty when I heard his Harley rolling down my street and into my driveway. "Are you fucking kidding me," I muttered, walking to the door prepared to send him packing. I opened it just as his foot hit the porch. He grinned and presumed to try to walk past me into the house.

"Uh-uh," I said, shaking my head and stopping him from inviting himself in.

He looked confused. "No? I thought we had a date."

I spotted his cell phone in his front pocket and unabashedly reach my hand inside to extract it. Then I held it up to show him the time. "See that? It's 10:37 p.m."

"Yeah," he replied. "I told you I'd pick you up late tonight."

"No, you didn't."

"I didn't?" He seemed surprised. "Well, I'm here now. What I want to show you doesn't start until late at night. I thought I mentioned that. If I didn't, I'm sorry."

His apology was genuine enough that I couldn't stay mad. I also couldn't explain why I wanted to go off with him to some strange destination at ten-thirty on a work night.

"You gonna invite me in, or should I leave and go off somewhere to lick my wounds?"

I pushed the door wide open and stepped aside. "Give me a minute to change."

He assessed my shorts and T-shirt. "You're dressed perfect for where we're going. Throw on some sneakers for the ride, but bring a pair of flip-flops. That's all you'll need." He had on a pair of loose jeans with several rips that appeared to be from age—not manufacture—and a tank top that showed off every ripple of his well-honed abs. "You can throw them in my backpack."

I looked over at his bike and spotted the bag on the seat. "Okay then." I changed my shoes and then grabbed my keys and followed him out the door. "Still not planning to tell me where we're going?" He just grinned and handed me a helmet and the backpack.

16

We rode through town and headed for the expressway. I'd been on the back of a motorcycle before, but I'd never been on the back of a Harley. As cliché as it seemed, there was something about riding on the back of one with my arms wrapped tightly around the waist of a rebel like Jackson Hunter, that was both scary and liberating at the same time.

The thick air turned into humid sea breeze as we drove over the Bull River and then coasted along the Savannah River toward Tybee Island. Around eleven-thirty, we rode toward the north tip of the island and I could see the Atlantic Ocean come into view in the distance straight ahead. In the six months I'd lived in Savannah I'd never made it out to the island, and I wondered what Jackson had planned for us this late on a Thursday night that required flip-flops and being outside. We were either having a late-night dinner at one of the oceanfront restaurants or going to the beach.

We rode south and finally stopped and parked the bike. He kicked his shoes off and stripped from his jeans, revealing a pair of shorts underneath. Then we exchanged our shoes for flip-flops and stuffed our clothes in the backpack.

"You're not worried about leaving your Harley parked on a strange street?" I asked, thinking about that bike parked on the side of my house.

He shook his head. "I know this neighborhood."

With the backpack swung over his shoulder we headed for the beach. I changed my mind about the flip-flops and carried them as we walked in the sand, the sound of the Atlantic filling my ears as the tide rolled gently under the bright moon.

"I don't know why I've never been out here before."

He glanced at me. "I don't know either. Not many people have all this less than an hour from their front door. Seems almost criminal not to enjoy it."

"Guilty," I sighed.

We walked without a word for the next half mile or so, completely comfortable in the silence as the beauty of the shore-line and horizon superseded small talk. There was an ease about Jackson that I suspected was lost on most people. His facade was both ominous and fascinating at the same time, the textbook stereotype of a dangerous biker. But beyond his long black hair and imposing size, there was a thoughtful man in there, one who reminded me to bring flip-flops for the beach and knew when to shut up and let the awe of the ocean speak for us.

We walked to a remote section of the beach. "Are we going to walk all the way around the island, or should we just dive in and swim to Florida?" I teased.

He pointed ahead to a sand dune covered with sea grass. "We're here." Then he opened the backpack and pulled out a small blanket, spreading it over an area at the foot of the dune. "Have a seat." I planted myself on the blanket and watched him curiously as he pulled out a couple of plastic cups and a thermos. "You like red, right?"

"Wine?" I asked. "Yeah, how'd you know?"

He grinned, and I remembered the row of red wine bottles on my kitchen counter. He must have noticed them when he helped himself to a second bottle of beer from my refrigerator the night before. "Consider this my version of box-o-wine." He unscrewed the thermos and poured the wine into our cups. "Glass in a backpack is a recipe for disaster."

"I have to come clean, Jackson. I didn't think you were capable of something so original. This, I mean." I motioned around the beach. "I thought we'd end up at one of those restaurants we passed on the way in. This is so much better."

He checked the time on his phone. "Then you're really gonna like what you see in about . . . ten minutes."

My eyes widened as I realized our beach blanket and wine was just the precursor to what he had planned for us. "What?"

"Patience, woman." He leaned back on his elbows and gazed out at the water.

Fifteen minutes ticked by as we lay on the dune staring up into the bright sky. He sat up and looked at the beach. "It's started, Katie."

I followed his eyes. Half a dozen yards away under the bright beam of the moon, the ground was moving. A scattered group of small creatures was traveling across the beach toward the ocean. I leaned closer and saw them emerging from under the sand.

"Turtles!" I gasped. "They're hatching!"

I must have been beaming when I looked at him, because he grinned back at me and laughed. "Loggerheads. It's nesting season."

My heart actually pounded from the surge of gratitude I felt to be witnessing something so amazing. "I can't believe you did this for me. I . . . don't even know what to say."

He leaned back on the blanket again. "Yeah, well, you haven't seen the best part yet."

I'd seen the stories on the news and in the papers about the Tybee Marine Science Center's conservation program to help the population of loggerheads, but the nests were usually marked to warn people of them. The little guys breaking through the sand a few yards away from us had no such marker around their nest.

"Hold on, Jackson." I cocked my head at him. "How did you know where the nest was? I'm even more curious about how you knew they would be hatching at exactly this time. You psychic or something?" The *or something* part had me anxious.

"Yeah, I'm a real mystery man." He motioned back to the beach. "You're missing the finale."

The dozen or so hatchlings had turned into hundreds, racing with their tiny flippers to make it to the water before the sun came up or predators got hold of them. Something moved in the middle of the brigade. I started to jump up as a flock of sea birds appeared on the beach in the soup of hatchlings and sand, seeming to pick them up and fly away. Jackson caught my arm and pull me back down.

"They're eating the turtles!" I yelled, trying to pull away from his grip so I could charge onto the beach to chase off the hungry birds.

He shook his head. "Look closer."

I focused on the commotion on the beach, not quite believing what I was seeing. The tiny loggerheads weren't being eaten by the birds—they were turning into birds and flying out to sea. One by one the little hatchlings sprouted wings and lifted off the sand and glided past the moon into the distance.

"Sea shifters," he said before I could ask the question. "They shift into sea birds to make it out to sea. They'll shift back into loggerheads once they land out there. Ordinary hatchlings are lucky to make it to the water or even past the shallows without getting eaten. But these little guys aren't ordinary. They come back to this same spot to lay their eggs, and they'll hatch on the night of the full moon at right around this time every month during nesting season. Like clockwork. They're fascinating creatures, Katie." A grin spread across his face as he continued to gaze at the water. "Just like you."

"How'd you find this place?" From what he'd told me he wasn't a shifter himself, and I hadn't picked up any evidence that he was lying to me about that.

"Kara brought me here a few years back."

"Kaleb's daughter?" I asked, surprised that they'd shared such an intimate secret. The same secret that he was now sharing with me. "I thought she was just some casual hookup."

He glanced at me with a slight admonishing look. "I never said that. You just assumed." And he was right. I just assumed that since he and his best friend both slept with her that she was just another conquest.

"Mmm, I see. So you're just passing this little treasure on to me, now."

His smile faded as he looked toward the last sea shifter disappearing toward the safety of the deep ocean. "Well, I guess if you want to think about it like that. A gift is a gift, Katie. The less people that know about this place the better, but I thought you'd like to see it. You're the only person I've ever shown it to."

I'd managed to offend him. I could see it in his profile as he continued to stare off and look at anything but me. "That came out wrong," I said. "I just meant—"

"Do you know why I wouldn't let you work on my arm the first day I walked into your shop?" he asked, saving me from saying something else obscurely offensive.

"Because you're a chauvinistic ass?" I joked.

He laughed quietly and gazed out over the water again. "Because you nearly knocked me off my feet with those eyes of yours." He turned to look at me and I felt the stir in my stomach grow into a hurricane. "You scared the shit out of me, and I don't scare easy."

My mouth was stuck. I couldn't think of a single thing to say. When I finally regained my mind, I said something less than poetic. "Then why do I feel like every time you look at me you want to get as far away as possible? Like I'm contagious."

"Because you are contagious and I do want to stay clear of you. You're the last thing I need right now, Katie." He leaned closer and paralyzed me with those unsettling green eyes and that sonorous voice. "You're also exactly what I need right now."

Before I could speak he kissed me. A soft, lingering kiss that turned me inside out and left me boneless and weak. Then he moved me back against the sand and rolled his significant weight over me, blocking the brightness of the moon. But he remained perfectly still, hovering inches from my face, the smell of his skin mingling with the salty breeze coming off the water. A second later he was on his feet and pulling me off the sand, gathering the empty cups and the blanket. Then we headed back up the beach, hand in hand, wordless again as we let the sea fill our senses.

When we got back to the bike, I climbed on behind him and rested my face against his back as we made the thirty-minute ride back to my house to explore all the reasons why we were perfect for each other.

JACKSON SAT his empty wine glass on the kitchen counter and took a steady breath before turning to look at me. "Just say the word, Katie, and I'll leave." Looking back at his beautiful green eyes, I knew where the night would end. My limbs were already warming up, and I felt that familiar quickening of my breath as Jackson touched the side of my face with his lips. It was a soft brush, followed by the barest flick of his tongue that nearly knocked the wind out of me.

"Jackson," I whispered, fighting the urge to let go. It had been so long since I'd been able to completely lose myself in a man. "I don't want to ruin this. Maybe it's too soon for—"

"Too soon for what, Katie?" He worked his mouth up to my

temple and across my eyelids, sending a ripple of heat all the way down to my toes as he ended his journey at my mouth. "We're just kissing," he murmured against my parted lips.

I stepped back and took a deep breath, debating the sanity of getting wrapped up in a guy while I was in the throes of hunting evil spirits and trying to keep a business afloat. Juggling all the loin-driven emotions that went hand in hand with infatuation meant one of those endeavors would suffer. He settled the debate by pulling me back against him and kissing me deeply.

A moment later we were in the bedroom, me discarding my clothes while he paused near the door and seemed to be considering my earlier comment. I climbed on the bed and shook my head, making it unmistakably clear that he needed to forget what I'd said. I wanted him.

His eyes heated as he read mine, and his lips parted as if a thought were edged at the tip of his tongue. "*Fuck it,*" he hissed. He pulled his own shirt over his head and released the zipper of his jeans, sliding them off with his shorts to reveal his impressive size that was in direct proportion to his impressive height. Stepping out of them, he climbed over me, caging me as his black hair fell over my face and cascaded against my breasts like water. He smelled like wine and sea, kissing me fully before working his way down my breasts and stomach, past my hips. I thought I'd disappear into the sensation of his hands and mouth and . . . that voice. He murmured something deep, sending a warm rush of breath over the sensitive skin between my legs.

"Jackson, *please.*" I reached for him and he slid his palms up my thighs and hips and gripped my hands tightly, forcing my arms to my sides to hold me in place while he sent a wave of pleasure through me, the small of my back arching off the mattress. The moment I settled back down he raised up and slid inside of me, gripping my waist to pull me closer and allow him to go deeper, barely interrupting the wave that was ready to send me over the edge again.

A powerful urge kicked in and I rolled on top of him, mounting him and riding out the climax until the lines on my back fought to break free. My eyes burned with heat as I gazed down at him, fighting the overwhelming drive to grind into him harder. Suddenly his own eyes changed, the brightness in them growing darker as I moved back and forth against him. My hands reached for his, pushing his arms above his head to pin him against the mattress, but all I could see were the talons beginning to protrude from the tips of my fingers and the glittering scales covering my arms. My jaws tightened from my growing fangs, and every inch of my body shivered from the beast exploding from within.

Jackson's eyes were fixed in fascination, caught somewhere between the intense pleasure and the pain of my claws piercing the tough skin of his palms. A thin line of blood seeped from the point where the tip broke through the surface of his right hand.

As quickly as the animal-like drive consumed me, the air left my lungs and my pleasure turned to fear. I rolled off him and sat at the foot of the bed, horrified. Glaring at my traitorous hands in disgust, I watched the scales return to skin and felt my fangs recede as I ran my tongue over the disappearing tips.

"Katie?" He straddled me from behind and pulled me against him. "Did I do something wrong?"

I turned and looked at him in disbelief. "Jesus, Jackson. I could have fucking killed you."

He tensed for a moment and then moved to the edge of the mattress to sit next to me, his hand running along the lines of the beast as it settled against the skin of my back. "It's okay to shift, Katie. This isn't my first rodeo." He laughed quietly. "I've got a little experience with chicks like you."

He was referring to Kara. I still didn't know what a Sapanth was, but I suspected they had claws, too. "You never told me exactly what Kara is."

"Sapanths are cats. *Big* cats," he added with an arched brow.

"Sex tends to trigger a shift. At least it does with cats."

"Yeah, well, I've managed to control it from doing that. Until now." It wasn't easy in the beginning, but I'd gotten good at keeping the beast quiet during intimate moments. At least with ordinary men. The last guy who met my dragon during sex wasn't human. God, I missed what that felt like.

Jackson laughed again. "What's so funny?" I asked.

"Maybe I should have qualified that comment," he replied. "*Good* sex triggers a shift. I think we're gonna have to get used to a little threesome with that beast of yours."

"Confident, aren't you?" When I glanced back up at him, his eyes were getting that look again. And by the way I was reacting to that look, so were mine.

"You can't hurt me, Katie." Maybe he was right. I suspected there were things about Mr. Hunter that were yet to be discovered. Then he kissed me, pushing me back against the bed so we could finish what we started.

I BOLTED STRAIGHT UP in bed and gasped for air, looking at my outstretched arms to see if I had wings. I was a sea shifter, flapping my wings under the weight of the water as I torpedoed toward the bottom of the ocean to get away from something.

Jackson's hand found the small of my back as he lay against the bed with his other hand resting between his head and the pillow. "You okay?"

I wiped a bead of sweat from my forehead. "Yeah. Bad dream." I left it at that, but it was more like a nightmare. I was flying over the ocean toward something that kept pulling at me. It was the moon, covered with an elaborate series of twisting lines that kept undulating and breathing. But the moment I realized what those lines were, I dove toward the waves. The moon was wrapped with a giant tattoo.

By the amount of light coming into the room, I estimated it to be around eight a.m. I flopped back down next to him, feeling a little uneasy about what we'd done a few hours earlier, mainly because it had felt so raw, so intimate. I barely knew him and here he was, shattering me to the point of uncontrollable bliss.

I hopped off the bed and grabbed the robe hanging on the back of my bedroom door. "I have to make a call. I'll be right back."

Instead of calling Sea Bass directly, I went into the kitchen and called the shop. It was at least half an hour before anyone would be there, which I'd anticipated. I left a message on the answering machine saying I wasn't feeling well and was staying home. None of them would believe the lie, but one of the perks of being the boss was that it didn't matter if I said I was sick or just taking the day off. All I knew was that I wasn't going anywhere near the shop after having just woken from another dream about a giant breathing tattoo. I'd just stay out of the line of fire for the next twelve hours until that dinner party at Lillian Whitman's house.

I was about to dial Fin's number to warn him about my latest dream when something moved behind me. Jackson was leaning against the hallway wall, naked. Everything about him was impressive, and if he didn't put some pants on, crisis or not, I was never getting him out of my house.

I cleared my throat and pulled my eyes away from his distracting features, turning to the cabinet to grab the bag of coffee. "Breakfast?"

He hooked me around the waist and pressed my back into the refrigerator door, leaning in and reminding me of just how small my five-foot-eight frame was against his. "I don't eat breakfast," he said in a rough voice.

"Didn't your mama raise you right?" I countered, trying to sound witty when all I wanted to do was melt into him. His hand ran under my robe and settled at the dimple of my back, pulling me into him. "Let me go," I whispered.

He stepped back, noting my serious tone, lifting my chin to look me in the eye. "We good?"

I nodded and smiled. The way he touched me was unnerving, the feelings he elicited from me with such ease. The last time I felt like this my head ended up in a bad place. It made me stupid and weak and cut my heart open. No one had ever gotten close enough to do that again. Not even Elliot could reach that place. "I need to get to the shop," I lied. His expression took a more serious note, and I knew he'd heard me leave that message stating the contrary.

Maneuvering around his arms, I kissed him quickly on the lips and headed for the toaster oven. "I'm making toast and you're eating a piece." But by the time I turned around he was gone.

"Should I come by after work?" he asked, emerging from the bedroom a few minutes later, dressed with his keys in his hand. "Or are we not there yet? It is Friday night."

It was that awkward stage where neither of us knew what the other wanted. I wanted him to stay all day, but I had deadly business to attend to and dinner at Lillian Whitman's house, a party I suspected was more business than pleasure. "I have plans tonight that can't be cancelled. Tomorrow? Lunch? Dinner? Midnight snack?"

His disappointed face brightened. "All of the above." He gave me a final kiss and headed for the door, with Jet under his feet before he reached it.

"Watch Jet," I warned. "I don't let him outside alone. Too many crazies looking for black cats."

"Sorry, little man," he said, bending down to run his hand over Jet's arched back. He gave me a last look that set my stomach aflutter. Then he maneuvered around the cat and headed toward his bike parked openly in the driveway, in the neighborhood he now apparently trusted.

17

I considered dialing Fin's number but chose to mull over it while I ate breakfast. I supposed it could have been just another dream, not some harbinger of another evil spirit gunning for my ass. The only way to find out for sure was to call Fin and ask if they were missing another one, but I suspected I would have heard about it by now it they were.

A cup of coffee and two slices of toast later, I dropped down on the sofa and turned on the TV. The morning news sobered me.

At this time, police have no reason to suspect foul play, but they are treating the disappearance as suspicious. An anonymous tip placed attorney Christopher Sullivan at a pub on the south side. Investigators are hoping to get answers after interviewing staff and witnesses.

My stomach felt like a right hook had just been delivered to it. I knew this was coming, but I wasn't prepared to see Christopher's name and picture plastered across the screen of my television. The police knew he was at MacPherson's the night of the murder, and that meant they were about to find out who he left with—if they didn't already know.

A loud bang on my door nearly made that toast and coffee come roaring back up my throat. "Fuck," I muttered, creeping toward the window to see if a patrol car was parked out front, lights flashing as Chatham County PD stood on my doorstep to take me away in handcuffs. A stupid thought crossed my mind for a second, but then the stronger voice of reason prevailed and convinced me that running out the back door would only delay my incarceration and tarnish my plea of self-defense. And there was always the insanity plea. I was about to pull the blinds back when I heard the patio door open.

"What the hell is going on with you, woman?" Sugar strode into the kitchen and poured herself a cup of coffee. "I told you to get a metal rod for that damn door, didn't I?"

I'd taken that advice, but apparently I'd forgotten to drop it into the door track before leaving for the beach with Jackson the night before. Note to self: *put metal rod in door.*

"Jesus, Sugar. Next time you knock on my door you might want to do it with a little less aggression." I glanced at the kitchen cabinet where I kept that little wooden box. "You know I've got a gun in that cabinet behind you." Not to mention the possibility of invoking the dragon.

She grabbed her cup from the counter and walked over to me, regarding my weary eyes with commiseration. "Baby, you in a world of trouble."

"Nah, I'm not in trouble, Sugar—I'm *fucked.* I'm a bona fide member of the *fucked* club." I walked back over to the coffee pot and poured myself another cup. "You know what I did the night before last?" I asked, although her family being honorary members of the Crossroads Society pretty much guaranteed she already knew. They were all in the secret club, maybe even had a secret handshake. I was about to find out just how good a friend she was. "I killed a man. Christopher Sullivan." Her unflinching stare confirmed what I suspected.

"Mm-hmm," she replied, glancing at the TV as the news was making its way back around to the story of the missing assistant DA. That's the thing about local news. If you miss it the first time, all you have to do is wait a few minutes for the top stories to recycle right back around. "Now you listen here," Sugar ordered, penetrating me with her best don't-fuck-with-me stare. "I know all about that. I also know what it was that you killed, and it wasn't Christopher Sullivan. Well, technically it was, but not until after that godforsaken piece-of-shit spirit tried to suck you dry. I guess the damn thing thought it could inhabit all this," she waved her hand up and down my body, "and spring that other spirit loose by itself. Bypass the middleman. Kinda like sucking its own dick." She smirked and downed the rest of her coffee. "But I guess it didn't get the memo about that dragon, now did it?"

I cocked my head at her, wondered why she was standing in my house at 9:17 a.m. "What are you doing here, Sugar?"

"I went by the shop first thing this morning to see how that little date of yours went with that bad boy last night."

"How did you know about that?" I hadn't even mentioned it to Sea Bass when I left yesterday.

"I know things, Katie B. When you gonna get used to that? I got the sight, and last night my sight was telling me you was fraternizing with that man you can't stand." Her expression turned sly. "Besides, I pulled up to your place right about the time you was disappearing around the corner on the back of that Harley. And since you decided to play hooky today, I figured I'd pay you a little visit. Now, I known you since the day that shop opened, and you ain't never laid out of work. Not one day. Hell, I seen you walk into that shop looking like Typhoid Mary."

Busted by my own compulsive work ethic. "I wish the two of us could just sit down and have a real nice girl talk about Jackson

Hunter, but as I said earlier, I'm fucked. I got more problems than I can handle, Sugar. Keeping my ass out of jail, for one. But right now I'm more worried about that tattoo I dreamed about last night."

Sugar's face went cold. "You mean like—"

"Yep. The tattoo looked different but the feeling it gave me was the same. I'd bet my right arm that the other spirit has busted free, or it's about to."

Without saying another word, she made a beeline for my bedroom. I followed and watched her rummage through my closet. "What the hell are you looking for, Sugar?"

"A damn suitcase," she answered. "I'm getting you out of this house before that spirit comes looking for you."

After what I'd done to the first one, I doubted this one would be stupid enough to try getting inside of me. After all, the spirits were separate but inextricable parts of the same entity, so I'm sure both of them understood the futility of trying to overcome the beast in me. My real value to them was in my ability to apply that tattoo to the host's skin. I just needed to avoid clients until that party tonight when I prayed Fin would tell me they'd discovered a brilliant method for capturing the spirits.

"I'm not going anywhere, Sugar. I just need to avoid the shop for a little while."

"The hell you ain't! I don't care if you turn into Godzilla. Mm-hmm, you got to get out of this house, baby."

"Stop!" I said, grabbing her arm before she yanked all my clothes off the rack. "I'm having dinner at Lillian Whitman's house tonight. I'm just laying low for the next ten hours until I can talk to Fin and sort all of this out."

She stopped and looked at me with a firm gaze. "Well, I ain't leaving. You got anything to eat in this place?" She headed out of the bedroom and I followed her to the kitchen as she opened the refrigerator and pulled out a carton of eggs. "All this drama is making me hungry. You got any bacon in here?".

163

"I'm out of bacon," I said. "Don't you have to go to work?"

She ignored me and turned on the stove burner, dumping a full tablespoon of butter into the hot skillet. "How many eggs you want?"

"I already ate."

She cracked two eggs into the skillet and flipped them with a shake of the pan after a few seconds. Then she slid them on a plate while refilling her coffee cup with her other hand. A real multitasker. Sugar was one of those people you wanted to stay close to during a catastrophe. She had that gift of knowing how to handle things. A proactive nature. I suspected that short of the Apocalypse, there was nothing that could defeat her.

I grabbed another cup of coffee and joined her at the counter while she ate her breakfast. The silence was beginning to get uncomfortable—for me—as Sugar chewed her eggs and stared into the space in front of her. "How do you do that?" I finally asked.

"Do what?" she replied without moving her eyes from the random spot they were fixed on.

"Make me feel like I'm being interrogated without saying a word or even looking at me?"

Now she glanced at me. "Why? You got something you need to confess?"

With a frustrated sigh, I headed for the living room and sank into the couch. Sugar finished eating, then washed her plate before following and sitting down next to me. "We went to Tybee Island and watched turtles hatch on the beach," I said, breaking down and indulging her curiosity about my date with Jackson, including the part about him leaving shortly before she arrived. Then we spent the rest of the morning and the afternoon watching talk shows and grazing on junk food, like a couple of stoners with nothing better to do than loaf and eat all day.

"I DON'T SEE why you're not invited. You're a member of the society."

"I ain't got no time for dinner parties," Sugar said, tossing clothing options from my closet onto the bed. "Lillian Whitman knows better than to waste an invitation on me. I'll invite myself if I feel the need for painful conversation." She dangled a red dress at me. "This one. Brings out them gorgeous eyes."

Without question, I took it and proceeded to strip off my shorts and T-shirt before slipping into the dress. "It would be a hell of a lot more fun if you went with me."

"I'll pass, baby. Besides, I got a show tonight." Sugar was a featured performer at the Blue Light Club. She also ran a popular blog that doled out advice that until recently I never suspected was anything more than that. But since learning about her family's deep connection to root work, I was beginning to suspect those suggestions for donations might be a clever front for payment rendered. Payment for a little conjure to help her followers solve all those problems they submitted to her for "advice."

"Now about them shoes," she continued.

I looked down at the black kitten pumps I'd stepped into. "What's wrong with them?" I rarely wore them because they were too conservative for my taste. But considering where I was spending the evening, I thought they'd be appropriate.

"Nothing wrong with them," she muttered, glancing at a more stylish pair on the floor of the closet. "If you're heading for church."

"It's dinner, Sugar. Not another ball."

"Baby, you in Savannah," she sniped. "Them shoes gonna be judged the second they step foot in that big ol' house."

I complied, kicking them off in exchange for the not-so-comfortable pair of four-inch black heels. A minute later my phone went off. It was a text from Fin's driver letting me know he was parked out front.

Sugar walked me to the Bentley and gave me a serious look before I got in. "You be careful out there," she warned. "Don't you forget I'm on speed dial if you need me."

"I know, Sugar. But don't you worry about me. I can be a real beast when I need to be."

She glared at the Bentley with contempt before heading toward her Eldorado parked in front of it at the curb. It was too big to fit in the driveway behind my car. "Damn waste of money, with all them folks starving around here." She yanked the heavy door open and started to climb inside. "You might be seeing me again before the night is up," she yelled over the yard. "In fact, I might just move in with *you* until that thing is back in the book." She shook her head. "Lord, what I won't do for my girls."

"I know, Sugar," I whispered, too low for her to hear me. "I know."

When I turned back to the Bentley, the driver was standing next to it holding the door open. I thanked him and climbed inside, savoring the experience of traveling in a car that cost more than that house I was renting. I could probably buy two or three for the price of that car, and throw in a brand-new Honda Accord to go with it.

We pulled away from the curb—or should I say glided—and headed for Lillian Whitman's palatial house. The driver smiled at me through the mirror, and it occurred to me that I didn't know what to call him. "What's your name?" I asked, studying the back of his well-manicured head. His hair was conservatively smoothed into a shiny dark cap, and I guessed him to be in his late thirties or early forties. His suit looked expensive, and I wondered if that was one of the perks of working for Fin Cooper, or if he had to shell out a month's salary to look the part. He smelled good, too.

"My apologies, Miss Bishop. I should have introduced myself the first time we met. I'm Joseph."

"Joseph," I repeated. "That's a nice name. You been working for Fin long?"

"Going on eight years."

The car went quiet as I struggled to think of something to keep the conversation going, to fill the awkward silence. But the moss-covered trees captured my attention as they did the last time I'd driven out to the house, the night I found out Victor Tuse was dead. It was nice to enjoy them from the backseat of the Bentley, without the distraction of driving my own car and having to keep my eyes on the road. The last time I was in the backseat of the Bentley a pair of black shades rolled across the windows to conceal the society's location. But now that I was an honorary member, I knew exactly where we were going.

"Joseph?" I said, still staring out the window at the trees lining the drive.

He caught my eyes through the rearview mirror. "Yes ma'am?"

"Are you a Savannah native?"

He nodded his head. "Born and raised. My grandparents migrated here from Louisiana. New Orleans area. But my parents are Savannahians."

"So you're familiar with hoodoo and root magic?" I was curious to get another perspective. One from outside the society, and he seemed normal enough.

Initially he remained silent, and I wondered if I'd overstepped my bounds with the question. Savannah was a town of fierce etiquette, after all. It only took one misplaced question to offend. Fortunately, a good drink was enough to mend fences around here.

"About as much as the next person," he eventually said.

I smirked at his evasion. Obviously I'd hit a nerve with the question, but I was talented at reading people's reactions where they might be too vague for others to notice. "I'm just wondering if you believe in all that stuff?" I looked directly at him through the mirror. No hiding from the question now.

"Well, Miss Bishop, it's my opinion that only a stupid man tries to refute what he knows nothing about. Or what he's seen with his own two eyes."

"Is that an affirmative, Joseph?"

He grinned back at me as we pulled off the main road and headed toward the big house. "Yes, ma'am."

F in was waiting on the steps as we pulled up to the house. Always the gentleman, he opened the door and extended his hand, assessing my dress as I stepped out. "Lovely as always, Miss Bishop." We hooked arms and climbed the double staircase leading up to the front door. "We're having lamb tonight. Hope you don't have any aversions to eating young creatures."

I smiled faintly at the thought. I did try to eat ethically, and normally chose foods that were on the humane side. And while delicious, lamb and veal weren't a regular part of my diet.

Lillian's beautiful house hit my senses—as it always did—the moment I walked through the front door. It was just one of those things I'd never get used to, the grandeur of the place, and the unattainable objects that only came to those with the good fortune of history and inheritance.

"Katie," Lillian greeted as we walked into the palatial living room. It was nice to hear that someone had finally dropped the formality and was addressing me by my given name.

"Hello, Lillian," I said in return. "It's nice to see you again."

She smiled slyly at me, betraying the professional circumstances of the gathering. "Fin tells me you've been a busy woman lately. Got some cleaning up to do. But we can talk about all that later." She walked over to the bureau and poured me a glass of scotch without asking my drink preference. The perfect hostess, she was. Just like a seasoned bartender memorizing a regular client's favorite drink, she presented it to me and motioned for me to sit.

A moment later I heard voices coming down the hall. Dr. Greene came into the room with Emmaline and Davina McCabe, all three sporting wide grins as they greeted me. Moses Greene was a tall man with puffy hands that made me question his skills as a cardiologist. Maybe he was retired from surgery, resigned to stress tests and consultations these days. With his graying hair and the deep definition to his facial skin, I estimated his age to be late fifties or early sixties. But then again, people of color tended to age more gracefully, so he could have been in his seventies for all I knew.

Davina sat across from me and winked. "That grandson of mine behaving for you?"

"He better," I replied. "He's my right hand these days."

"It's nice to see you again, Katie." Emmaline came over to the sofa and sat next to me. "I always feel so insignificant at these things," she whispered with a faint smile. I imagined she was referring to her youth, and since we were close in age she wasn't the only one in the room who was still on the biological upswing.

"I see your point," I whispered back, trying to sound commiserative but not really feeling the same level of *insignificance*.

The door opened and in walked José, the flamboyant hair-stylist to the wealthy. He froze in his tracks halfway into the room and glanced at his watch. "Am I late?" I could tell by his expression that the thought mortified him. This man was all about image, and being the last one to enter the room must have made him question his lack of promptitude, a mark of imperfection.

"Damn fool," Davina muttered under her breath, revealing her intolerance for the man.

"Calm down, José," Fin said. "You're punctual as ever."

His tightened shoulders visibly deflated as he continued into the room and helped himself to a drink. With Joan Crawford flair, he swept across the room and dropped into one of the wingchairs, crossing his leg and swinging it like a pendulum as he regarded me from the other side of the table. I regarded him back, refusing to surrender to his glare.

"Unfortunately, Alma and Pete won't be joining us tonight. Prior engagements that couldn't be avoided." Lillian looked displeased by that, like a woman who wasn't used to being refused. Behind all that genteel manner I imagined she could be a real snake when necessary. I respected that as long as she never aimed her venom at me.

A woman with black hair tightly slicked back into a chignon announced, "Dinner is ready." One of Lillian Whitman's staff, she wore a gray sheath dress and conservative black shoes.

"Thank you, Claire," Lillian said, standing up. "Shall we?"

Everyone stood and followed Lillian into the dining room. The rectangular table was big enough to accommodate fifteen people, at least. The far end of it was set for the six of us. We sat where Lillian instructed, in a carefully orchestrated order that put me at the end corner with Fin at my immediate left. She took the seat at the head of the table near my right. I noticed an extra place setting directly across from me, on her other side. When she saw me looking at the empty chair, she explained. "It appears my granddaughter lacks the punctuality gene. But I'm sure she'll be joining us shortly."

Claire came into the dining room with a large platter of rack of lamb in her hands, followed by two men carrying the rest of the meal. She placed the platter in the center of the table. The men did the same with the sides. The wine was already on the table when we arrived.

"Who wants red?" Fin asked, standing up and reaching for the bottle of Pinot Noir. He examined the label. "Oregon. Humph. I prefer a New Zealand, but this will do."

Lillian smirked. "It's bad enough I collect my Sauvignon Blanc and meat from the other side of the world. It's the least I can do to support the American economy."

He proceeded around the table, filling our glasses with the wine. José was the one dissenting party who blocked his hand, preferring bourbon over grape. When he was reseated, Lillian nodded toward the food in the middle of the table. "We serve ourselves around here," she said, glancing at me. "I hope you don't find that offensive."

I shrugged. "Not at all. I prefer it."

Since no one wanted to be the first, Dr. Greene reached over the table with his plate and grabbed a couple of lamb ribs with the tongs resting on the edge of the platter. Then he offered them to Emmaline, who reminded him that she was a vegetarian.

"I had the asparagus and roasted potatoes prepared just for you, Emmaline," Lillian said.

We'd all just about filled our plates when our missing dinner guest popped into the room. "Sorry, folks. Minor catastrophe at the pub." Fiona MacPherson planted a kiss on Lillian's cheek and took her seat. She glanced at me as she shook her napkin open and placed it in her lap. "Hey, Katie."

Without answering, I just stared at her. Seemed like a significant oversight for her to fail to mention who her grandmother was. I'd gotten to know her well over the months, and surely she was aware of my relationship to the Crossroads Society. I guess that explained her cautious response when I asked her about Blackthorn Grove. It also explained why Fin didn't seem concerned at all when I mentioned Fiona as an eyewitness to me leaving MacPherson's with Christopher Sullivan the night of the murder.

Nobody will be laying a hand on a MacPherson in this town, he'd said. And now I knew why.

"Well," I began. "I'm just going to throw the question out there before I get too deep in this plate of food. The MacPhersons are family?"

Lillian placed a small bite of lamb in her mouth and chewed it thoroughly before swallowing and answering my question. "Fiona's mother was my daughter." There was a hint of sadness in her tone, and the reference to *was* explained why. "Her daddy, on the other hand—"

"Grandma, please," Fiona quietly interrupted.

Lillian relented and resumed eating, while the rest of the table averted their eyes and acted like they weren't party to the conversation. The MacPhersons were clearly a sore spot in this house, and I wondered what skeletons in the family closet created the rift. A conversation for another day.

"We might as well get down to business," Fin said. "Address the elephant in the kitchen, so to speak."

"More like a goddamn whale," Davina commented, jabbing a spear of asparagus with her fork.

Fiona lowered her head to stifle a snicker. She must have been well-seasoned in the snide conversations around this big house, having probably lived around her grandmother's circle all her life.

"As you are all aware," Fin continued, "Victor Tuse is dead, and the spirit has moved on to a new host. What most of you don't know is that it made a very bold attempt to possess Miss Bishop the other night." A muffled gasp went around the table as all eyes levelled on me. "But as you can see, it failed. It did, however, manage to possess Christopher Sullivan, one of Chatham County's esteemed assistant DAs."

Emmaline's fork fell to her plate and bounced onto the table. "I just saw his picture on the news this morning. He's been missing for a couple of days."

I glanced at the one individual who could identify me as the last person to be seen with him. Fiona was staring back at me with a slight grin. Fin or Lillian must have prepped her, because she looked unfazed by the news.

"Mr. Sullivan is dead," Lillian interjected. She looked at me but spoke to the room. "I'm afraid Miss Bishop had no choice in the matter. It was her or the spirit."

I felt sick from the way they were all looking at me, like I was a monster. "Christopher and I were seeing each other. It chose him because of that, and I'll never forgive myself for what happened. I'm sorry—"

Fiona's face turned bitter. "Don't you apologize for what that thing did. If it wasn't Christopher, it would have been someone else. It could have been Sea Bass, or Elliot if he was still in the picture. It was baiting you, Katie."

"It tried to kill me." I felt somewhat relieved that I had at least two allies in the room.

"No," Lillian countered. "It wouldn't have killed you. That would have defeated the purpose. It wants to *become* you, Miss Bishop."

We were back to formalities and last names, and I suspected that meant I was about to hear some difficult things. I guess there wouldn't be a better time to segue into my latest news. "I had another dream last night. Another dream of a tattoo. I think the other spirit is trying to break free." And if it did and it managed to get that tattoo inked into its host's skin, it was all over. The bones would be unearthed from their crossroads grave and some pretty nasty things would be unleashed on Savannah, and then the rest of the world. "Maybe we should all go down to that dungeon to make sure it's still in the grimoire," I suggested, glancing at the floor where it was imprisoned somewhere under the house.

Fin's face froze. I couldn't tell if he was confused or considering it. The loud, boisterous laugh that bellowed from his mouth clarified it for me. "Well, you go right ahead, Miss Bishop.

Maybe you can take a bag of peanuts along to feed it. Like an elephant at the zoo."

"That's not necessary, *Fin*," Fiona spat. "Jesus, you can be an asshole sometimes."

I guess I just assumed it was protected behind some hermetically sealed dome. "Yeah, Fin. Why don't you let me in on the big joke," I said, getting irritated myself with his sarcasm. I was the one taking all the risks, and he had the nerve to ridicule me for suggesting something perfectly reasonable.

He sobered from his amused spell and leaned into the table. "Miss Bishop, there's a good reason the grimoire is buried a hundred feet underground. The architects of that tomb would have dug deeper if they hadn't hit a shelf of stone. Only a fool with a death wish would go down there unprepared."

I looked back and forth between Fin and Lillian. "Are you telling me no one is going down there to check on that book to make sure it's still there?" The thought almost made me laugh.

A muted snicker escaped José's mouth. "What? Do you think we're idiots? Ignorant Southern bumpkins?" His cowlick bounced off his forehead as he huffed and turned back to his plate.

"Cameras," Lillian said, shooting José a dirty look. "We monitor the book with cameras. It's much safer that way. We do send someone down there periodically, but not without proper preparation which includes a rather extensive ritual involving the bone. A magical shield of sorts."

"Fire with fire," Fin added. "The way to control something otherworldly is to fight it with its own power. Legvu is a master of the bone, which also means he's ruled by them." He took a bite of lamb and chewed it leisurely, staring at me unwaveringly for an uncomfortable minute before continuing. "The way to catch a bone god is with the bone." He looked at Lillian thoughtfully. "*Have* we checked the grimoire today?"

Lillian seemed annoyed by the question. "What do you think, Fin?" After a moment, her relaxed expression returned.

"Of course. Everything looked to be in order when I checked it this afternoon. But I can assure you we'll be keeping a closer eye on it now that Miss Bishop has had her little premonition."

I didn't like the way she dismissed my dream, my "little premonition." "That would be wise, Lillian, seeing how my last dream turned out to be a reality."

Her condescending attitude changed. "I mean no disrespect. It's a stressful time for everyone, and I tend to deal with stress in a cavalier fashion."

Davina put her fork down and clanked it loudly against her plate, drawing everyone's attention. "I guess this would be a good time to explain why we're all sitting around Lillian's table eating her fancy food and drinking her overpriced grape juice." I nearly looked away in embarrassment as she reached into the neckline of her dress and continued farther down into her cleavage, extracting a small satin bag. "Always keep what's precious close to your heart," she said. "No one's getting their hands on this without killing me first."

She tossed it across the table. I hesitated as it landed next to my plate. "What's in it?"

"Open it up and see for yourself."

I glanced at Fin who nodded his approval. The bag weighed nothing, which made me wonder if there was anything at all inside. But when I untied the string and shook the contents into my hand a thin, flat object settled into the center of my palm. A light current of energy traveled over my skin toward the tips of my fingers. "I still don't know what this is."

"That's the weapon you're gonna use to catch the son of a bitch," Fin announced, coming up short of actually clarifying anything.

I snorted and tossed the object on the table. "Yeah, right."

"Watch your mouth, girl!" Davina spat, nearly coming across the table before Fin put his hand on her forearm to keep her in place. "You don't throw the bone like it's a piece of trash."

The tone in her voice shook me. I'd already pegged the Ozark woman as something fierce disguised under the guise of age, and the ferocity of her voice successfully commanded my attention. I reached for the bone and gently picked it back up. "I'm sorry. I didn't realize—"

"That wasn't very polite of me," she interjected, settling back into her chair. "Please accept my apology, Katie."

Fin sighed deeply and combed the top of his head with his fingers. "Now let's all just settle down and start this conversation over." He gestured to the object in my hand. "As insignificant as it looks, Miss Bishop, that little piece of bone in your hand is a powerful weapon. Took us a while to figure it out, but better late than never." He turned to Davina with a steady look. "The floor is yours, Davina. Just remember who you're speaking to and try not to interject any threats. We don't want to give Miss Bishop's beast a reason to come out, now do we?"

"I'd like to see the dragon," Emmaline said with a glint in her eyes. She smiled at me but quickly receded back into her seat when the rest of the table admonished her with their glares. Fiona grinned at me devilishly, clearly finding the whole spectacle entertaining. "I'm sorry, Katie. That was rude," Emmaline apologized.

Davina continued before I could reassure Emmaline that I wasn't offended. "It's a bone charm. Ideally it would be made from the same bones as the ones Legvu buried at the crossroads. But in light of the fact that we haven't found them yet, a hyena bone will have to do. A trickster for a trickster. It will be weaker, but that charm will stun old Legvu enough for us to suck him right back inside that book."

"Legvu?" I repeated.

Fin clarified. "You see, as soon as the second spirit is freed from the grimoire, and based on the latest dreams you've been having we can assume that's either happened or about to, the first one will join it. They'll reunite in the same host. The next time you meet that host, Miss Bishop, you'll be looking at Legvu himself. He'll just need that final tattoo to fully manifest his power and show you his true form."

Great. I was no longer up against half a god. My next battle would be with the almighty Legvu himself. "How are you going to get him back inside the book?" I was skeptical about how the whole business of capturing him was going to work.

"Don't you worry about that," Fin said. "As soon as Legvu is 'stunned', as Davina put it, he'll leach right out of his host and climb inside that bone charm that'll be calling his name. A fly drawn to shit, as they say. After that, all we have to do is toss the charm in the room with the grimoire and that book will take care of the rest."

It all sounded too easy, and I knew better than that. "So all I need to do is wave the charm in the host's face and voila?"

"Well, it won't be that easy," Fin said.

"You have to get it inside of the host," Davina clarified. "Then we'll cut the bone charm out of him—or her—once Legvu is trapped inside of it. We'll have a small window of time before he recovers and finds his way back out."

Short of a laugh, I snorted. "Oh, well, is that all? You mean I have to get the host to eat that piece of bone?" Yeah right. *Here you go, Mr. Host. Chew on this.*

Fin's expression hardened. "Shove it down his goddamned throat or up his ass. I don't give a damn how you do it, Miss Bishop."

"Fin!" Lillian admonished. "Watch that foul mouth of yours at my table." Fiona finally broke down with that laugh she'd been suppressing since the conversation began, which only made Lillian more agitated. "You might as well leave, Fiona," she told her granddaughter. "You've been looking for a reason to get up from this table before you even sat down."

Fiona finished her glass of wine in a single gulp and stood up, smirking at me with her hand to her ear in a call-me gesture as she walked out of the room. I had a feeling our friendship was about to jump to the next level now that my secrets were out. I also had a feeling she'd known about those secrets since the day Fin walked into my shop. Every time I stepped inside that bar and she served me a drink, she knew exactly what I was. Now she had the green light to acknowledge it.

"You're a smart woman," Davina continued. "I'm sure you'll figure it out." She leaned into the table and pinned me with her wise and seasoned eyes. "I don't care if you have to sleep with that damn thing to get close enough to cut him open, just get that bone inside of that host."

19

When I walked into the shop the next morning, Sugar was sitting in the chair behind the front counter. She barely glanced up from the magazine she was reading, pretending very poorly not to pay me any mind. I walked past her toward the coffee pot.

"You know what you need?" she asked as I poured a cup.

"No, but I'm sure you're going to tell me."

She dropped the magazine and joined me at the coffeemaker that cost all of fifteen dollars. "You need one of them fancy express-o machines. Class the place up a little bit."

I stirred a pile of generic creamer into my cup and headed for my station. "It's espresso, and I don't have money to burn on frivolous gadgets. Besides, something like that would ruin the unique ambiance of this place."

"Yeah, you probably right," she agreed, pouring her own cup. "Wouldn't want folks to think they walked into Chez L'Ink instead of this fine establishment." She followed me like a puppy dog and dropped into a chair to watch me prep my station. "Well?"

"Well what?" I asked.

She deadpanned me and took a sip of her coffee before getting to the obvious point. "You gonna tell me about that bone charm Davina gave you last night?"

I finished fiddling with the bottles on the table and gave her my full attention. "You knew about that?"

"Mm-hmm." She crossed her legs and pursed her lips. "Well, I didn't know until I talked to Mama last night."

"How did your mama know?"

"Well, where the hell you think they got that bone?" she retorted as if I'd missed the obvious. "You think a hyena just dropped dead in Davina's backyard?" I was living in a town full of root doctors, and Davina had links to her own brand of Ozark magic. I guess the bone could have come from any of them. "Bone like that takes some extra special connections."

Sea Bass came through the back door and gave me a concerned look. With a few long strides he was at my side, considering me like I was some injured bird that needed gentle handling. "You all right, Katie?" He glanced at Sugar as if she might know the extent of the illness that kept me home for the first time in the history of the shop.

"*Jesus.* I call in sick for one day and everyone thinks I'm dying, or something tragic is happening." I shook my head and headed for the autoclave to dump a load of tools inside to be sterilized. "I'm fine, Sea Bass. I just needed a day off."

When I turned back around, Sugar was chastising me with her eyes while Sea Bass was sweeping the pristine floor. "Now you be nice to that boy," she said. "Sea Bass is your best friend—after me—so you better start reciprocating before he decides you ain't worth his love and devotion." She glanced at him and puckered her lips. "I'd treat you better than that, baby boy."

"Damn it, Sugar, stop doing that," he moaned. "It's embarrassing."

"All right!" I said, if for nothing more than to get the two of them to cut it out. "I had another dream."

Sea Bass went still. "You mean—"

"Yeah. I'm expecting someone to walk through that door any minute now with a drawing of the tattoo I saw in my head." If that happened I had only two choices: apply the tattoo or somehow get that bone inside of the unfortunate host. The former option wasn't really a choice at all, because the second I finished the tattoo, Legvu would manifest completely and probably kill me before going straight to the bones at the crossroads to unleash all hell. Hence my desire to stay home behind a locked door that probably wouldn't do a damn bit of good anyway.

Sea Bass threw his hands up. "All right, all right. We're intelligent people here. Let's just think this through and come up with a plan." Sugar and I stared at him, waiting for this miraculous plan to materialize. His head bobbed up and down as the wheels turned in his head. "Well, maybe you're right," he finally said. "Maybe the best thing for you to do, boss, is to lay low for a few days."

"Forget it." I continued prepping for the day, lacking the luxury of wallowing in fear while I waited for the inevitable. "It doesn't matter if I stay home for a day or a month. It'll just wait." A part of me realized it was better to let it come for me at home. At least there my dragon could come out without an audience, and if it tried to kill me it would definitely meet the beast. But I knew it would wait for me at the shop because that's where the ink and equipment was. No use trying to get me to apply that tattoo on top of my kitchen counter.

Mouse was listening to the whole exchange, looking nervous and well . . . mousy. "I–I can screen the customers," she stuttered. "Maybe I can warn you if it comes in so you can slip out the back door." She grabbed a piece of paper and a pencil from her station. "Can you draw the tattoo?"

"Thanks, Mouse, but I'm not going anywhere. If it comes in the shop I'll think of something." I glanced around the room, noting the lack of business. "Where is everyone?"

"Uh, Katie," Sea Bass said. "It's only 8:40 a.m."

We weren't even open yet. The only reason Sugar was inside was because she came in with Mouse. It also explained why Abel was missing. He came in around noon on Saturdays, because of his moonlighting job as a bouncer on Friday and Saturday nights. I needed to sit down and get my head screwed on right. No use putting ink to someone's skin if I couldn't even think straight, and I had customers walking through that door in twenty minutes.

The door opened and everyone in the shop jumped. "I'm sorry," the man apologized as he witnessed our startled looks. We must have scared him with our beady gaze because he turned around to leave.

"Can we help you, hon?" Sugar called out, like she was an employee. "We ain't open just yet, but don't go running off." She glanced at me and muttered something about a possible paying customer, which she was right about. We needed as many as we could get.

He looked at the sign on the door, clearly flipped to the CLOSED side. "I'm sorry. I was just wondering if you know where Hawthorne Automotive is."

My shoulders slumped. "Two blocks down on the right. Can't miss it."

Sugar sized up his bare, skinny arm as he reached for the door to leave. "You know, a big old tattoo would dress up that arm nicely. Attracts them women like flies."

"Thanks, Sugar." I rolled my eyes and walked back to the coffee pot for another cup. Then I settled in for a long day.

———

JACKSON KNOCKED on my door shortly after nine p.m. My head rolled around my tight shoulders as I greeted him, crackling like a bowl of Rice Krispies. I motioned him in and headed for the kitchen without a word, grabbing a bottle of red wine and two glasses on my way toward the patio. "There's beer in the fridge if you're not in the mood for wine."

"Wine is fine." He followed me outside and pulled a chair up to mine, bracing my foot on his knee and slipping off my sandal to rub the spot under my toes. "Why are you so tense tonight?" he asked.

As good as it felt I tried to retract my foot, but he gripped my ankle and held it in place with ease. "Doesn't that gross you out?" I asked. "Rubbing someone's foot? Who knows where it's been."

He smirked and continued with the massage, hitting the sensitive spots like a pro. "How do you know I don't have a foot fetish?"

"Do you?" I asked wide-eyed. "Because that's a deal breaker for me."

He laughed softly, putting my foot back down to reach over and kiss me. "I can assure you the only fetish I practice is good old-fashioned fucking."

I feigned surprise. "You didn't really just say that, did you?"

"Why? Does blunt honesty make you uncomfortable?"

No, but the intensity in his gaze made me want to melt into the chair. "I'm fine with honesty," I replied. "It's just that there was nothing old-fashioned about what we did the other night."

"I'm gonna assume that's a good thing, Miss Bishop?"

I held his stare and nodded my head. "Oh yeah, Mr. Hunter. That's a very good thing."

We sat across from each other in silence, letting the heat snake back and forth between us until it gripped me so tight I thought I might fall out of my chair. It would have been easy to cut to the chase and end up in the bedroom, but I really liked Jackson and figured I owed him a little more disclosure about what he was getting into if he chose to tangle with me. He deserved to know what a mess my life was, even more than his.

I shook it off and reached for the bottle of wine. "Look at us.

Two people with a perfectly good bottle of wine, and here we are ignoring the poor thing." I poured us both a glass and kicked off my other sandal before propping my feet up on the table. "Don't get any ideas," I warned, glancing at my toes.

He smiled and relaxed into his own chair. "Seriously, Katie. Something has you wound tight tonight. If it's about the other night—"

"It isn't," I insisted before he could continue. I nervously twirled the stem of my wine glass. He picked up on it, and I could sense the tension in me leaching into him. "There are things you don't know about me, Jackson."

"And there are things you don't know about me," he countered. "It's called getting to know each other." He set his glass on the table and leaned his elbows on his knees. "Look, Katie. I'm not the kind of guy who comes back for a glass of wine after a night in the sack, but something tells me you're not the kind of girl who does that either. I like you."

I tried to change the subject. "Okay. Let's get to know each other better. What do you do for a living?" I'd been wondering that since the day he first set foot in my shop. Not that I cared how much money he made, but it would be comforting to know he didn't pay his rent with drug money, or with some other sordid source of income that outlaw biker clubs were notorious for.

"Nothing right now." Sensing my concern, he added, "Let's just say I'm financially set for a while."

It made sense for him to stay under the radar, seeing how he had a band of outlaw shifters looking for him.

"Now quit changing the subject, Katie. Tell me about these things I need to know about you."

My lungs inflated at the thought of telling him about the sticky details of my parentage and the prognosis of my future, hinging on the success or failure of capturing a couple of rogue spirits before they could manifest into a god of destruction.

"Obviously you have an idea about what I am," I began.

His brow arched. "An idea?"

I huffed at the absurdity. I'd concealed my true self from Elliot for two and a half years, never once allowing him to see the dragon. But here I was with this new guy, and all it took was a barroom brawl to shove me into the light. Granted, he had his own secrets and a little experience with shifters, but I wasn't what he thought I was. I wasn't your average shifter.

"You're used to something different, Jackson. I don't sprout soft fur and whiskers. What you saw the other night is just a glimpse before the real beast comes out."

He looked amused and confused at the same time, as if nothing I said could sway the concrete impression he had of me. With his right hand, he took me by the wrist and ran his thumb over my pulse, examining the pale skin covering the faint blue vein where my blood was beginning to pump faster. "All I see is a beautiful woman with a big heart who likes turtles and red wine, who's earned friends who would cut my balls off if I hurt you. You bleed just like everyone else. That's what I see."

With a sharp jerk, I pulled my wrist away. "I'm a beast!" I blurted out. "Not like the shifters you left in Atlanta." His amused grin started to fade, and I could tell by the way he sat straighter that he knew I wasn't fucking with him. "You had sex with a dragon, Jackson, and it was amazing."

He just sat there staring at me, wordless. When he finally moved, it was to nod his head several times. "Okay then. I guess if I can weather a relationship with a shifter who turns into a panther, I can handle a dragon."

"Before you get all comfortable with bedding a dragon, you need to know the risks." He needed to know what happened to the last man I slept with. I had to assume that if the spirit tried to get to me through Christopher Sullivan, it could try to do the same with Jackson. Even though I was confident it wouldn't be stupid enough to try that again, I had no right to assume that risk for him.

Before I could say another word, he got up and headed for the patio door. "You got anything stronger to drink?"

"In the cabinet above the stove."

He came back out with glasses and a bottle of scotch and poured us both a shot. Then he eased back in his chair with his legs spread and his drink dangling in his hand draped between them. "Now, you were telling me about this risk."

I debated whether it was worth the pain of explaining Legvu and his divided spirits, or if I should just end our fledgling relationship before it went any further. His eyes made the decision for me. Hopelessly smitten with the man sitting in the chair across from me, and considering his own unusual past, I figured he could handle it. If not, he was welcome to move on to someone less complicated.

"There's this thing after me."

"Thing?" he repeated with slight amusement in his voice. "What kind of *thing*?"

"A spirit that likes to take up residence in unsuspecting hosts. Well, there are two of them, actually. I haven't met the second one yet, but with my luck it'll show up soon."

He deadpanned me, clearly not taking me seriously. I couldn't blame him. But considering what he knew about me already and the fact that he ran with a pack of shifters in his former life, it wasn't as farfetched as it sounded. In fact, it should have been right up his alley.

His cocky grin went flat when he realized I wasn't being dramatic. "You're serious?"

I nodded. Then I dumped the whole sordid story on the table, leaving out the part about killing Christopher Sullivan, because I thought that little detail might be premature. He listened to every word without balking and seemed unfazed by the prospect of getting involved with a mess like me. Or maybe his plan was to finish his drink and walk out that door and never see me again. He didn't seem like an asshole or a coward though.

Eventually he stood up and polished off his scotch, setting the empty glass on the table and regarding me with a question on his face. "A friend of mine is having a party tomorrow afternoon. A barbeque. Just good people and good food."

When he didn't follow that statement with an invitation, I cocked my head. "Is that an invitation, or are you just gloating about how much fun you're going to have without me tomorrow?"

20

Jackson made no attempt to get me into bed the night before. Maybe he was a good actor and my story did set him back a bit. I figured I had a fifty-fifty chance of being stood up for this barbeque thing, but he showed up at my house at two o'clock sharp. Fortunately, my schedule was pretty open at the shop. Nothing Sea Bass and Mouse couldn't handle while I took another day off. I promised them both an extra vacation day for covering for me twice in one week.

He hopped on his bike and handed me a helmet. "You sure you don't want to take my car?" I asked, wondering how we'd get home after a day of food and drink. "I can be the designated driver."

"I'll stay sober," he assured me. "Get on."

"Sugar's going to have a coronary," I muttered, fastening the helmet and climbing on the seat behind him.

"What was that?"

"My friend, Sugar. She's going to freak when she finds out I'm not at the shop. She worries about me. You met her the first day you came in."

"You mean the one who was giving me the stink eye."

"That's Sugar."

He fired up the bike and yelled over the engine. "Better call her when we get there. Let her know that the big bad wolf hasn't had his way with you."

I laughed as we pulled away from the house, clinging to his waist and enjoying the small bit of peace that would end the minute the day was up and we got home. We rode for thirty minutes south of Savannah and turned down a dirt road lined with houses about a quarter mile apart. It was the kind of area where you could get a house on ten acres of land and still have a reasonable commute into the city. We took another turn onto a road that served as a long driveway up to a sprawling ranch with a well-manicured yard.

"Wow." I climbed off the bike and removed my helmet, looking at the yard that edged up to the woods. "Nice spread."

"Cairo put a lot of work into this place. Built the house himself."

"Cairo?" I asked, suddenly wishing I knew more about the people I was about to meet.

He surveyed the property like a hawk, and then brought his eyes back around to mine. "He's like a brother to me. Covered my ass when Kaleb and his crew came sniffing around here." With my hand swallowed in his, we headed for the side of the house. "Come on. They're probably out back."

Before we got to the corner of the house the sound of voices amplified from the backyard. I glanced around but only saw a couple of cars parked in the driveway. As soon as we walked down the hill and rounded the side of the house, I saw where everyone else had parked. At the rear of the large backyard was a river with a row of motorcycles parked along its edge. There must have been at least two dozen parked in a neat double row.

"Well shit, man," someone said as we entered the crowd. "Where the fuck's your bike?"

"Parked in the wrong place, obviously," Jackson replied.

The guy gave him a bear hug with the appropriate fist pound on the back. "Ugly as ever," he said, grinning at Jackson from ear to ear. He was a good bit older than Jackson and had a rusty beard running halfway down his neck, its tip settling just above the neckline of his worn black T-shirt with JUDAS PRIEST written in faded silver letters across the front. He suddenly realized Jackson wasn't alone and turned to me with an even bigger grin. "Who's this?"

"This is Katie," Jackson introduced.

Cairo reached out and pulled me into him as I extended my hand. "We don't shake fucking hands around here," he informed me as he crushed me to his chest. Checking himself, he pulled back and quickly apologized. "Pardon my potty mouth, Katie." With a quick glance at Jackson, he finally gave himself a proper introduction. "I'm Cairo. I own this zoo."

Zoo pretty much summed it up. I counted at least five dogs lounging around the backyard, and if I wasn't mistaken, those were llamas fenced in a large corral near a barn on the right side of the property. "Are those llamas?" I was dying to bypass the crowd and make a beeline straight for the charming creatures. But I guess that wasn't the polite thing to do.

Cairo shook his head and corrected me. "Alpacas. Not as ornery as llamas. Make nice sweaters, too. At least that's the bullshit my wife used to justify getting the damn things. Haven't seen any wool collecting yet though."

"They're beautiful," I said. "Can I go up to them?"

Cairo sobered up a little. "Sure. Let me give you a little advice though. If they pin their ears back and start looking at you funny, you better duck. They may be nicer than llamas, but they can still spit."

"Okay," Jackson interrupted. "Why don't we mingle a little bit first before you get cozy with the wildlife."

He led me into the crowd and started introducing me around. I couldn't possibly remember all their names, but some of them were hard to forget. There was the woman with the blonde hair and oversized blue eyes named Tinker. Based on her unusually tiny frame and Barbie-doll figure, I was pretty sure I knew how she got her name. All she was missing was a set of dainty wings. Then there was the guy with the flaming copper hair that they called Red. But there were more Bobs and Marys than I could remember.

"Hungry?" He nodded toward the crown jewel of barbeque fare displayed on a table near a smoldering pit. Most of the barbeques I'd been to served hamburgers and chicken, but Cairo had gone big and smoked a whole pig. I guess it was no worse than carving up a whole turkey or a chicken, but something about looking at the animal's face turned me off to the idea.

"I think I'll stick to something boring," I said, heading for the less dramatic offerings next to the grill while he headed for the smoked swine on the table.

"That pork is about the best thing you'll ever put in your mouth," Cairo commented as he joined me at the hamburger table.

"I'm sure it's amazing. I'm just not a big fan of pork," I lied. "A good old burger is just fine with me."

His cocky grin gave him away before he asked. "So, you and Jackson . . .?"

I smiled while I loaded my plate. "I'm not sure what we are. We're still working on that part."

"Well, I'm biased, but he's a good guy. He can be an asshole sometimes but he's honest. He'll let you know exactly where you stand with him."

"That's good to know," I said. "I'd rather get my feelings hurt than be lied to."

"What kind of bullshit are you telling her, Cairo?" Jackson approached with a plateful of pork and potato salad. He took a bite of the meat and nodded his head. "Yep. It was worth the ride."

Cairo looked across the yard and then grabbed my free arm. "Come on, Katie. Let's go say hello to Jasper before Dottie wanders over." He motioned toward a brown alpaca standing at the fence, staring at the party like he wanted to jump the corral and join in. "He's the friendliest one of the herd, but Dottie doesn't like to share him with anyone. She gets jealous and tends to nip."

Jackson offered to guard my plate while I took a few minutes to meet the sweet-looking beast. I followed Cairo over to the fence where Jasper was eagerly waiting as we approached. I swear the animal was smiling. He ignored Cairo and came over to me so I could run my hand over the soft tuft of fleece on the top of his head. "Oh my God, is he cute," I gushed, momentarily losing my mind while I envisioned a space for one in my backyard.

"Yeah, they're cute all right," he snickered. "But I could do without that one." He motioned to the larger cream-colored female headed toward us.

"I guess that would be Dottie?"

"Yeah, and I'm not in the mood to wash spit off my face."

We turned to head back to the party. Jackson was still standing next to the table where I'd left him but he had company. A tall brunette with teeny-tiny cutoff shorts was leaning into him, laughing at his comments and rubbing her hand up and down his arm, the way you'd expect a man like Jackson Hunter to be fawned over. It shouldn't have bothered me as much as it did, but we were here together and it was a date.

I shoved my displeasure down my throat and formed a wide saccharin smile as I approached them, saying nothing as I retrieved my plate from the table. He wasn't my property, and I guess it was good to test the waters around other women early in the stages of our relationship, before I found out he was a womanizing prick.

After a very uncomfortable moment, I felt his hand on my waist. I could feel both of their eyes on me as I took a massive bite of the burger and looked anywhere but in their direction. My appetite had gone from ravenous to nonexistent, and for the life of me I couldn't manage to swallow the food in my mouth. I thought I might have to run for the nearest bathroom to spit it out.

"Katie, this is Angela," he finally said. The large lump of burger slipped painfully down my throat as I turned to meet the beautiful woman with her arm wrapped around my date. "Cairo's wife."

Shit.

I wiped my hand on a napkin and extended it, but like Cairo said, there was no *fucking* handshaking around here. She gave me a brief but genuine hug and smiled with her perfect teeth. "Jackson was just telling me about your shop." She turned around and lifted the back of her shirt to show me the six-inch wide tribal mark on her lower back—undeservedly dubbed the "tramp stamp." She lowered her shirt back down and grimaced. "Too many margaritas one night. I need to get that damn thing removed." Her eyes brightened. "Hey, do you do removals?"

"Sorry," I said with a sympathetic, limp smile. "I just put them on. If it makes you feel any better, I kinda like them." Of course, I didn't have one on my own lower back, but I hated the idea that some asshole thought they had the right to put a derogatory stigma on the position of a woman's tattoo. No one seemed to have a problem with penis ink.

Cairo joined us and Angela shifted her attention to him, wrapping her arm around his waist and kissing his cheek. "I hope my husband warned you about Dottie over there. She can be sweet when she wants to be, but she can be a real bitch a second later."

"So, you and Cairo . . ."

"Are married." She glanced at Jackson with a knowing look. My discomfort must have been written all over my face until he'd said the magic words that released me from my awkward state.

She grabbed a couple of beer bottles from the ice bucket next to the table and took me by the wrist with her other hand. "Come on, Katie. You and I have things to discuss." Jackson's face took on a look of worry as Angela delivered the threat.

I looked at the bucket and then back at him. "Don't forget who's driving."

We walked down to the river and sat on the edge of a small dock. "How long have you known Jackson?" she asked, opening the bottles and handing me one.

"Not long. He came into my shop a couple of weeks ago and managed to make my blood boil in record time. The man doesn't have a filter, does he?"

"That's Jackson," she confirmed, taking a deep swig of her beer. "He doesn't get attached very often. To women, I mean. But he sure likes you."

My heart skipped just a little when she said it. I don't know how he managed to make me feel that way after knowing him for such a blip of time, but damn it, that man had a hold on me. "Really. How can you tell?" I tried to ask the question casually, but she seemed to be a smart woman. I'm sure our mutual attraction was obvious, especially after my poor attempt at hiding my disappointment when I saw her with him, before I found out she was married to his close friend.

Something wet touched my skin, and then a head wedged into the gap between my arm and ribcage. An oversized mutt with a shiny sable coat practically knocked me off the dock as it insinuated itself into my space.

"See. Even his dog likes you."

I raised my arm to accommodate the dog's large body, getting a wet muzzle in my face in the process. "This is Jackson's dog?"

"Well, that's debatable. She lives here now, and I've gotten pretty attached." She explained how Jackson had stayed with them temporarily when he first arrived in Savannah and asked them to "dog sit" while he set up house in the city. "He'll have to fight me to get her back. That's a country dog. She doesn't belong in the city. It was Easter Sunday. Found her eating out of a trash can behind a gas station. That's her name—Easter."

The dog shoved her cold nose into my face a couple more times and then turned and ran back to the party. I watched Jackson drop down on his haunches to greet her, wrestling her wiggling body to the ground. "I don't know him very well," I said, staring at the reunion. She was grinning when I looked back at her. "What are you grinning at?"

"Nothing." She shook her head and leaned back on her palms. "It's just good to see him happy. This whole Sapanth thing has been tough on him." She turned to look at me. "Has he told you about them?" When I didn't answer immediately she frowned. "I'm sorry. I shouldn't have said anything."

"It's okay. He told me." I failed to mention the circumstances around him feeling compelled to share his background with a group of shifter bikers in Atlanta. No need to out myself to a stranger who I'd known for less than an hour.

"Then you know about Kara?" she asked.

"Yeah. Along with the fact that he's on the run."

She laughed. "Is that what he called it?"

I was about to interrogate her about that last comment when a loud noise came from behind us. We both looked back at the party as a chair went sailing across the yard. It stopped in mid-air and fell straight down to the ground, as if an invisible barrier had been thrown up in front of it. If I was seeing things correctly, a grizzly bear was standing on its hind legs and heading straight for the smoked pig on the table.

"What the hell?" I said as I scanned the crowd and spotted another one lashing its huge paw at a guy standing near the grill. Its deadly claws slashed across his face, tearing open his skin in a series of wide bloody streaks that were visible even from a distance.

"*Fucking animals!*" Angela spat, climbing to her feet. "Stay here—" she began, but the look in her eyes suggested the dragon was already beginning to emerge. With fascination, she cocked her head at me and whispered, "Well, I'll be damned."

I climbed to my own feet and gazed at her astounded face for a moment, feeling my eyes shift from blue to green. Then we both turned back to the mayhem in the backyard. The bear heading for the pig stopped in its tracks, a wall of bricks forming around its feet from all sides and growing taller by the second until it completely encased the animal in a cell of clay walls.

Angela grabbed my wrist as my claws protruded and the texture of my skin began to change. She wasn't frightened when I turned to look at her. She just shook her head and motioned toward Jackson. I whipped my head around just about the time he was smashing his fist into the other bear's snout and sending it flying a good thirty feet across the yard. He'd knocked it out cold.

"It's over," she said. "I'm getting real tired of strangers coming into my *fucking* house and ruining my *fucking* parties."

"They're shifters?" I asked, feeling my dragon recede.

Her brow raised. "Well, aren't you?"

I had no time to explain the subtle differences between me and those bears in her yard. By the time we ran back from the river, the mysterious brick wall had disappeared and the bears had shifted back into a couple of stunned men. Even the guy with the slashed skin was beginning to heal.

"Okay!" Angela shouted across the yard. "Show's over. Eat the goddamn pig!"

I glared at Jackson, who was helping Cairo clean up the spilled bucket of beer. When he looked up at me his eyes were full of heat. I knew what that heat felt like, because mine felt the same way after almost emerging back on that dock.

"You and I need to have a talk," I said. "Now take me home."

21

I liked to sleep a little late on Monday mornings since it was the one day of the week the shop was closed, so the knock on my door at seven a.m. was not appreciated. The more I tried to ignore it, the louder it got.

"*What?*" I barked as I opened the door, not caring who was on the other side.

"Before you slam the door," Jackson said, "hear me out."

Instead of having an argument when we got back from the barbeque the evening before, Jackson had simply dropped me off and left without a word, leaving me standing in the driveway with my jaw hanging down to my knees. I thought it was over and I'd never see him again. In fact, after he unceremoniously dumped me off in my driveway, I didn't *want* to ever see him again. At least that's how I felt at the time. This morning I just felt sad, like I'd lost something important.

I swung the door open and stepped aside. "Fine. Come in."

He sat at the kitchen island while I started the coffee. Nothing was getting settled until I got some caffeine in my system. In the interim, I tolerated the awkward silence by shoving a bagel into the toaster oven while he just sat there staring at my backside. "Would you like one?" I asked stiffly without turning around.

"No, thanks."

I threw the tub of cream cheese on the counter and swung around. "What the fuck was that yesterday, Jackson?"

"You mean the bears?" he replied, skirting around the fact that he'd knocked one of them clear across the yard. Last time I checked, human beings didn't have that kind of strength.

"You told me you weren't a shifter." He gazed at me for a moment before responding, and I got the impression he was weighing his options to determine the best way around the truth. Seemed unfair since he knew what I was. Did he really think I would judge him for being a shifter?

"I'm not a shifter," he finally said. "I just have . . . abilities."

"Like superhuman strength?" I said with sarcasm and disappointment in my tone.

His head slowly nodded. "Something like that."

I glared at him, debating whether to kick him out or give him a chance to explain. He'd been lying to me by omission, and that was a killer for even a well-established relationship. "What happened to blunt honesty?"

"I wasn't trying to lie to you, Katie. I was planning to tell you, but—" He shut his mouth and considered his words. I got the feeling he was trying to figure out how to explain what he'd probably worked so hard trying to hide from the world.

"Jesus, Jackson! I'm a fucking dragon! Trust me, I can handle whatever this is."

"I had an accident when I was sixteen," he finally said. "We had a freak winter that year and the lake froze." Before continuing he looked me squarely in the eye and shrugged. "I got careless and stepped on a thin patch of ice and fell into the water. It took them forty minutes to find me and pull me out."

One of my worst fears was drowning under a frozen lake. Even if you managed to find an air pocket under the ice, hypothermia would most likely kill you in minutes, and here was Jackson recounting that very scenario. I had to stop myself from physically shuddering at the thought. "My God, Jackson. How did you survive?"

His eyes glanced at the counter and then raised back up to mine. "I didn't. They pulled a corpse through the ice. By the time the ambulance got to the hospital I was pronounced dead. My parents—" He stopped, the words hitching in his throat for a moment before he was able to continue. "An hour later I hopped off the gurney they left me on while they waited for someone to wheel me down to the morgue. Then I walked out of the room. Just about gave everyone a heart attack. I still don't remember a thing past waking up that morning." He laughed quietly. "I had some pretty powerful skills I wasn't even aware of until I went to the gym a week later. Almost threw a two-hundred-pound barbell through the roof when I went to lift it."

The bagel started to smoke in the toaster oven. "Oh, shit!" I burned my finger dragging it off the rack. When I turned back around he was grinning at me.

"What's so funny, Superman?"

"I don't know," he mused. "Here you thought you were the biggest freak in the room."

"I still do. I'm a dragon, and all you can do is throw a bear across the yard. And what the hell was that brick wall all about?"

"Most of the people you met yesterday *were* shifters. The bears got a little carried away by that pig. Cairo should have stuck to chicken and burgers if he knew they were coming. But I don't think he did. They were guests of guests, just like you."

Suddenly I remembered my dragon peeking out in front of Angela. "Shit," I muttered. But I guess if she threw barbeques for shifters, it really didn't matter. I was more concerned with her level of discretion. "Angela saw me start to change while we were on the dock watching you wrestle with the bears."

"I know. She called me last night to congratulate me on my

taste for shifters." I knew what Angela meant. She was referring to his previous relationship with Kara, and now with a dragon. "I cleared a few things up and asked her to forget what she saw."

"And will she?" I asked.

"Your secret is safe. What the hell do you think she is, Katie? The woman turns into objects, for God's sake."

The statement almost blew right over my head. "What do you mean she turns into *objects*?"

"Cairo and Angela are not your garden variety shifters either. They're Dimensionals." He waited for the strange word to sink in. "Their whole clan is. Where do you think that brick wall came from?"

"Dimensionals? Does that mean what I think it means?" I asked curiously, remembering what I witnessed at the barbeque. "They turn into . . . brick walls? What the hell for?"

He grinned. "Good thing one of them did. I don't know if I could have taken both of those bears. But seriously, Katie, why does a shifter change into anything? Who the fuck knows? And it's not just walls. I've seen Cairo flatten into a makeshift bridge to get his car over a flooded street."

I went back to slathering my charred bagel with cream cheese and took a bite as I turned back around. "All right. I'm over it. But no more secrets. I don't want to know how many women you've slept with or your ATM pin, but I sure as hell don't want to find out through the grapevine that you're Spiderman, or some other super hero," I said, suppressing a grin.

"Agreed," he conceded. "And by the way, that goes both ways."

"Of course."

He got up to leave. "I'm heading out of town for a couple of days. A little unfinished business in Atlanta. I'll be back by Thursday night." He stared at me for a minute, considering his next offer. "You could come with me."

Wow. I didn't expect that. "I'd like to go but I can't leave the shop. Especially after taking a couple of days off this week."

He walked around the counter and kissed me. "I know, but it would be nice to have you on the back of my bike for a few hours."

Sugar came flouncing into Lou's at 12:40 p.m., ten minutes late. Her sunglasses suggested she'd had a rough Sunday night, and the jumpsuit she was wearing was zipped a little too low, exposing some of the hair on her chest.

"You're showing," I warned, nodding toward the tuft of dark curls peeking out.

She glanced down at it. "Yeah, I need to get that shit ripped off. Ain't got the tolerance for that kind of pain today though." She pulled her zipper higher and slid into the booth. After picking up the menu and pretending to peruse it for a minute or two, she tossed it on the table and folded her arms. "Where the hell you been?"

"I'm sorry, Sugar. I—I was planning on calling you," I groveled. "Things got a little crazy yesterday and it slipped my mind."

Her expression turned a little hostile. "Crazy? I'll tell you what crazy is. Crazy is me thinking that damn spirit finally got hold of you. Crazy is me trying to have a good time last night without worrying about you every five minutes."

She looked like a human fly, penetrating me over the table with her shiny dark lenses. "Can you take those things off." She whipped the glasses off and glared at me with her bloodshot hazel eyes. "You know, you could have just called *me*," I muttered.

Her eyes widened as she dared me to repeat what I'd just said. "What was that?"

All she had to do was pick up the phone, but I knew Sea Bass had let her know I was taking the day off to spend it with Jackson. And there lay the problem. She didn't quite trust him yet, and her feelings were bruised because I'd put him before her yesterday. "I really like him, Sugar. If he wanted to hurt me, believe me, he had plenty of opportunity to do it by now." Noticing the scorned look on her face, I offered a truce. "We need a girl's night out."

"Damn right." Her expression softened a little from the white flag I'd just waved at her.

I slipped out of the booth to get some food. Lou's didn't have wait service. If you wanted to eat, you ordered at the counter and carried it to your table. "You hungry? It's my treat."

She glanced at the menu. "Get me a bowl of tomato soup. And some crackers," she added as I walked away.

I carried our food back to the table five minutes later. "I got you crackers *and* a biscuit." That put a smile on her face. "So, what did I miss yesterday? Anything exciting happen around here?"

She dunked her biscuit into the creamy orange soup and bit into the soaked edge. "I don't know about right here," she mumbled around her mouthful, "but I been getting a head full of noise since you been gone."

My spoon stopped halfway to my mouth, knowing better than to assume that little statement was benign. Sugar had "the sight", as she called it, and that meant something was coming. "What kind of noise?"

"Oh . . . Mama's been bleeding into my head, sending me messages."

I waited for her to continue because I knew she was holding something back. She glanced up at me over her bowl but went mute, slurping the soup off the edge of her spoon. "Uh-uh," I said. "You better start talking, Sugar."

"There ain't much to talk about. You heard what Mama said: Better get them bones before them bones get you. I just keep hearing them words in my head, and that usually means they gonna be coming to fruition real soon." Before the spoon made it to her mouth, she stopped and dropped it back into the bowl. "You thought any more about how you plan to get that bone charm inside of that thing?"

I shook my head, frustrated by the whole situation. "I have no idea." The thought of even getting that close to Legvu made me lose my appetite.

"You sure I can't convince you to move in with me for a while?" She asked. "I can move in with you, baby, but you got to make me some serious room in that closet of yours."

"That's not happening, Sugar. I'll be fine." I patted the dragon over my shoulder. "Besides, I can't hide forever."

A second later her concern was challenged by curiosity. "You know what? We been sitting here for a whole twenty minutes and you ain't said one word about that man of yours. Come on. Tell Sugar all about that little date yesterday."

Seeing how she was privy to all things strange and unnatural in this town, I saw no reason to be discreet. I did leave out the names though. "Let's just say it was a real eye-opener. Jesus, Sugar, is anyone around here normal?"

She dug back into her biscuit. "All I got to say is if you come to Savannah and you ain't touched, you will be before you leave."

I decided to cut right to it. "Have you ever heard of something called a Dimensional?"

She swallowed her bread and shoved the soup bowl away. "You mean them folks who turn into things like chairs and sidewalks and all kinds of other useless things?" She leaned back into the thick vinyl seat and fiddled with the restricting zipper concealing her wayward chest hair. "If you gonna shift into something, you might as well turn into something fun like an eagle or a lion. What the hell good is turning into a goddamn dining room table?"

"Those are the ones," I said. "I met a couple of them yesterday, not to mention the more traditional kind." Actually, that little talent had been anything but useless at the barbeque. Had it not been for Cairo and his clan, the afternoon might have turned into a free-for-all. I'm sure there were plenty of good reasons for their existence. You know what they say, God doesn't make junk.

With squinted eyes and a raised chin, she asked, "Jackson? I read people pretty good, and I didn't read him as the boring type."

On the contrary, Jackson Hunter was one of the most interesting men I'd ever met. "There's nothing remotely boring about Jackson, and he's not a shifter. But he has some eclectic friends." I considered my next words carefully, not because I didn't trust Sugar completely, but because I didn't want to hear about it if she didn't approve of me dating someone who could possibly break my dragon like a twig—*could he?* "Let's just say he's stronger than the average guy."

"I see. Strong as in . . ." she prompted, rolling her hand and head in conjunction to move me along.

"Really strong." When she pressed further with her annoying glare, I obliged her. "He threw a grizzly bear across a yard yesterday. Well, actually he punched it and it sailed about thirty feet."

She gave me one of those deadpan looks she was so good at, pointing her toothpick in my direction. "Mm-hmm. I can't say I'm surprised. A woman like you would attract something like that."

"A woman like me? What the hell does that mean?"

She cocked her head. "That was a compliment, baby. Boys like that are looking for something special, not some high-maintenance, whiny little ass thing. You got that effervescence about you."

"Well, does Jackson have your approval?"

She rolled her eyes and sighed. "Honey if you don't jump on that man, I will."

22

I liked Tuesdays. It was Wednesdays that usually had us all working our tails off for enough revenue to pay the utilities, if we were lucky. I vowed to do away with two-for-one Wednesdays as soon as the shop was turning a decent profit. But something had the hair on the back of my neck standing at full attention all morning and the pit of my stomach felt floppy, like something was fighting to push its way out.

"Uh, Katie," Sea Bass said, pulling on the other end of the broom handle I had in a death grip as I stared blankly out the front window. "May I? Unless you want to actually use it."

I let go of the handle and continued with my nervous puttering while I waited for my one o'clock appointment to show up. He was ten minutes late and I had a feeling he wasn't coming, which was fine with me considering my distracted mood. Lucky for my earlier client I snapped out of it long enough to put that salamander on her right shoulder. I always told myself that the day I did bad work because of personal issues was the day I turned in my equipment and became the silent manager.

The phone at the front counter rang. "Katie," Abel called across the room. "Your one o'clock just cancelled. Car trouble."

Relief washed over me, even though it was the final session of a large tattoo that would have brought in some decent revenue for the day. I paced around the shop trying to walk off some of my excess adrenaline. Mouse was working her way down a client's sleeve, adding the fierce talons of an owl that wrapped around his arm just above the elbow.

I glanced at the coffeemaker. "I'm going to the deli for a cup of peppermint tea. Anyone need anything?" Caffeine would just make it worse, and Lou's didn't sell anything without it. With no takers, I grabbed my wallet and headed for the front door. As I reached for the handle, a woman with blonde hair pushed it open from the outside. She stopped in my path and pinned me with her violet eyes, refusing to let me pass. "Can I help you?" I asked, dread pooling in my gut as she smiled at me and refused to budge.

She replied in a steady voice that fueled the squirrels already trampling around my innards. "I'd like a tattoo."

I took an involuntary step back, meeting her stare as she proceeded forward. Had I not stepped to the side, I'm sure she would have barreled right over me. "We're a little busy today," I lied, glancing at Sea Bass who was about to open his mouth and correct me. His jaw half opened before he caught on to my strange reaction to her and snapped it shut. "Do you have an appointment?"

She gave me something between a smirk and a smile and glanced around the half-empty room. "You don't look very busy."

Call it instinct, but I knew I had to get out of there. Without debating those instincts, I maneuvered around her toward the door. But as soon as I started to move, she grabbed my forearm and shook her head. The dragon stirred.

Sea Bass glanced down at the woman's hand gripped around my arm like a vise. He must have picked up on the message I was sending him or the flash of green in my eyes. "I can do it," he said. I stared at him in disbelief. An honorable but stupid gesture;

he was trying to protect me. He knew damn well what would happen if the woman was the host and he started working on that deadly tattoo.

"No!" I blurted. "You have a client coming in at two o'clock. I'll do it."

He headed for the door but she blocked his exit, motioning for him to get back. Then she walked over to my station and made herself comfortable. She reached into her bag and pulled out the drawing. Sea Bass, Abel and I all held our breath as we waited to see what was on that sheet of paper, to confirm if indeed she was the host. Even Mouse's hand went still as she looked up to see.

I took the paper from her hand. Just as I suspected, it was the same tattoo from my latest dream. The second spirit was free, and now the host housing both of them—Legvu himself—was standing in my shop.

"Do you want to make any changes to the drawing before we begin?" It was a standard question, but in this case it was meant to stall until I could figure out what to do. Everyone in the shop was at risk if I didn't cooperate. "Maybe a little more color?" The drawing was round and geometric, similar to a mandala but with imagery behind it that disturbed the peaceful rhythm of the design. For reasons I couldn't quite explain, it was difficult to look at for more than a few seconds, which begged the question of how I could apply it without becoming uncomfortable—or even ill—while I worked on it.

She gazed back at me and said what I already knew. "It must be applied exactly as it appears on the paper. Not a mark out of place." The faint grin on her face vanished. "Because that would be very bad, Miss Bishop."

A thought hit me like a wave of water, sucking the breath back into my lungs and making it difficult to breathe. Maybe that's why the others died before they completed the tattoo. Had they accidently deviated from the drawing? Maybe it had nothing to do with my dragon at all, and the only reason I was still alive was my ability to color between the lines.

"That's ridiculous," I muttered.

The host looked at me oddly. "Did you say something?"

"Nothing. I'll just go over there," I pointed to the scanner, "and make a stencil."

She was watching me like a hawk, so calling Fin was out of the question. The rest of the shop was in her sights, too. Basically, Sea Bass and the rest of the team would be under house arrest and helpless to do anything but watch as I made the stencil and then applied that tattoo.

I took my time but finally had no choice but to walk back to my station to begin, the whole time my brain trying to work out a plan to get me out of the shop without causing a riot. Legvu's host could cause a lot of damage if I didn't cooperate, and to make matters worse my eyes were starting to burn again. Everyone in the shop was about to meet the dragon and get caught in the cross fire if I didn't find a peaceful way out of there.

The front door opened and in walked Sea Bass's two o'clock client, an hour early. "Hey, man," he said to Sea Bass. "I was hoping we could start early so I can get out of here by four." A regular and an old friend of Sea Bass's, he glanced around the half-empty shop and raised a questioning brow. "That okay with you?"

Sea Bass glanced at me for direction. "Sorry, Sean," I said. "He's helping me with my client right now. You'll have to come back at two o'clock." Disappointed, he looked to Sea Bass who seemed a little frozen in place. "Sea Bass, tell your client to come back."

Sea Bass came back from la-la land. "Y-Yeah, Sean, you're gonna have to come back in an hour."

The second Sean walk back out the door, the host stripped off her shirt and lay on the table facedown. I pointed my finger into the middle of her back. "Here?" I asked, knowing exactly where to put it, the same spot where Victor Tuse asked to have his applied. She nodded and lowered her head, dropping her arms to the sides of the table. I steadied my trembling hands and applied a small amount of gel to her back before carefully pressing the stencil down. The thought of making a mistake before I ever put a needle to her skin seemed almost laughable, but a real motivator to get every detail right.

Stop shaking, I told myself, my thoughts running rampant as I tried to visualize a way out of the impossible situation. Then I remembered the bone charm Davina had given me—neatly tied up in that little satin bag, stuffed inside a drawer in my kitchen. *Fuck!* I'd forgotten the damn thing. I'd been so wrapped up in Jackson Hunter I'd left it in a drawer like a spare set of keys.

For the next hour I traced the stencil with the finesse of a bomb specialist, inking the lines with painstaking precision, beads of sweat seeping through my brow and into my eyes. I was beginning to think the best idea was to run out the back door and hope she ran after me. At least it would create a diversion so the others could escape out the front.

"I need to take a break," I said. "My hand is—"

Sugar walked through the front door and took one look at Sea Bass's frantic eyes staring back at hers, and I swear her cinnamon skin blanched. I could see his mouth moving, silently telling her to *get out* as his eyes targeted the woman on my table.

My eyes must have been screaming, too, because she stopped in her tracks and turned back toward the door. "I guess this ain't Le Petit Gateau," she stated, referring to the bakery a few blocks away, hurrying out of the shop and disappearing out of view.

The host turned her head at an unnatural angle and glared at me suspiciously. I held her stare and refused to let her see my nerves, praying that Sugar had figured it out and was calling Fin Cooper from around the corner. My hand started to work again, retracing the lines I'd already done in an attempt to stall for more time. The tattoo would take hours, but the dragon wouldn't wait if I didn't calm myself down and get on with it.

I got about five more minutes of work completed before the inevitable rush hit me. It was too late. I could feel my eyes shifting, the brilliant green smashing through my blue irises. I couldn't hold my eyes shut for long, and I was a minute away from revealing my dragon in full glory for everyone to see. Well, I guess being outed was better than being dead. I hoped the same was true for the rest of the folks in the shop.

"What the fuck!" Abel blurted, feeling the floor tremble as my dragon stirred and a growl resonated through the shop.

A siren somewhere in the distance drowned out the growl, growing louder as it turned down a nearby street. I caught myself thinking about how fortunate we would be if it turned down our street. Then it did. The siren blared, getting louder by the second, assaulting our ears with the excruciating sound. The fire engine reached our block, but just as I expected it to fly past the front window it came to an abrupt stop in front of MagicInk and the siren went mercifully quiet. It was almost surreal, watching a crew of firemen jump out of the bright red truck and head straight for our front door.

It took the host about two seconds to grab her shirt and turn to me. "We're not done!" she hissed, gazing at my burning eyes with fascination. Then she walked right past the firemen and out the front door. I, on the other hand, ran for the back door and slid down the exterior wall of the building, praying I'd have enough time to recover before anyone came out after me. Thank God it was Sea Bass when I looked up at the person hovering over me.

"Katie!" He took my face in his hands and looked into my otherworldly eyes. "That's it. Just calm down and think good thoughts. Think trees and birds and . . . butterflies."

I sucked in a massive lungful of air and felt my adrenaline simmer back down to a manageable level. After a minute or two,

Sea Bass informed me that my eyes were back to bright blue, right about the time one of the firemen stepped through the back door.

"You all right, ma'am?" he asked, hunching down to feel my wrist. "I can call an ambulance."

"No, no! I'm fine."

He stood back up. "Someone called in a fire at this address. Any idea who might have done that?"

I shook my head and gave him my best bewildered look, which wasn't too difficult considering the circumstances. "I have no idea."

He glanced around the cars parked in the rear lot and then walked back in the shop. *Sugar*, I mouthed to Sea Bass.

"Fuck yeah, it was. Remind me to give her a big kiss when I see her." He helped me up and looked around for signs of the host. Then he reached into his pocket and pulled out his keys. "Here. You're staying at my place for a while."

"I'm going home, Sea Bass."

As he started to object I cut him off. "To call Fin and pack a bag. There's only one safe place for me now. I guess I'm moving into Lillian's house until this is all over with. I hope she likes cats, because I'm not going anywhere without Jet."

"Roger that, Katie, but what if the host is waiting for you when you get home?" He gave me his classic pointed stare, the one where his forehead creased and his eyebrows lifted into tight question marks.

"I guess I'll find out, won't I?" I doubted that would happen. The spirits may have acted on impulse at times, but I had a feeling Legvu wasn't as stupid as his individual parts seemed to be. Cornering me in a public place where my dragon wouldn't be provoked as easily was a smarter strategy. And besides, it needed that tattoo and this was where the ink was. "I'll call Fin on my way home. He'll probably be waiting for me by the time I get there."

"All right, but you call me and let me know where you are," he insisted.

I agreed and headed for my car. As soon as I hit the street I picked up my phone and dialed Fin's number. It rang five times and then rolled to voicemail. "Damn it, Fin!" I growled at the phone before tossing it on the console. I must have called his number six or seven times before I reached the house, each time rolling to voicemail. I was beginning to wonder why that was, seeing how my number popping up on his phone should have triggered an immediate answer. Six or seven calls in a row should have had him alerting the National Guard.

Being late afternoon made it a little less creepy to walk inside the house, and Jet would be a good barometer of anything strange going on inside. If he met me at the door with his tail up in the air, I'd know that the house was clear. "Hey, baby," I greeted him as he brushed against my legs. "Anything interesting happen around here today?" I did a sweep of each room and then reached into the kitchen drawer for that bone charm that shouldn't have left my side.

My cell phone rang, nearly sending me through the roof. Expecting to see Fin's name across the display, I grabbed it off the kitchen counter and deflated a little when I saw Sugar's name pop up. "Hey, Sugar," I said, waiting to hear all about that false alarm I knew she was responsible for reporting.

"Hey yourself," a voice said back. It wasn't Sugar. The voice was cold and steady, just like the one I'd heard less than an hour ago in my shop. "Sugar has caused me a lot of trouble, Katie Bishop. I'd like nothing more than to slit that thing's throat from ear to ear. But that would be like burning all my aces, now wouldn't it?"

I steadied the tremor in my hand as the phone rattled against my ear, trying to sound unfazed and in control. Never let your opponent see you sweat. "If you've got her, you'll have to do better than that. And I'll need some proof that she's okay."

The sound of a deep breath came through the phone. "*Okay* is a relative term," he snidely remarked. "But I'd be happy to provide proof of life. In fact, I think I'll put together a little home video for you."

I cringed because my time was up. "Let her go and I'll do whatever you ask."

"Her?" The host laughed on the other end. "I bet there's a flaccid little dick under that skirt. You know what? I think I'll take a look after I hang up this phone."

I don't know why I bothered to frantically shake my head. Only Jet could see it. "If you touch her, you'll never get that tattoo," I warned. "Now stop fucking with me and tell me what to do."

There was that laugh again. "You just sit tight," he instructed. "I'll be coming to you."

The call ended. I stared at the screen as I waited for the proof he was about to send. Then I heard the telltale ping announcing a text message. There was a video attached of Sugar with her hands tied, suspended from a beam above her head. Her mouth was taped, and I could see the fear in her eyes as he approached her with the phone camera, his hand coming into view and reaching for her skirt.

I closed the video without watching it all the way through. Then I made one last call to Fin, leaving him another message that I was going to hunt him down and murder him if he didn't pick up his goddamn phone. With my gun retrieved from the box in the cabinet, I slid down to the kitchen floor with the barrel pointed toward the door while I waited to see who would get to me first.

23

I'm not sure how long I sat on the floor with my arm propped on my knee and the gun dangling from my fingers. I decided to keep the safety on, figuring I could have it off in less than a second. No need to kill anything from a nervous jolt every time the icemaker dropped a load of cubes, or an unfortunate bird hit the glass patio door.

Jet seemed amused by the whole sitting on the floor thing, winding himself under and around my propped knees and climbing halfway up my shoulder to sniff my face. "Just stay out of the gun sight, Jet. Fin will knock on that door any minute now."

The room was getting darker. Since it was late afternoon when I took my position, I hadn't bothered to turn on any of the lights. Probably a good idea since a lit room would only give an intruder the advantage.

Thank God the safety was on, because the gun hit the wooden floor when my cell phone rang. Fin's name displayed across the front as I reached for it. "Where the hell have you been?" I answered without a greeting. He seemed relieved by the fact that I was intact and barricaded in my house. Then he justified his lack of response by alluding to the woman lying next to him. Good to know that the one thing that could keep him distracted from matters of life and death was sex. He instructed me to stay put with the lights off. "You better identify yourself first, Fin. I got a loaded gun pointed at that door."

I hung up the phone, feeling a little relieved but knowing damn well what could happen in the blink of an eye if he didn't get to me first. It felt like an hour had passed before I heard the faint sound of a car pulling into my driveway. Jet padded over to the front door, his ears pinned back and a low growl coming from his throat. "Get over here, Jet," I coaxed quietly, patting my thigh to get his attention. He shot under the sofa in the living room instead.

Heavy footsteps came down the sidewalk, accompanied by voices. They paused before hitting the front step and knocking on the door. My heart raced wildly. Fin would have been more deliberate in his approach, and he would have come alone. And he sure as hell would have announced himself before he knocked, on account of that gun he knew was aimed at the door.

The knock came again, only this time much louder "Police! Open the door, Miss Bishop!"

Police.

My chest felt like it had dropped into my gut. It could have been a trap, but I could hear the faint sound of breaking voices coming from a police radio on the other side of the door. There was only one reason I could think of why the police would be here. And even though Fin had supposedly gotten rid of Christopher's mutilated body, there was still a chance it had been found and the evidence led straight to me.

Without thinking rationally, I creeped toward the door with the gun still dangling from my right hand. Through the peephole I could see two uniformed officers. "Can I see your badge?" I said. Anyone could rent a uniform. A Chatham County Police badge appeared through the lens of the peephole.

Suddenly realizing the gun was still in my hand, I stashed it in the hall closet before opening the door, hoping Fin's car was right behind them. It wasn't.

"Katie Bishop?" one of the officers asked.

"Yes," I nodded. "Is this about the false alarm at my shop earlier today?" It was a long shot, but worth a try.

The second officer spoke up. "Miss Bishop, we'd like you to come with us down to the station."

My eyes darted back and forth between them. "For what?"

"For questioning related to the disappearance of Christopher Sullivan."

"What?" I asked in a quiet voice, more from shock than in search of reasonable cause. "Am I being arrested?"

"Not yet, but we'd like to ask you some questions. We have an eyewitness that placed you with Mr. Sullivan the night he disappeared."

Never so much as having a speeding ticket before, I had no idea how to respond. But the police station was probably the safest place for me anyway.

"Let me get my bag." They watched me like a hawk as I nervously grabbed it from the kitchen counter. As I was shutting the door, Jet slipped out and ran for the side of the house. "My cat!" They ignored my protest and escorted me to the patrol car. "Is this necessary?" I asked, staring at the opened rear door where criminals usually sat. "I can follow you in my car."

"I'm afraid not, Miss Bishop. Please step inside."

Not wanting to fuel the trouble I was already in, I complied. As we drove out of the neighborhood I decided to discreetly text Fin to have him meet me at the police station, but as I rooted around my purse I realized my phone was still sitting on the kitchen floor. "Shit," I whispered.

The officer in the front seat turned around. "There a problem, Miss Bishop?"

"I left my cell phone at the house. I don't suppose either of you have a phone I can borrow?"

"You can make a call from the station," he replied, turning back around to respond to a voice on his radio.

When we got to the station I was immediately escorted to a questioning room where a detective was waiting. He was wearing a gray pinstriped suit with his tie loosened around his neck. "I'm Detective Ryan. Please have a seat." He motioned to the folding chair on the other side of the table that I'm sure was designed for discomfort. "I hope you don't mind," he continued, stretching the knot even farther away from his throat. "The air conditioner is only working at about fifty percent in here."

I guess that explained why sweat was dripping down my neck like condensation on a bottle of beer. I prayed it wouldn't start rolling down my face next, like I was guilty or something. Of course, speculating on who—other than Fiona—could have identified me with Christopher that night was enough to make me sweat blood.

"I was told I could use a phone," I said, desperate to get a message to Fin.

"Plenty of time for that after we've had a chat, Miss Bishop." He gave me a curious look and added, "Unless you have something to hide."

I refused to say another word. In return, he sat straight in his chair and leaned into the table, pinning me with a glare that probably worked on more meek suspects. But I prided myself on intelligence, and there was nothing remotely intelligent about waiving my right to remain silent.

"That phone?" I requested again, making it perfectly clear I was going to place that call before I opened my mouth.

The door opened and another detective waved him over. They spoke for about a minute before he returned and retook his seat with a smug look on his face. "Your lawyer has arrived." He leaned back and crossed his right ankle over his left knee, folding his hands on his stomach just above his belt. Not once did he take his eyes off me as we waited for this lawyer who claimed to be mine.

"Okay then," I announced, nervously wondering what the hell was going on. It had to be Fin who sent him. But how did Fin know I'd been taken to the station for questioning? Maybe he'd spotted me in the back of the police car driving out of my neighborhood. Or maybe I'd been assigned a public defender, but I was pretty sure I had to be charged with a crime first and then ask for legal assistance.

The door opened again, and in walked a man wearing a sharp looking suit and carrying an expensive briefcase. Court appointed attorneys probably didn't dress that well. He dropped the briefcase on the table and took a deep breath through his freckled nose before turning to look at me. He made me uneasy as he held my gaze with his intense blue eyes, eventually turning to Detective Ryan with an extended hand. "David Brady. I'm Miss Bishop's lawyer. Now, before we go any further with this interrogation, I'd like to know exactly what my client is being charged with."

As soon as Detective Ryan began to speak, David Brady pulled out one of the rickety chairs, sliding the leg across the hard floor until the metal squealed. Ryan stopped talking and glared at Brady. "My apologies, Detective Ryan," he said as he took his seat. "You were saying?"

Ryan exhaled and continued. "No one is under arrest. Yet."

"Then why is my client being detained for questioning?" Brady countered before Ryan could get another word out.

"Mr. Brady, as a member of Savannah's legal community, I'm sure you're familiar with the disappearance of Christopher Sullivan from the Chatham County DA's office." Brady nodded. "A witness has come forward who can put Miss Bishop in Mr. Sullivan's company on the last night he was seen alive."

"Alive?" Brady said. "Are you telling me you have evidence to support that Mr. Sullivan is in fact dead?"

Detective Ryan smirked, clearly familiar with the game. "No, Mr. Brady, we haven't found a body yet, but our witness saw Miss Bishop with Sullivan the night he disappeared."

David Brady made no indication that he was impressed with the detective's statement. He just sat there as if waiting for the real evidence to be revealed. "And this witness," he finally said, "has been questioned by you?"

Detective Ryan lost his cocky smugness. "Well, not yet. He—"

"What do you mean by not yet?" Brady interjected.

The detective looked a little uneasy. I could tell by his body language that his defenses were up. "He's agreed to come in tomorrow to give a statement."

"And his name is?" Brady pushed.

Now, Detective Ryan looked downright embarrassed. "We don't have that information yet. The tip was called in from an untraceable number, but as I said, he agreed to come in and make a statement."

David Brady stood up abruptly, sending the chair a few feet back. "I'll be taking my client home now." He handed Ryan a card. "When you have legitimate cause to haul Miss Bishop back down here for questioning, you let me know."

There was nothing Detective Ryan could do but sit there and watch us leave. I'd been taken in for questioning, in the back of a police car no less, based on an anonymous tip.

We exited the police station and head for the parking lot. "Did Fin Cooper send you?" I asked. He kept his eyes straight ahead as if I hadn't spoken. "I don't care who sent you. I'm just glad they did. But I would like to know who to thank."

We rounded the corner of the building and headed for a black sedan parked at the far end of the lot. I struggled to keep up with him as each of his long strides equaled two of mine.

From behind, his bright red hair reminded me of something, but it was the way he bounced his foot nervously against the pavement as he opened the door that jogged my memory.

I turned around to confirm where I'd seen his face before. The red mohawk was gone, but the piercing eyes were just as blue as they were the night he sat at the bar next to me at MacPherson's.

"I know you," I began as reality set in and a sickly feeling overwhelmed me. Before I could step out of his reach, he draped something over my head that rested around my neck and hung down to my cleavage. The weight of it was too much for my legs to bear, clouding my mind like an anesthesia coaxing me to sleep. I touched the necklace, the bone fragments studding the chain every few inches, and Pearl May Mobley's words filled my mind: *You got to learn to see him, else he'll come right up on you and put the bone to you.*

Legvu had finally won.

A bright ray of light hit my face when I opened my eyes. For a moment, I forgot what happened the night before and how I ended up on a cold floor in a room that wasn't a room at all but a cavernous enclosure that seemed to go on forever. It looked more like an airplane hangar, with its mile-high ceiling and echoes bouncing off the walls from the slightest move I made. But then the memory of the police station and the bones draped around my neck came crashing back like a freight train. The ramblings of an old conjure woman had come true, and Legvu had done exactly what Pearl May Mobley had warned me about. Sugar had to be somewhere nearby.

I pushed myself off the floor and propped up on my right elbow, nearly falling back down from the crushing pain inside my head. My vision was so blurred that I could barely make out the figure across the room. I could hear what sounded like thunder rolling in the distance, booming quietly twenty miles away, but as I regained my focus I spotted a large sheet of metal near the dilapidated roof, bouncing up and down from the wind like a bird's wing. There were tall steel posts positioned along the length of the space and rusted strip lights suspended by wires from the tall ceiling. It must have been a warehouse or a deserted factory.

"Head hurt?" he asked, his head cocking at me from across the room where he sat on a rusted table. He hopped off and took his time approaching me. "Aspirin would probably help with that."

I replied cockily, "Why? Do you have any?"

"Unfortunately, I do not. But I do need a steady pair of hands today, so perhaps a little hair of the dog that bit you will do the trick."

I thought that only applied to a hangover, and I hadn't been drinking. "And what exactly was it that bit me last night?" I asked.

"Just a little bit of the crossroads. I can give you more if it will relieve your symptoms." He noticed my face light up at the mention of it and quickly quelled my hopes that the bones had been unearthed. "Don't get too excited, little dragon. I haven't resurrected the mother lode—yet. Those bones around your neck were just enough to take down the beast and keep it sedated. And if you're thinking, *hmm, why don't I just lift this necklace of bones from around my neck and toss it away*, it won't work. Only the doctor who applies the medicine can reverse it."

"I'll pass, but thanks for caring so much about my well-being." I felt for the bones to see if they were still hanging around my neck. They were, but lighter feeling than before when I thought a ship's anchor had been dropped over my shoulders. *Bone warfare*, I thought, remembering the charm Davina had given me, the one I stuffed inside my bra minutes before the police came knocking on my door. That little trick I adopted when she pulled it out of her own bosom the night she gave it to me, because I knew it was the perfect place to retrieve it in a pinch. Today's quandary definitively qualified as a pinch. If he could sense it, he wasn't letting on. I suspected the bones around my neck were too powerful to let a little hyena bone stand out.

He clasped his hands behind his back and began to stroll in a wide circle around me as I remained on the floor. "Did you know that this mill was built over the very spot where I was tricked into that grimoire, Katie?" he stopped and regarded me with a raised brow. "You don't mind if I call you Katie, do you? Miss Bishop is so cold and formal, and I think our relationship has earned us a first name basis, yes?"

"What do I call you?" I asked in return, banking on a little friendly psychology to defuse the situation. Humanize the victim, the experts say. I guess it couldn't hurt to humanize the predator, too, even though there was nothing human about a wayward god whose purpose was to flood the earth with evil for the sake of power.

He seemed amused by the question, shaking his head stiffly as if the obvious had been lost to my thick brain. "Call me Master."

So much for informality.

A loud noise echoed through the place. It sounded like a metal bucket had been kicked across the room, or one of those metal ceiling flaps had fallen to the floor. Legvu's eyes darted toward a door on the far end of the mill. "Shut up!" he shouted. "Or I'll slit your fucking throat!"

I gasped. "Sugar?"

He turned back to me and scoffed. "This is your fault. If you'd done your job and given me that *fucking* tattoo, your friend in there wouldn't be hanging from a rafter like a side of meat." Suddenly his sneer turned to amusement. "Shall we go see?" He yanked me off the floor and practically dragged me down the long room toward the door. My heart sank when we turned the corner. Sugar was dangling from a beam, her feet thrashing wildly about a foot off the floor. The duct tape wrapped around her mouth looked tight. I could see a spot of blood where it had worn her skin away around the edge of her lip, probably from stretching her mouth to try to scream.

I shook my head discreetly as she began to get more agitated at the sight of me, trying to get her to shut up for her own good. "Get that damn bucket back under her feet," I demanded, spotting the source of the loud noise on the other side of the room. She must have kicked it out from under her feet. To the left of Sugar's dangling form were two tables, the smaller one covered with an assortment of tools that I assumed were meant for me. Next to a box of plastic gloves and a few jars of ink, there were several bamboo sticks that looked like thick paint brushes. No tattoo machine. No power source.

"Is that what I think it is?" I motioned to the table with a flick of my head.

Legvu grabbed the bucket and took his time walking back to where Sugar was dangling painfully from the rope around her wrists. He slid it back under her feet. "Do that again and I'll let gravity have its way with you. Then I'll disembowel you in front of your friend."

Not stupid and not wishing for death, Sugar's feet found the top of the bucket and went still, her eyes bulging and frantic—or was that a look of seething hatred she was sending him? Good thing her mouth was taped, because I had no doubt she'd get herself killed if she had the use of her wicked tongue.

The Japanese art of tebori tattooing wasn't for the faint of heart—or the untrained. It was a traditional form of hand tattooing that I wasn't qualified to do, especially when a single mistake could cost me my life, not to mention Sugar's.

The look on his face answered the question. "Are you out of your mind?" I spat. "I don't know how to do that. What you're asking me to do is suicide."

He glanced around the room and circled back to meet my incredulous stare. "Do you see a power source around here? I'm afraid this is the best I can do under the circumstances. You'll just have to be careful."

Legvu walked over to the longer table next to the tools and removed his shirt. I was surprised to see the unfinished tattoo I'd started on the female host earlier that day now on his back. "Shall we begin, Katie?" He held out a copy of the design and waited for me to comply. I considered refusing, but he'd kill us both and find some other oblivious tattoo artist unless I picked up that bamboo stick with the row of fine needles at the end and began puncturing the ink into his flesh. The technique involved dipping the row of needles into the ink and jabbing his skin in successive movements. Not unlike a machine, but with less control and a hell of a lot slower, which increased the likelihood of error but bought me more time. One wrong jab and Sugar and I were dead.

He lifted himself onto the table, face down. I gazed at the tattoo I'd started on the woman, but now I could see the one from Victor Tuse's back underneath it. It wasn't actually under the latest one, but a part of it. Separately, it was impossible to see how they complemented each other, the second one an extension of the first. Where the lines of one ended, the other seemed to organically pick up. I was building a master design. One that would open the prison gates and allow Legvu to shed his earthly chains and walk free.

"Stop wasting time!" he demanded.

With a deep breath, I slipped on a pair of gloves and picked up the tool with the thinnest set of needles along the edge. I figured less needles meant less ink to botch. Then I dipped the tip into the blue ink and held it just above his skin. I'd seen the technique performed a couple of times, but until I'd actually done it myself there was no way to know how much force was necessary to puncture his skin. In his case, I didn't give a shit about minimizing the pain. In fact, I hoped it hurt like hell.

"Do it!" he growled, startling me and sending the bamboo stick sailing to the floor.

I growled back, "Yell at me again and I swear I'll stab that thing in your carotid artery!" It wasn't a bad idea, just a stupid one.

He relaxed back into the table and waited. I picked up a new tool and got down to business, testing the technique in the center of a large section where I couldn't make a mistake. Awkward at first, the pressure and rhythm required to apply the ink got easier as I worked. But I made sure it didn't get too easy, because time was money, and I still had no idea how to get that bone inside of him.

Sugar's eyes were beginning to look weak when I glanced up at her. The stress of being strung up like slaughtered livestock with only a wobbly bucket to support her weight was starting to take its toll on her body and mind. *Hold on*, I mouthed to her. But I could see it in her eyes, the white flag she was waving in the back of her head, the surrender to her maker she was willing to concede.

Without my phone I had no idea of the time, but I guesstimated that I'd been working on the tattoo for about an hour before I finally decided I needed a break, if for nothing else but to stall for more time and see about getting Sugar untied from that rafter. It was a reasonable request.

"What are you doing?" he asked as I put the bamboo stick down and stood up.

"I need a break."

He pushed up from the table to looked at me and shook his head. "No breaks."

"You want it done right?" I asked. "Because my hand is sore from jabbing your skin, and nothing more is going to happen until I get the circulation back in my limbs." It wasn't a lie. My right hand was starting to go numb from the repetitive motion. "It was your idea to do this in an abandoned building without power," I reminded him.

"Very well," he conceded. "Five minutes."

"Fifteen," I countered.

He sneered. "Ten."

"Twenty. We can do this all day," I threatened. "Do you want me to fuck up that tattoo? Because that will just put you back to square one, stuck inside that host indefinitely while you look for another patsy who can survive finishing it." I was beginning to lose some of the fear and garner more of the power I had in this little scenario because he needed me.

"Twenty," he agreed.

I motioned to Sugar. "She needs a break, too. Cut her down until we get started again."

"No." He sat up and went to the window. I started to argue but he cut me off. "If you push me another inch, I'll start to disassemble that thing hanging from the rope, piece by piece." That nervous habit with his leg started up again, and the look in his eyes as he turned around to face me sent a chill up my spine. "Trust me on this. You don't want to see what I'm capable of to persuade you, Katie."

He made it brutally clear that there wouldn't be another warning. Sugar would have to muster every ounce of strength she had to endure the torturous hanging, while I took my time finishing that tattoo on his back. The only thing that would save us was a miracle.

25

JACKSON HUNTER: WEDNESDAY, 5:56 P.M.

T he minute Jackson walked into MagicInk, three sets of eyes focused on him as he searched the shop for Katie. His eyes traveled to the flash art framed on the right wall, all the work they'd done since opening the shop, and some that was still waiting to find a spot on someone's skin.

"Where is she?" he asked Sea Bass, who was glaring at him suspiciously. "She's not answering her phone. I checked her house. She's not there."

Sea Bass tried to stand eye to eye with him, but it was difficult for the average person to measure up to Jackson's considerable height, even those considered gifted by stature. "I was about to ask you the same thing," he replied, bobbing his head in a cocky display of bravado. "You know anything about that?"

Jackson glanced at Abel and then back at Sea Bass. "About what?" A sickening feeling fell over him as the question left his mouth. His trip to Atlanta had been cut short with a nagging feeling that something was wrong, bringing him back a day early to find out his instincts were right. He'd called her a dozen times the night before, but every one of those calls had gone to voice-mail. When he rode into town late that afternoon his gut feeling sent him straight to her house, only compounding his fear by the sight of Jet sitting outside on the patio table. Katie never left her cat outside, and after easily popping the sliding door open—without the metal rod installed—his fear had escalated.

They all stood there staring at him, mute and accusatory. "Someone needs to tell me what the hell is going on."

"She's missing," Abel finally said, strolling up to Jackson to glare at him side by side with Sea Bass. "When's the last time you saw her?" Ingrained habits were hard to break, and Abel's former cop was resurfacing in droves. "You said you checked her house? How did you do that? Break a window?"

"Wow!" Jackson said, throwing up his hands in surrender, realizing he was a suspect in the eyes of the people standing in the room. "You're way off base, man." He couldn't blame them. If he were in their shoes he'd think the same thing. But he also knew that something was after her. Some spirit with a hard-on for a particular tattoo. She's told him everything the night before the barbeque at Cairo's. Without knowing how much of her secrets the rest of them were privy to, he tiptoed around the subject. "I saw her Monday morning, just before I left for Atlanta."

"Atlanta?" Sea Bass repeated, squinting his eyes. "What were you doing in Atlanta?"

"Nothing you need to concern yourself with." He left it at that and carefully broached the subject of the spirit. "She told me something's been following her."

"You mean the spirit?" Mouse said, quickly covering her mouth with both hands as her eyes bugged wide. "I–I mean—"

"It's okay," Jackson said, putting her out of her misery. "She told me about this Legma or Larma something."

"That would be Legvu," Fin corrected as he walked through the front door. "And you are the distraction that's had her so preoccupied and careless lately." Jackson refused to take the bait and stood silent as Fin examined him, eyeing his considerable height before settling his gaze on the fresh tattoo Katie recently put on his arm. "Nothing to say about that? Mr. Hunter, is it?"

Jackson nodded slightly. "And you are?"

"My name is Fin Cooper." He extended his hand. Jackson took it.

"Mr. Cooper owns half the town," Abel said. "I'm surprised his name wasn't engraved on your welcome package when you moved here. You're a big deal around here, aren't you, Fin?" He made no attempt to hide his distaste for Finley Cooper.

Fin scoffed. "Abel and I go way back to the days when he wore a uniform and a badge." He walked up to Abel, stopping uncomfortably close to the ex-cop. "But you don't wear that badge anymore, do you?"

"All right!" Sea Bass interjected. "We got more important things to worry about than a pissing contest." He shook his head and pulled his lips tight. "What do you know, Fin?"

Fin inhaled sharply and continued. "She was taken in for questioning last night by the police."

"Questioning?" Jackson said. "About what?"

"Apparently, there's been some misunderstanding about her involvement in the disappearance of an acquaintance," Fin said. "Someone called in an anonymous tip putting her at the scene of his last known whereabouts on the night he disappeared, at MacPherson's Pub on the twentieth."

Jackson tried to hide his shock. Katie had mentioned Christopher Sullivan. She described him as an ex, and said the spirit had possessed him in an attempt to get to her. It was meant to be a warning, but she'd failed to mention the fact that Sullivan had gone missing. His mind went back to the night of the brawl at MacPherson's. Reconciling the date, it was the twentieth, the same night Katie showed up in the middle of the fight and ended up showing him her claws in the parking lot. He considered stepping forward as her alibi, even if he'd only seen her earlier in the evening. The cops didn't know that though, so it would be his word against an anonymous tip.

"Mr. Hunter? *Mr. Hunter?*" Fin repeated, trying to pull Jackson back to the here and now.

"Did they arrest her?" Jackson asked.

"Now that's where the story gets real interesting," Fin continued. "A man showed up out of the blue and claimed to be her lawyer. I suspect she thought I sent him. He seemed to know a bit about the law though, because he managed to get her out of there. Then the two of them disappeared. Got camera footage from the parking lot behind the station showing her getting into a car, but if you ask me it looked more like she was dumped into that car. Plates are registered to a Thomas Frazier, but I suspect that man posing as her lawyer was in fact Legvu's latest host."

A walk-in customer entered the shop. The woman looked at the five of them congregated in the center of the room and waited for someone to acknowledge her. "Are you open?" she asked. When no one answered, she pointed toward the sign hanging on the door. "The sign says you are."

"Mouse, why don't you—" Sea Bass motioned toward the woman and Mouse took her cue, steering the woman to her station across the room.

Sea Bass and Fin kept glancing back and forth at each other, having some silent conversation. "Mr. Hunter," Fin finally said, "may we have a word?" He looked at Abel. "In private." Jackson followed Sea Bass and Fin out the back door. "How do I put this?" Fin said, exhaling with a heavy sigh as he studied the ground. He looked back up at Jackson and proceeded. "How much do you know about Miss Bishop? I mean, her talents?"

Trying not to divulge more than he should he scrutinized Fin, working just as hard to dance around the question. "You mean her . . ." His hand waved in a circular motion, trying to move the conversation along and coax Fin into giving up more information before he answered.

"Well, yes," Fin acknowledged. "I think we're alluding to the same thing."

"Oh, for Christ's sake!" Sea Bass spat. "We ain't got time for this. The goddamn dragon! Do you know about the dragon?"

Fin rubbed his forehead. "Well, he does now."

"About her being a shifter?" Jackson asked, for lack of a better way to describe it.

Sea Bass rolled his eyes. "Thank you, Jesus!"

"Well, there you go," Fin said. "Now we can cut to the chase and get past all this sidestepping shit." He proceeded to relay the events of the previous day, starting with the spirit walking into the shop and the fire department showing up, and ending with the phone conversation instructing Katie to stay put until he got to her house. "Here's what we know. The police must have shown up shortly after we ended the call, because I went straight over after hanging up. Couldn't have been more than fifteen minutes, tops."

Jackson listened until Fin finished. Then he turned to go back inside and out the front door to his bike parked on the street. "Where the hell are you going?" Fin called after him.

"To her house."

———

FIN FOLLOWED Jackson back to Katie's house. "I don't know what you think you're gonna find in there," he said as Jackson performed the maneuver of lifting and opening the patio door. Good thing he didn't put that metal rod in the track when he showed up earlier, because he didn't relish the idea of breaking one of her windows.

"Why?" Jackson asked. "You know where she is?" He slid the door open, catching Jet before he could slip outside again. After tossing the cat on the couch he started turning the place over, careful not to destroy anything as he looked for clues of what might have happened in the house before the cops showed up. It may not have had any bearing on what happened later at the police station, but it bothered him that she'd left Jet outside on her way out. In the confusion of having the police haul her out of her own house, she probably didn't even realize he'd gotten out, just like she'd forgotten to secure the useless patio door with that metal bar. Regardless of the reasons for either, it got his hunches stirred up and he intended to find out why.

There was nothing out of the ordinary. And why would there be? If the police had taken her away, clearly nothing had happened to her prior to them knocking on her door. Even Jet's bowl was still half-full of food. But years of living side by side with a pack of shifters had its benefits. He'd developed some pretty sensitive instincts over those years, including a hunch-driven psyche that never relented when there was something to be found.

The refrigerator door whined as Fin opened it. "I doubt you'll find her in there," Jackson said.

"Maybe not, but I could use a cold beer, seeing how I doubt there's any bourbon in this place. That girl's a scotch drinker. Never developed a taste for peat." He grabbed two bottles, offering one to Jackson who shook his head. "Suit yourself," Fin said, placing the second beer back on the shelf before shutting the door and leaning back against the kitchen counter. He bent down to retrieve the bottle cap he'd dropped and spotted something on the floor, hidden under the lip of the cabinet. "Well, fuck me." Jackson froze and turned to look at Fin, who was standing in the kitchen waving Katie's cell phone in the air. "Looks like your instincts were right, Mr. Hunter."

Jackson wasted no time striding over to Fin and snatching the phone from his hand, pressing the home button repeatedly but getting nothing but a blank screen. "Fucking phone is dead."

"Forget your manners, boy?" Fin glared at him before looking around the kitchen for a charger. "Now where would I keep a charger if I were a woman?"

Jackson headed for Katie's bedroom and found the charger next to her bed. He came back into the kitchen and plugged it into the wall. Eventually the home screen appeared. "Goddamn phone is locked!"

"What's that cat's name?" Fin asked.

Jackson enter "JET" into the keypad. It was too short, but "JET1" was the magic password. "She's gonna have to change that," he muttered.

The log showed dozens of calls the day before, both in and out, most of them incoming from Jackson or outgoing to Fin. He checked the text messages next, just another one of those hunches that paid off. The latest one was from Sugar's phone—with a video attached. His nostrils flared with anger as he hit the play button and watched Sugar struggle with her hands tied above her head and her mouth taped shut.

"Let me see that," Fin said, grabbing the phone back from Jackson. At first he seemed as uncomfortable about what he was watching as Jackson was. But as he replayed it several times, his expression went from disturbed to curious. He kept watching the video over and over again, hitting the pause button repeatedly to study the image. Eventually a sly grin crept up one side of his face. "Well, son of a bitch."

"What are you seeing in that video?" Jackson demanded, ready to play tag with the phone again, but thinking it wiser not to disturb the carefully adjusted image that took Fin so many attempts to pause just right.

Fin set the phone on the counter and pointed to a spot in the video, something directly behind Sugar's strung-up form. "You see that?"

Jackson looked closer, squinting at what Fin had his finger on, shaking his head in confusion. "A window?"

"It's a window, all right. But I'm more interested in what's just outside of that window." Jackson looked again, this time noting a series of faded words written in white letters on a red background. It was a large sign. The kind you used to see on stores and building decades ago. The kind collectors paid good money for. In the distance behind the building was a huge faded sign that said COCA COLA.

Jackson leaned back and scoffed. "Jesus, Fin. You do realize we're in Coca Cola country." Collector's items or not, Coca Cola was part of Georgia's heritage, the world headquarters located about two-hundred and fifty miles west in Atlanta. There must have been hundreds of those old signs around the state.

"That is true, Mr. Hunter. But I know what's dead and buried right under *that* particular one," he said, pointing to the sign in the paused video. "One thing you can always count on in the good old USA—progress."

"Your point?"

He motioned to the video again. "My point is that the building we're looking at is an old mill. It's been abandoned for decades. Built right on top of an old plantation. We just covered up the past with brick and mortar. It also happens to be the very spot where the grimoire was found." Fin shook his head slowly, recognizing the serendipitous discovery. "Legvu has taken them back to where it all began, to the very spot where he sprung from his first host and was subsequently imprisoned in the grimoire. He's taken Miss Bishop back to where he was born. Well, reborn."

Jackson took another look at the video. "You sure about this?"

"Well, Mr. Hunter, there's only one way to find out."

26

KATIE BISHOP: WEDNESDAY, THE OLD MILL

I continued the slow process of manually piercing his skin with the ink covered needles, taking extra caution as my margin for error quickly evaporated each time I worked toward the edges of the design. Either that stroke of genius I needed so badly was about to surface, or Sugar and I were dead women.

"How did you do it?" I asked. "Escape the grimoire?"

"Small talk, Katie? I wouldn't think you were inclined to such a waste of words."

His tone was dismissive, but I knew men—mortal or not— couldn't resist impressing women with their accomplishments. I was curious to know how he'd done it, because if I won and found a way to stuff him back in that book, I needed to know how to prevent him from escaping from it again. "Actually, I'm curious." I waited for him to bite. When he didn't, I sweetened the pot. "I'll make you a deal. Tell me how you did it and I'll shut up and cooperate with anything you ask me to do."

His head turned toward me. "Anything?"

After getting a whiff of the innuendo in his voice, I changed my mind. Men were men, and apparently even a god wasn't above lechery. "Forget it."

He continued anyway. "You know, humans are a predictable species. Lust, greed, power—so many ways to sway one's moral compass. It was quite simple, getting that fool to serve as my bridge."

I seized the opportunity. "Fool?"

"That narcissistic embarrassment to your kind." He rolled his head forward and rested his chin on the back of his folded hands. "The one who makes his living chopping off other people's hair."

My mind worked, trying to put together the pieces. "José?"

"Yes, that's the fool who thinks he's worthy of elevation to the next world." His tone took on a more amused note. "If you ask me, he isn't worthy of the one he's in right now."

The revelation floored me. Who would have thought that pompous, vain man would even have the capacity to dream up a plan to let the spirits out of the book? He seemed too self-absorbed in his own little world to even venture out. But then again, he was a board member of the Crossroads Society. I guess I always assumed his membership was simply by default, seeing how they were all direct descendants.

"But why?" I asked, needing to know what had turned José into a traitor.

"Simple greed," he continued, appearing to enjoy boasting about the way he manipulated the man. "I offered something he wanted—immortality."

José didn't strike me as a particularly smart individual. He was far too obsessed with himself to expand his mind and think outside of his own little bubble. Which begged an even bigger question. "How did he do it? How did he get you out?"

"There's a reason the grimoire is buried a hundred feet underground. The magic in that book is very powerful, but in order to maintain that power it must remain as focused as a laser. The smallest distraction is like an inclusion in a diamond, a tiny flaw in the dome encasing the book." He glanced sideways at me and read the confusion on my face. "All it took was a second of distraction. That fool made the mistake of getting too curious. And true to his stupidity, he took the elevator down to the tomb where the grimoire is enshrined. Thought he could just take a peek and no one would ever know."

Only a fool with a death wish would go down there unprepared. Fin's words made perfect sense now. Even José had made a snide remark the night of the dinner party when I questioned whether anyone was going down there periodically to check on the book. *We monitor the book with cameras. It's much safer that way*, Lillian had explained. I wondered how José got past those cameras. I suspected he was the one monitoring them on that particular day.

"As soon as that elevator door opened, it was too late. The armor was momentarily cracked," Legvu continued. "My left half slipped right out of the grimoire." He turned back to the wall and took a deep breath. "Unfortunately, he got back on that elevator just in time to refocus the magic and keep my other half from escaping. I'm surprised the magic didn't kill him. But as you can see, I found a way to make that little idiot go back down there to set my other half free."

"So he was offered immortality in exchange for going back down there to let the other spirit out of the grimoire," I said, knowing the answer.

He laughed. "Unfortunately for him, I won't be keeping that bargain. If I do I'm stuck with him for eternity, and that is a torture I refuse to bear."

No integrity. What a surprise. I realized the only reason he was being so candid was because he never intended to let us go. Whatever bargain he offered would be worthless.

"Do you know why I brought you here, Katie?"

I glanced around the cavernous space: the debris-scattered floor, the tall windows with the broken panes of glass, the rusted light fixtures hanging at random around the room above where tables or machinery used to stand. It was as good a place as any to commit his crimes, barring the lack of electricity.

"I was born here," he informed me. "Well, reborn is a more accurate term. The year was 1764 and I'd barely managed to climb aboard a slave ship leaving the west coast of Africa. I had planned to hitch a ride inside the strongest man on the boat, but then I saw an opportunity lying on the floor in the back corner. A woman who looked to be about a breath away from losing her unborn child. So you see, I was doing her a favor by replacing the dying child's spirit with my own. A win-win for both of us."

The building was old, but not that old. Lillian had told me the story of the pregnant slave, so I assumed he meant he was born on the land beneath the building. "What was this place?" I asked, noting the wide look in Sugar's eyes.

"The plantation where I was born. The slave quarters were located directly under this building. It's also the very spot where my freedom was taken from me, so I thought it might be a fitting place to get it back. Come full circle, as they say."

Sugar struggled against the ropes, a garbled muffle coming from her taped mouth as her eyes burned. At first I thought it was fear, but as I studied her face I realized it was a look of contempt. Her ancestors were from the same plantation, lived in the same room where the grimoire was found. It was entirely possible she was related to the woman who'd given birth to Legvu's first host, the innocent child of a slave. This place was a part of her, too.

"Finish the damn tattoo," he demanded, his reminiscing coming to an abrupt end as he followed my eyes back to Sugar's venomous glare.

I dipped the needles back into the ink and continued to press the fine tips into his skin. In thirty minutes to an hour it would be done, and we'd meet the real demon living behind the guise of the man with the red hair. My mind was so distracted with looking for a way out that my hand nearly jabbed the outside edge of the tattoo. "I need another break," I said, dropping the bamboo stick and stripping off my sweaty gloves.

My heart skipped when he grabbed my wrist, his strength catching me off guard as he held me in place effortlessly. "No more stalling, Katie." His eyes softened, and I recognized a look that made me more uncomfortable than the cold gaze he'd worn since the moment he walked into that interrogation room of the Chatham County PD. Even his voice changed. "We could share this," he said. "I would share all of it with you, Katie. We would be unstoppable." He turned and looked at Sugar's suspended body. "I might even allow you to save your friend."

It hit me all at once that I could see Sugar die today, all because of a circle of bones hanging around my neck that seemed to have more power than any of us.

Sugar made another strangled sound as I resumed the task.

"Shut that *fucking* mouth!" he spat, whipping his head around and nearly colliding with the needles at the end of the stick.

"I'll do it!" I yelled. "I'll finish the goddamn tattoo and do anything you want. Just let her go."

Legvu abruptly turned back to me with a look of both surprise and satisfaction on his face. "Really? Anything?"

"Anything," I repeated. It was better than watching him kill Sugar before he killed me. I'd allow him to enslave me because I knew I'd eventually find a way out. I'd have to do some unpleasant things along the way, but I'd find a way to suck him back inside the grimoire someday, and when I did I'd find a way to destroy that book, unlike my predecessors.

I went back to work on the tattoo, only this time I was eager to complete it. No more games. It was time to meet the real Legvu. With painstaking care, I finished the last line and filled in the final drop of red ink to complete the masterpiece. Then I stood up and took a step back to wait for the grand finale.

His amusement showed. "Well, I don't bite, Katie. Not yet." He stood up and stretched his half naked body like a leopard waking from a lazy nap. His muscles rippled as he contorted and grew taller, reaching a height that stopped a few feet from the ceiling. But I knew I was about to see the real transformation when his skin began to change color. The fair complexion of his Irish host went nearly black, like a cup of espresso with a drop of coconut oil shining and glazing over the surface, and his blue eyes turned into black star sapphires. Except for his fangs and the shining light coming from the center of his eyes, he was a tower of darkness. Even his scent was of rot and death. By the time the change was complete, he was half man and half beast, towering over the room with a set of fingers terminating in sharp claws that could kill Sugar or me with a single swipe.

He turned his head at an exaggerated angle, popping the vertebra loudly as the bones loosened and aligned with his unusually long neck. Then he turned and sized up his prisoner squirming against the ropes.

"You agreed to let her go." I found myself inching into the space between them, glancing back and forth between his leer and Sugar's terrified face.

His head shook slowly as the words hissed along his black tongue. "Not yet. I want to see the dragon first. But to make sure you behave I'll hold on to my collateral a little longer."

Is he crazy? I thought. *He's going to let me change?*

It seemed like suicide, but then I got a little nervous. Maybe I was no match for him now that he'd manifested into his true form, and he knew it. Individually the spirits were weak against the beast, but a true god could hold his own against just about anything, including a full-fledged dragon.

Legvu reached out toward my exposed skin. With a swift movement, he flicked the bone necklace over my head and drew a single claw across my neck, slicing my tender skin and releasing a river of blood from my jugular. My breath caught as I felt the rush of magic and the shock of pain from the sizable cut gaping at my throat. I reached for the wound and felt the warm blood seep down my neck as it covered my chest. But as my fingers felt along the opened skin, another pain struck me. It was my own talons digging deep into the gaping wound.

His irises elongated and flashed with excitement. "Magnificent," he said, leering back at my burning eyes. "You know, Katie, we'd make quite a team. The devil and the dragon. I might keep you."

Suddenly we were eye to eye, his height no longer having the advantage as mine quickly caught up. Sugar wasn't squirming anymore. Instead her eyes were transfixed on the two creatures standing a few feet away. I supposed the fear of being caught in the cross fire between us was a legitimate concern, and it was the first time I'd changed in front of her.

A sound echoed off the walls, thundering from one end of the room in a circle until it returned around the other side. I recognized it as my own steady growl. My voice. Inch by inch I felt the familiar stretch and pull of my skin as my fair flesh took on layers of shiny scales that moved in a perfectly articulated suit of armor. The fading daylight illuminating through the tall windows was eclipsed by a giant wing passing over the room, and I lifted several feet into the air and lunged at Legvu.

"Delightful!" he roared, lifting his arm and blocking me with some invisible force that sent me flying backward until my wings crashed into the far wall, nearly breaking them.

I climbed back to my clawed feet and decided to try a simpler strategy. Maybe he was stronger, but I had a secret weapon. The floor shook from my weight as I marched back across the large expanse of the room, determined to end the battle quickly. Fire projected from my jaws, travelling the ten-foot distance between us. It bathed Legvu's head and torso in a blanket of blue flames, licking at his flesh, cracking and popping as it scorched his skin.

There we go, I thought. *Game over.*

When the flames died down Legvu's form remained standing, still and charred like an incinerated marshmallow skewered over an open pit. But before I could claim victory, his blackened eyelids flipped back open and his bone-colored fangs gleamed back at me. "That was fun, Katie." He flashed a wide grin and cheered, "Do it again!" After a moment of silence and my humbling at the thought that Sugar and I were completely fucked, his grin flattened. "You can't kill the incorporeal with fire any more than I can kill a dragon with it. Now, I think we've had our fun, Katie. Don't you?"

I shuddered as the bones settled back over my neck and the dragon retreated. "Why bother with the bones?" I asked as he stepped away and smiled at me, gloating. "I'm no match for you."

"Because it lessens the drama and makes you more agreeable. Besides, I prefer complete and utter control of my slaves. You'll get used to them."

"I held up my end of the deal." I motioned toward Sugar. "Now let her go!"

"Don't worry, I'll release your friend," he said with a cold stare. "When I'm good and fucking ready."

27

JACKSON HUNTER: WEDNESDAY, 8:46 P.M.

Jackson climbed into Fin's Mercedes, barely clearing the door of the overpriced roadster. "I don't understand why anyone pays this much money for so little car."

"Well, I ain't about to climb on the back of that," Fin said, nodding to the Harley parked in Katie's driveway. He glanced at Jackson's knees crunched against the dash. "I can call my driver and have him bring over the Bentley? Or you can follow me on your bike."

"Yeah, that would be real inconspicuous," Jackson replied. "I'll manage, thanks."

It was getting dark outside, which was a good thing considering what they were about to do. The objective was to confirm that Legvu had indeed taken Katie to the old mill as Fin suspected. How they proceeded from there was still a work in progress.

The property was located near the Savannah River about twenty minutes north of Katie's house, in an area littered with abandoned buildings that turned into a ghost town after dark. They turned the headlights off a few blocks south of the building and pulled the car off the road.

"This would probably be a good time to establish a few rules, Mr. Hunter."

Jackson turned to Fin with a flat stare. "Rules?" he repeated. "The only rule I can think of is finding Katie and getting her out of there alive. And since you're the one who essentially put her in that hell hole, you'll have to forgive me if I don't place a lot of weight on your next statement."

"Legvu was after her long before I introduced myself, Mr. Hunter. I'm just the man who put it all into perspective for her. And may I remind you that if it wasn't for the Crossroads Society I imagine Legvu would have taken her sooner, possibly before she ever laid eyes on you."

Jackson shut his eyes tight and calmed his urge to rip Fin Cooper's head off his shoulders, something he was perfectly capable of doing. "Let's just get out of this car and find her."

"We're gonna do that, Mr. Hun—"

"You call me 'Mr. Hunter' one more time and I'll put you to sleep in that seat you're sitting in."

Fin arched his brow. "It's dangerous for a man your size to be so touchy." He unbuckled his seat belt and reached for the door handle. "Shall we, Jackson?"

They got out of the car and headed down the street, toward the battered white building with the cracked and broken windows. The challenge was to get in undetected and confirm that Katie was there. What they did with that information was debatable, because taking on a god like Legvu wouldn't be as simple as rushing in with guns.

Surprisingly, most of the doors were locked, which made no sense considering the place had been abandoned for decades. Breaking it down would only cause a loud ruckus, alerting anyone inside that they were coming in. The back of the building proved to be more useful as they came across a gaping door merely secured by a half inch steel chain.

"Well, fuck," Fin said. "What now?"

Jackson reached for the heavy chain through the six-inch gap and quietly twisted it. The steel links seemed to melt into fragments in his hand, releasing the door. He pushed it open quietly and walked inside.

"That's an impressive talent you got there," Fin commented, gawking at the chain that was now dangling broken against the open door. "Ever considered joining the society?" he asked, following Jackson inside.

Jackson ignored the remark and put his finger to his lips to silence Fin. He pointed toward a door at the far end of the room. They crept toward it but stopped when they heard voices coming from somewhere overhead, on the second floor of the building. One of the voices was Katie's.

Fin grabbed Jackson's arm as he took a hasty step toward the door. Jackson whipped around and glared at the fingers pressing into his flesh. "You want to take that hand off me?" he warned.

Fin dropped his hand, remembering how the thick steel chain had melted away in Jackson's grip. "Not only are you gonna get us killed," Fin whispered, "you'll get Katie killed in the process."

Jackson conceded, nodding to Fin. They climbed the steps to the second floor, careful not to make a sound. The voices got louder. Jackson was tall enough to peer over a horizontal window above a closed door. He nodded toward the room, indicating that Katie was inside. Then he motioned Fin back to the staircase.

"He's in there with Katie and Sugar," Jackson said as they reached the bottom of the steps.

Fin seemed surprised. "Sugar is alive?"

"He's got her strung up to a beam, the same one from the video." Jackson rubbed his face with his hand and glanced around the first floor. "Son of a bitch looks like a monster."

"That's because he *is* a monster," Fin declare with a dark, even tone. "Now, I'll admit I'm impressed by your strength, Jackson, but we are no match for an angry god."

Jackson nodded his head. "Right. But I know who might be."

28

KATIE BISHOP: WEDNESDAY, THE OLD MILL

The room was dark, the only illumination coming from a few working streetlights outside the building. Legvu was a creature of the night, blending in with the darkness even after the burns I'd deliver had healed miraculously. He'd been sitting in a chair a few yards away, silently staring at me for what seemed like hours.

"I don't suppose you have any candles?" I asked. It was small talk to take my mind off the pathetic scenario that was eating away at my resolve. Poor Sugar. She was barely hanging on—literally. Her legs had gone weak, and I could see her silhouetted shadow sagging toward the metal bucket that no longer braced her feet, but still managed to keep her from completely dangling in the air. Another hour of mindless waiting for Legvu to make a move and I was afraid her arms would suffer irreparable damage.

He surprised me with the gift of light. With a flick of his hand several of the rusted strip lights cracked and flickered, the blown-out florescent tubes firing up as if they'd just been replaced. "Benefits of being a god," he said.

"How long are you going to keep us here?" I asked,

conceding to myself that he would never let Sugar go. "We're hungry, and I have to take a piss."

He stood up and approached my chair, a cocky grin on his face. "Be my guest."

"What?" Then I realized he'd just invited me to squat in the middle of the room. "You'd like that, wouldn't you?"

Returning to his chair, he picked up a glass of water, hesitating as it touched his lips. "Where are my manners?" he said, feigning the hospitable host. "Would you like some?"

My mouth was a desert, but water would only exasperate my overflowing bladder. "No," I answered, looking at Sugar who was begging for that water with her eyes, "but she could use some."

He regarded Sugar, and for a moment I thought he might have the decency to offer the glass to her. "No," he mused after a few seconds of thought, shaking his head. "I'd have to remove all that tape and then wrap it around her mouth again."

That was the end of the small talk. The room went silent again as he dragged out the excruciating wait, deciding what to do with us. I was about to give up and piss on the floor when I heard a sound coming from outside the room—voices.

Legvu's cocky expression went cold as the sound got his attention. He looked back at me and raised his finger to his lips, glancing at Sugar as a warning for me to shut up. He rose swiftly out of his chair and headed for the door. I was amazed at how a creature of his size could move so elegantly without making a sound, completely naked, with claws for feet that walked over the debris of broken glass on the floor as if it were a soft lawn grass.

A trickling sound pulled my eyes away from Legvu's disappearing backside. It was the sound of liquid running down Sugar's legs, dripping over the edge of the bucket and landing in a pool on the floor. Our eyes met, but I quickly glanced away to hide my own terror from seeing her so vulnerable and to allow her the dignity she deserved.

My eyes traveled around the room and stopped on a pile of

wood tossed in the corner. Next to it was evidence of squatters or teenagers looking for a party spot in the abandoned building: a torn backpack, scattered cigarette butts, cinder blocks probably used as makeshift seats. One of the blocks was broken into several pieces. I glanced at the glass of water and then back at the concrete pieces of the cinder block.

"Shit, Sugar," I muttered as an idea whirled around in my head. I crawled over to the broken concrete block and pulled the bone charm from the cup of my bra. Sugar's eyes went wide as she moaned. "Shhhh," I silenced her. That little piece of bone was our only shot at getting out of the building and sending Legvu back where he belonged, and he'd be walking back through that door soon.

The muffled voices continued, assuring me that the unfortunate trespassers in the building hadn't run into Legvu yet. I cringed at the thought of hearing screams when they did, but right now I needed to focus on saving the two of us. The cinder block was broken into several pieces small enough to pick up and use as a hammer. I placed the bone on the floor and waited for an opportunity to smash it. The volume of the voices went up as Legvu must have had a face-to-face with the intruders. As quietly as possible I brought the piece of concrete down on the bone, listening for signs that he'd heard it and was rushing back. The commotion continued. The end of the bone broke off into a small pile of coarse fragments. With the edge of the cinder block, I ground the smallest pieces into fine dust. If I could mix some of it into his water he might drink it. Not as good as getting him to swallow the entire bone, but I suspected it would at least throw him off a bit and possibly give me the upper hand. My hands shook as I swept the small pile of dust into my palm.

Legvu came back through the door with two men dangling from his hands. I stood up abruptly, forced to leave the larger piece of the bone on the floor. The intruders were alive, but he had a tight grip around their necks that suggested they wouldn't be for long. By the looks of their clothing and dirty faces, I assumed they were a couple of homeless men who'd made the unfortunate mistake of seeking shelter for the night in the wrong place.

With my shoe, I concealed the larger piece of hyena bone on the floor, careful not to put my full weight on it.

"Look what I found." He dropped them to the ground. "Boy, are you two going to regret walking in here tonight," he mocked, delivering the dire news to the stunned men. One of them regained his senses and tried to stand up. Legvu didn't stop him, and by the predatory look on his face I could tell he was eager for the man to run. But instead of running he stood frozen in place, staring at the giant mutation glaring down at him. Legvu's eyes were frightening to look at whether you knew what he was or not, but to see something so demonic, with his coal skin and half-beast form, was enough to send the heart into arrest.

Legvu lost interest quickly when neither of the men scurried for safety. "*Fuck*," he hissed with a disappointed sneer before grabbing the standing man's neck again and swiftly snapping it until he sagged like a rag doll in the beast's grip. Then he tossed the body across the room and reached for the second man. This one he slammed hard enough against the floor to break bones. "Humans are so fragile and resilient at the same time," he commented, nudging the poor man with his clawed foot. "Look at him. The damn thing refuses to die." With a quick snap, he repeated the murderous move that ended the man's life.

With an exaggerated draw of breath through his nose, his mouth twisted in disgust. He seemed annoyed by the whole encounter, like it was a waste of his precious time to expend energy on a couple of vagrants. He glanced at the spot where I'd been standing before he left. "What are you doing over there?" he asked, looking suspiciously at me like I was up to something, which I was.

I couldn't help it. My eyes went to the water glass on the table behind him. He followed my gaze and then looked at the hand I was holding behind my back. Putting two and two together, he stomped toward me and reached for my throat. I stumbled back, taking my foot off the bone on the floor, seizing the only opportunity I was going to get.

"What's this?" he asked, almost laughing as he spotted the bone next to my foot.

Without losing a speck of the bone dust trapped in my hand, I dodged his lunge and fell to the floor. When I looked up, all I could see were his furious eyes fixed on mine as he descended on top of me. The lights flickered for a moment before extinguishing, leaving only the illumination from the waning moon as a dark shadow hovered above the room, crawling over the ceiling and descending on top of Legvu. The shadow seeped over his dark form like black oil spilling over his body, wrapping around his waist and pulling him off me.

I gazed at him as he floated a few yards away. On one side, he was held by a man with dark skin, his face furrowed from age and his bare back scarred deeply. On his other side was a woman wearing a long brown dress with a white apron, and a scarf wrapped snugly around her head. She was weeping, and as I looked closer I could see something swaddled in a sling against her chest. It was the still, lifeless form of an infant.

The two apparitions multiplied, and within minutes Legvu was surrounded and nearly engulfed by a sea of ghostly slaves. Their incorporeal eyes turned in my direction, and I realized they were waiting for me. Time seemed to stop as the room fell silent. Even the snarls coming from Legvu's mouth muted into nothing, and Sugar's frantic thrashing hit a moment of pause as she calmed herself and gazed at the vision filling the room around us.

I climbed to my feet and approached the trapped god, holding my hand out to unfold my fingers and expose the precious powder. A thin layer stuck to the sweat of my hand, but there was enough to set free. Then I blew it into the air and watched it whirl into a tiny cyclone. The bone dust appeared to dance under the dim moonlight as it traveled through the thick night air and landed in his eyes.

Legvu stopped fighting the army surrounding him, his face stuck in a fixed gaze of horror as his mouth opened and closed but made no sound. He turned to look at the larger piece of bone lying on the floor as if resolved to his fate. They released him and he began to grow smaller, his body disappearing into fine mist in the shape of an extinguishing tendril of smoke, the bone sucking him inside.

The ghosts dissipated as quickly as they'd appeared, and the phantom lights flashed bright again. I reached for the chain of bones that seemed dead and powerless without Legvu's will to control them and ripped them from my neck. It wasn't much, but I'd managed to get some of that bone inside of him through the membranes of his eyes. Before he had a chance to regain his power and fight his way back out, I threw the necklace across the room and grabbed the charm from the floor, shoving it in my pocket.

There was no easy way to do it. I stood on one of the chairs and ripped the duct tape from Sugar's mouth.

"*Ow!*" she spat. "*Goddamn motherfucker!*"

I nearly fell off the chair from the force of her growl. But time was of the essence, and if I didn't get her down from that beam soon Legvu was going to find his way back out of that small piece of bone and make us both regret we were ever born. She'd struggled so hard against the rope that the knot had tightened to the point where it would take a knife to cut her loose.

"Check them dead boy's pockets," she said.

As usual, she was right. One of them had a switchblade in his pocket. I cut the rope and she sagged to the ground, spreading her arms and legs like a snow angel while she got her circulation back.

"We have to get out of here, Sugar!"

She jumped up, her wig nearly flying off her head. "Give me that goddamn bone!" she ordered. "I'm gonna teach that son of a bitch some manners!"

I could feel the bone vibrating in my pocket. Either Legvu was fighting to get out, or some other wicked force was about to explode from it. "Not now, Sugar." I grabbed her arm and steered her toward the doorway just as the building started to shake. Tiles from the high ceiling came raining down around us, and the floor started to split from the spot where we were standing all the way down to the closest exit. The lights swayed, flashing and popping as the phantom bulbs exploded and sent very real shards of thin glass ricocheting around the room.

"Come on, baby," Sugar said, finally getting the picture and bottling up her need for vengeance. "We goin' straight through that door and out this hellhole."

We were about halfway across the room when the crack in the floor turned into a parting sea of old wooden beams. The floor lifted on both sides and sent us tumbling sideways down the slope toward the exterior walls. By the time we regained our senses and looked up, the upper floor was caving in and about to come crashing down on top of us.

"Lord Jesus!" Sugar prayed, tracing a cross over her chest as she curled into the fetal position and waited to meet her maker.

"Hell no!" I yelled. "Get your ass off that floor and follow me!" We weren't dying today, not after everything we'd just survived. We scrambled toward a window and prepared to jump. But as we pulled at the unyielding pane and started smashing out the remaining glass pieces, the entire structure of the building started to collapse inward, pulling us down into the rubble like sand being swallowed by the tide.

My eyes shut instinctively and then popped back open. There was a brick wall to my left where a minute ago all I could see was a hurricane of construction debris flying in a whirlwind around us. Then there was another one starting to form on my right.

Brick by brick the walls went up in a flash of architectural magic. To make the whole scene even more surreal, I looked closer at the makeshift wall and caught a glimpse of a face staring back at me.

"Sugar?" I swung around and saw her standing behind me, safely confined in the tight space with her eyes fixed on the same wall I was just looking at. "You okay?" I asked.

"I'm fine," she replied. "I'm just hoping that face over there in that wall is a friend of yours."

I turned back to the camouflaged eyes that were now more pronounced in the texture of the brick. "Cairo?"

IT TOOK ABOUT twenty minutes for Jackson, Fin, and a whole arsenal of Cairo's clan to dig us out. But had it not been for Jackson's strength, I imagined it would have taken a lot longer to get through all the rubble of a collapsed four-story building. Lucky for us, because even though the area was deserted at night, the police and fire department had probably already gotten wind of it and were on their way. Besides, I could feel Legvu growing stronger inside that tiny piece of bone tucked in my pocket.

I handed the charm to Fin. "It was José," I said. "Legvu promised him something he couldn't refuse if he helped get the second spirit out of the grimoire. Imm—"

"Immortality," Fin said before I could get the word out.

"You knew?" I glared at him for lying to me by omission.

"Now before you get all fired up about it," he said, staving off my wrath, "let me just say that we only had our suspicions. In fact, while we were digging you out Lillian called to let me know that José confessed, probably about the same time Legvu got himself sucked inside this piece of bone I'm holding. He called Lillian in a panic after looking in the mirror and noticing his hair was falling out in clumps. Had open sores forming all over his face. That man's skin was literally sliding off his flesh."

"I don't get the connection. Is he sick?"

Fin smirked and bit off the tip of a cigar before lighting it. "I guess you could say that. It appears that José is a little older than he looks."

"How much older?"

"Say . . . more than a century. Apparently, he's been forty-five for about a hundred years. Sold his soul to the devil more than once, but that debt always comes back around to bite you in the ass. Seems he was overdue for a little rejuvenation and decided to offer his services to Legvu in exchange for a little magic nip and tuck."

I laughed bitterly. "What will happen to him, now? His age will eventually catch up and send him to the grave?"

Fin's face sobered. "I'm afraid it already has, Miss Bishop."

29

The shop was busier than usual when I walked through the front door. Fridays were relatively slow, with the weekend crowd preferring to get their tattoos on Saturday.

"Hey, Carl," I said to my business neighbor sitting in Mouse's chair, giving him a cordial smile as I headed for the front desk. He owned the thrift shop three doors down and had a habit of drawing out a single-session tattoo into two, usually with me applying them. Sea Bass was convinced he had the hots for me since he always insisted I be the one to do the work. But today I had more important business to attend to.

His eyes visibly brightened. "Hey there, Katie. I was hoping you'd be in this morning." He glanced at Mouse. "No offense, Mouse. It's just that Katie usually takes care of me." Mouse snorted but said nothing, focusing back on the American flag she was wrapping around the cap of his shoulder.

"Sorry, Carl. I had a breakfast date with my boyfriend." It was a lie, but it was kinder than shooting him down when he inevitably asked me out. I guess it wasn't a total fabrication, seeing how I did eat scrambled eggs and toast on the kitchen counter with Jackson before leaving for my meeting with a *real* lawyer.

Carl's expression sagged. Maybe now he'd move on to someone who would reciprocate and show a real appreciation for his devotion.

The morning after the mill collapsed, Fin made a call to his attorney's office to set me up with legal representation. There was still the matter of an eyewitness seeing me with Christopher Sullivan the night he disappeared. But since that anonymous call had been made by a demented god who was now safely imprisoned back in the grimoire, there was no evidence that I'd been anywhere near Christopher the night he vanished. On top of that, they'd never actually found a body—thanks to Fin and his accomplices—so there were no legal grounds for the police to bother me any further. For all intents and purposes, I was a free woman.

"That's right, Carl," Sugar added. "Katie B got her a big ol' boyfriend who ain't gonna appreciate another man sniffing around his woman."

I glared at her and cocked my head, begging her to be kind to the man. Sea Bass was hunched over her chest, tattooing a four-leaf clover a few inches above her left breast. Despite hanging for dear life from that beam for an entire day, Sugar seemed relatively unscathed. Even Dr. Greene had been astounded by her miraculous recovery. Though a little sore, she was back to her usual self, and I couldn't help but think that Pearl May Mobley's juju had something to do with that. A powerful conjure woman for a mama came in handy.

"Humph," I said, examining the tattoo. "Feeling a little lucky, are you?"

"Luck of the Irish," she replied.

"Since when are you Irish, Sugar?"

"Since I be sittin' here with my ass intact. I figured a little good luck charm ain't gonna hurt."

Indeed, I thought. We were all lucky to be here.

The front door opened and in walked Fin. "That meeting go well, Miss Bishop?"

"As well as I could hope, Fin. I think the worst is over, at least for now." One thing I learned early on in life was to never underestimate the power of karma. While killing Christopher Sullivan was an act of pure self-defense, I knew deep down that as long as his body wasn't put to rest in the family plot, there would always be that threat in the back of my mind that old ghosts would resurface and the police would come knocking on my door again. That was an unpleasant possibility I had to live with.

"I have something for you," he said, holding out an envelope.

"What's this?" I opened it and extracted a set of papers. It was the deed to the building we were standing in.

"Signed and notarized," he pointed out. I was listed as the grantee. He'd promised me the deed if I joined the Crossroads Society and helped them recapture Legvu, but I never really thought he'd make good on that offer. I figured without a legal contract, he'd find some sleazy way out of handing over a whole building.

I looked up at him. "I thought—"

"You thought what, Miss Bishop?" The look in his eyes as he waited for me to question his integrity made me question my own. "That I would renege on a deal?"

My shoulders slouched as I smiled back at him. "No, Fin. I'm just a little stunned right now." I glanced around the room and shook my head at the thought of what I'd just been handed. "This may be a little hard for someone like you to understand, Fin, but most working folks don't have the luxury of not worrying about the rent. You just liberated me."

He laughed quietly. "Well, then today is a good day." He turned to leave but added a remark before walking out the door. "I'm sure you'll more than earn that deed with the next calamity the society has to deal with."

"N—next calamity?" I called out to him. "What do you mean by *next*?"

"The crossroads, Miss Bishop." He glanced back at me and pulled a cigar from his pocket. "We still need to find those bones."

I DODGED a few cars and headed for Lou's to grab lunch. For the first time in God knows how long I felt a little peace, and the freedom to just sit in one of the old vintage booths by myself without a care in the world that couldn't wait. Fin had just changed my life with a piece of paper, and I decided there'd be plenty of time to worry about the bones tomorrow. Today was mine.

The grilled cheese sandwich on the plate in front of me disappeared in record time, along with a pickle and a hefty serving of greasy fries smothered in ketchup. I was debating between a sugar cookie or a brownie to top it off with my cup of coffee, when my eyes rolled around the room and stopped on a woman sitting at one of the booths against the far wall. It was the woman who'd been stalking me, with the blonde hair and large glasses. She was staring back at me.

"That's it," I muttered, getting up to confront her before she disappeared again. I walked across the room to her booth. "Why the hell are you following me?" I asked without an introduction. If she was so interested in me, I figured she already knew my name. She sure as hell knew where I lived. She smiled and motioned to the seat across from hers. "Hold on," I said, going back to grab my coffee and purse while keeping an eye on her to make sure she stayed put.

I slid into the seat as she smiled and took a sip of her coffee. Her eyes were concealed behind the dark lenses of her sunglasses. "I was wondering if you'd come over," she said. "I guess I could have come over to your table or knocked on your front door the other night, but it was best that you came to me. It's much more likely that you'll stay and hear me out since you initiated the exchange." Her voice was soft and disarming. Clever if she meant me harm, because she had my interest and the proximity to pounce. My breath caught when she pulled the large frames from her face, revealing her bright emerald eyes. A memory flashed in my mind and then disappeared as fast as it came.

"Do you remember me?" she asked. "It's Katie now, right?"

I gazed at her familiar eyes, allowing an unexplained emotion to wash over me. "Now?" I repeated.

"The last time we met," she continued, "you still went by your given name, Katarina."

In an instant, the oxygen seemed to vacuum from the room. *Katarina, Katarina, Katarina,* my father called. I was four years old, standing in the middle of a valley circled by a range of mountains that were green at the bases and snow-capped at the tops. The air was warm and smelled of wildflowers each time the breeze picked up and carried the scent through the valley. But as I stood with my bare toes cushioned against the grass with a gust of wind almost lifting me off the ground, I realized it wasn't the wind at all. I looked up at the blue sky, clear of even a single cloud. The voice echoed from the sky again, *Katarina, Katarina, Katarina.* My father sailed through the blue, casting a giant shadow over the valley as he passed over my head. *Fly with me!*

A sharp gasp left my mouth, nearly sending me over the edge of the seat. As I refocused on the woman sitting across from me, smiling with a graveness that suggested it was more condolence than pleasantry, I remembered where we'd met.

"You came to see me a long time ago." The encounter was vivid in my mind. I was seven or eight when she walked up to me as I was leaving school. She was standing on the sidewalk, blocking my path and gazing down at me. Then she took a deep breath and told me she was my aunt. I was adopted very young and had no memory of my birth parents, and certainly no memory of any other relatives. My adoptive mother acted very strangely when I got home that afternoon and told her about the encounter. She said the woman was crazy and reminded me about the rule of never talking to strangers. But to this day I knew that woman wasn't a stranger.

She nodded. "I'm your aunt, Marianna. I think I mentioned that when we first met. Do you remember me asking you to show me your tattoo?"

"I remember you. And I remember you showing me yours." She had a tattoo like mine. Hers was slightly different, but the colors were the same. "You ran your hand over my back, and then you just turned around and walked away. So why are you here now?"

"Katarina," she sighed, "I've always been with you. In New York and now here in Savannah. But it's time for me to leave. Right after your twenty-fifth birthday."

"I don't know what's happening here," I said. "I don't know you, and I think you owe me the courtesy of cutting through the bullshit. So why don't you just tell me what you want and what my birthday has to do with it."

She stood up and walked over to the counter to order two more coffees. She returned and placed one of the cups in front of me. "I'm sorry. My nerves are frayed and I've gotten quite dependent on caffeine to keep them calm. Ironic, yes?" She took a deep swallow of the piping hot drink and proceeded to answer my question. "Katarina—"

"My name is Katie," I corrected.

"Of course." She took a deep breath and continued. "Do you know what you are? What *we* are?"

I'd been called a couple of things lately—creature, shifter—but I preferred to just refer to myself as a woman who happened to host a dragon on her back. To me they were two separate things that managed to coexist and borrow from one another on occasion. "I like to think I'm a woman with an unusual pet," I snickered. "But I suppose you're going to finally put a name to it."

"No, Katie, you are not a woman with a dragon on her back —you are a dragon when the beast is awake and a woman when it sleeps. But make no mistake, you are the dragon first."

I put my cup of coffee back down on the table before I dropped it as her words ran through my head on a loop, trying to decipher what part I'd heard wrong. "I'm not sure I understand what you're telling me."

"The transformation will take place on your twenty-fifth birthday, when you will become the dragon permanently. Then you will rejoin your father at Mount Triglav in the Julian Alps."

I laughed in a short, mocking way. "That's absurd."

"No more absurd than the girl sitting across from me who grows claws when she's threatened, or sprouts wings and flies across skyscrapers."

Until a couple of days ago when Legvu slashed my throat, I hadn't completely changed into the dragon in over two years. And since leaving New York I'd managed to control the beast fairly well. I had to admit though, it was showing unpre-dictability lately.

She leaned across the table for discretion. "I know about Christopher Sullivan and what was inside of him," she whispered. "Your strength is impressive. The dragon is waking up."

My coffee cup tipped over and nearly fell to the floor as I pull away, shocked and shaking. "How do you know that?"

"It doesn't matter, Katie!" Her eyes turned fearful, almost desperate in the way they raced back and forth between mine. "You have to believe what I'm telling you before it's too late!"

"What if I don't want this?" I asked, shaking my head because deep down in my gut I knew she was telling me the truth.

"It's our birthright, Katie. It happens to all of us."

"All of us?" She had a similar dragon on her back, and I was pretty sure she was a lot older than twenty-five. "You're my father's sister?" From what I'd been told, my mother was an ordinary woman from Russia. My father was the dragon in the family.

"Half-sister. Same father, but my mother was human. I'm just like you, Katie—a dragon's child. We have a choice." Her eager expression gave me hope. "We'll always be dragons, but we can choose which form will dominate after our transformation. Do nothing and the choice will be made for you. But if you know how to play the game the choice is yours. In fact, that's the reason I'm here. All women should have choices, Katie. I did, and so do you."

"I'm in," I said without hesitation. "Just tell me what to do."

A sly grin edged up the side of her face. "Well, my dear, if you want to live your life on your own terms, all you have to do is die."

READ KATIE BISHOP'S BACKSTORY TODAY!

Want to know more about Katie? Read THE FITHEACH TRILOGY and find out where it all began.

THANK YOU TO MY READERS

A book means nothing without someone to read it. Thank you for that. I hope you'll consider taking a few minutes to leave a brief review, even if it's just a sentence or two. Feedback is always appreciated and vital for authors.

ALSO BY LUANNE BENNETT

THE FITHEACH TRILOGY

The Amulet Thief (Book 1)

The Blood Thief (Book 2)

The Destiny Thief (Book 3)

THE KATIE BISHOP SERIES

Crossroads of Bones (Book 1)

Blackthorn Grove (Book 2)

Shifter's Moon (Book 3)

Dark Nightingale (Book 4)

Bayou Kings (Book 5)

Conjure Queen (Book 6)

Dirt Witch (Book 7)

HOUSE OF WINTERBORNE SERIES

Dark Legacy (Book 1)

Savage Sons (Book 2)

King's Reckoning (Book 3)

Sign up for news and updates about future releases!

LuanneBennett.com

ACKNOWLEDGMENTS

I owe an ocean of gratitude to the Katie Bishop Beta Reader Group for reading the book and providing priceless insight that simply made the book better.

Thank you to my family and friends: my mom for holding her tongue when I decided to walk away from my former career to write silly little stories all day. Jen, Debra, and Linda for all your support. Jen, you are a tireless proofreader and seer of hidden story opportunities.

Thank you to my spiritual kin: Sonja, Tabitha, Joshua, David, and Derrick for donating your precious time and talent, and for always having my back. That kind of loyalty is priceless.
Thank you to my incredible betas around the globe: Gina, Davina, and Susan.

And of course, Little Bear and Miss Lila for treading across the keyboard when it was way past time for a break, and for curling up in my lap on cold winter mornings in that back room.

ABOUT THE AUTHOR

LUANNE BENNETT is an author of fantasy and the supernatural. Born in Chicago, she lives in Georgia these days where she writes full time and doesn't miss a thing about the cubicles and conference rooms of her old life. When she isn't writing or dreaming up new stories, she's usually cooking or tending a herd of felines.

I love to hear from readers. Contact me at:
www.luannebennett.com
books@luannebennett.com
facebook.com/LuanneBennettBooks

.